It was *freezing* out here.

Maybe Aaron had trapped Stephanie on the porch deliberately so that she'd agree to his terms quickly. "What's your grandmother's stake in the business?"

"She owns the whole shebang. I'm basically acting as her business manager."

"So only she can fire me."

Aaron opened his mouth to form an objection, but then closed it. "Yes. She's *our* boss."

It must've killed him not to have seniority over her. If anything, *she* should have seniority over *him*.

"All right," she said, holding out her hand. "Consider me your new assistant manager."

Relief flooded Aaron's stormy eyes. As he squeezed and pumped her hand, a pulse of something thick and hot blew through her.

Oh, no. *Hell*, no. She was *not* attracted to Aaron Caruthers. They weren't just out of each other's leagues; they were playing different sports.

FICTION

Dear Reader,

Welcome back to Everville, New York, the town where my second book, *Back to the Good Fortune Diner* (Harlequin Superromance, January 2013), was set. I've gone back in time to a few months before Tiffany arrived to tell the story of how the county's best roadside bakeshop became the very popular Georgette's Bakery and Books.

Everville's motto is The Town That Endures. To me, enduring means accepting change. As the wife of a civics nut, I enjoy learning about what makes communities work. As the town evolves, so, too, do the lives of Aaron Caruthers and Stephanie Stephens—the bookworm and the cheerleader who never thought they could be a match.

I love to hear from readers! Visit me on Facebook, Twitter (@VickiEssex) and my website, vickiessex.com, and watch out for more stories from Everville!

Happy reading!

Vicki Essex

VICKI ESSEX

A Recipe for Reunion

HARLEQUIN® SUPERROMANCE®

MAY 2 1 2015

Recycling programs
for this product may
not exist in your area.

ISBN-13: 978-0-373-60902-4

A Recipe for Reunion

HARLEQUIN®
www.Harlequin.com

Printed in U.S.A.

Vicki Essex likes eating baked goods, but isn't great at baking them. She loves books, and isn't a bad hand at writing them. To be showered with cookies, say hello to her at vickiessex.com, find her on facebook.com/vickiessexauthor and follow her on Twitter: @VickiEssex.

Books by Vicki Essex

HARLEQUIN SUPERROMANCE

Her Son's Hero
Back to the Good Fortune Diner
In Her Corner

Visit the Author Profile page
at Harlequin.com for more titles

I'd like to thank my agent, Courtney Miller-Callihan, for being awesomely supportive and for really grokking me. *cookies*

Thanks to my editor, Karen Reid, whose insights are always, always helpful.

And as always, thank you to my darling, brilliant husband, John, whose magnificent brain inspired Aaron's eclectic tastes and polymathic genius. I couldn't do this without you, magoo.

CHAPTER ONE

Two months ago...

N o o n e w a s eating her goodies.

Stephanie racked her brain trying to figure out why. She'd baked all the treats herself, tailoring each recipe to meet her friends' varied preferences and dietary restrictions: gluten-free chocolate cupcakes and dairy-free carrot muffins; nut-free cookies, a plate of soy-free bite-size brownies and three different pies because Lilian didn't like lemon meringue, Susan loathed pecan and Karen thought apple was "boring."

The last time she'd seen all her high school girlfriends together had been Christmas four years ago. Yet, instead of being excited, a weird sense of disappointment had dogged her all evening. While everyone else was busy chatting, talking over each other like a gaggle of geese, she got the feeling that if she waded into the fray, she'd be nibbled and pecked to death.

But she had volunteered to host this holiday shindig, so she couldn't hide behind the food forever. Steph brightened her smile and picked up a plate of sugar cookies, painstakingly frosted in B. H. Everett High's blue and gold. Brandishing the treats and armed with good cheer, she circulated. She might not be the best convocation…conservation…talker, but she was a damned good baker.

"Well, it's not like I *don't* want to come back to Everville," she heard Janny say wistfully. "But Mark's job is in Cleveland, and my business is flourishing. I wouldn't have clients here."

"Yes, nice as it is to come home, I'd never move back," Cristina proclaimed. "Rumor is the property values in town are taking a dive. I'm not sure about the new mayor, either—I mean, I wasn't the biggest fan of Bob Fordingham, but at least we knew what to expect from him."

"Cookie?" Steph thrust the plate out. Janny and Cristina each politely took one.

"Steph, we were just talking about the new mayor," Cristina said. "Cheyenne Welks, right? What's she like?"

She shrugged. "What's to tell? She comes to Georgette's every day at eight for a large black coffee and usually gets a plain croissant."

"But I mean what are her policies like?" Cristina clarified. "I've heard that she's been spending a lot on infrastructure—like that big water main project."

"Oh, I don't really follow politics," she said. She'd noticed all the construction in town, of course, but she didn't have to drive through it on her way to work so she didn't pay it much attention. "But she's really nice."

Cristina touched her arm. "Thanks for hosting, by the way. It's nice of your parents to let us hang out here, considering all the times we've trashed their home."

"As long as we don't throw up in the pool again," Janny added jokingly.

"Like old times, eh? Glad to know some things'll never change." Steph found herself inexplicably irritated as Cristina bit into her cookie. "Mmm. This is good. Catered?"

Steph perked up. "I baked them."

"Oh." Her long lashes flickered. "Still working at Georgette's then?"

"Yeah."

Silence dropped between them as heavily as an anchor. "She's still…around?"

"Oh, yeah. I don't know anyone who's as energetic as she is at her age. She'll outlive us all." She laughed a little too loudly. This was the third time she'd answered this question today. In fact, if her friends' queries were any indication, her life could be summed up in three statements.

I work at Georgette's.

I've been there five years now.

Yes, Georgette's still alive.

"So, what are you guys up to?" she asked to relieve the silence that stretched between them like yeasty dough.

Cristina launched into the story of her life—college, husband, career in interior design, a vacation in Hawaii, plans for kids. Janny's story was nearly as glamorous—two daughters, a house and a massage therapy practice in Cleveland.

Steph took it all in with a smile, clutching the plate of cookies as she suppressed her envy. Years ago she would've lightly punched her friends in the arm and exclaimed, "So jealous!" It was hard to joke about it now.

As she moved off, she reminded herself it'd been her choice to stay in Everville, that her family was here and that she loved the town and working for Georgette. Okay, so she wasn't living in the big corner house on King Street that Mr. Merkl owned, the way she'd always dreamed, with three kids, a dog, a cat and a swing set. But it hadn't been her fault that Dale hadn't kept his promise to marry her after college. Still, everything she needed was right here in her hometown. She should be happy.

She *was* happy.

"I'm catching the red-eye back to LA," she overheard Cindy say as she approached. "With the wedding coming, my condo renos *and* my practice on the go, I've got way too much happening to stick around here."

"You're going to have a heart attack if you keep up this pace," Teri warned.

Cindy snickered. "I live for interesting times. I can sleep when I'm dead."

"I don't know how you do it," Steph interjected, passing the cookies around. "I like my sleep way too much."

Cindy tipped her head side to side, declining a cookie. "You have to keep moving if you want to stay on top. LA's not like Everville."

Steph quirked an eyebrow. "What do you mean?"

"Oh, c'mon. You've been all over the place. You know that small-town upper New York State isn't exactly a busy cultural and business hub. Frankly, I'd go nuts if I had to come back here permanently. I mean, everything here opens at ten and closes at six."

"I'm up at four every morning to bake," Steph said stiffly, belatedly realizing her schedule had nothing to do with the rest of the town's business hours.

Cindy's smile was toothy and unflinching. "Good for you."

It was her tone that had grated on her, Steph concluded much later, after everyone had gone home and she was left to clean up the half-empty wineglasses and leftovers. Everyone had con...condo... condensation...

Given me that pitying attitude, she huffed. They'd all used that tone that said, "You poor thing, working like a dog, stuck in Everville and not even married!"

It was ridiculous, she knew, to even think any

of her friends thought that about her. She couldn't know for sure what any of them felt.

And she hadn't expected those strange, sorry looks. The girls of the cheerleading squad whom she'd once considered sisters had all grown up, branched out and moved on. They'd changed, and they saw her as still living in the past. She'd always thought she was a good judge of character, but she didn't know them anymore, and they didn't know her. Why had she insisted on this reunion? Nostalgia? Loneliness?

"Leave those." Helen Stephens nodded at the empty glasses in her hand. "I'll call Lucena and have her clean up."

"I can do it, Mom." Stephanie loaded the stemware into the dishwasher. "I'm not dragging Lucena in on her day off. *I* had the party here, so *I'll* be the one to clean."

Helen's brow furrowed as if she was worried her only daughter might trip and fall on a wineglass. "I just don't want you to wear yourself out." Her expression eased as she beamed around the house. "You did such a lovely job with all the decorations and food—" she gestured toward the console table in the foyer "—but you forgot to hand out your treat bags."

Steph sucked in her lower lip. As everyone was leaving, there'd been so much chaos as her friends scrambled for their coats and purses that Steph had nearly forgotten all about her take-home party favors. Many of her friends had refused anyway because they were on diets or "couldn't have those around the house." The statement baffled her. Who couldn't have cookies around the house? But she didn't press the matter. She wasn't about to admit she'd taken their rejection personally, either.

"I'll bring them to the seniors' home tomorrow," Steph said. Then she pictured the residents reaching for the plates only to remember their blood pressure, their sugar intake, their weak stomachs and numerous food allergies. The nurses probably would have to throw out the treats to ensure no one tried their luck.

Steph had spent three whole days baking twelve dozen cookies, all of them her original recipes.

They were her life's work—and they'd been rejected. Dismissed.

Like Steph.

"Sweetheart, what's wrong?" Helen laid a hand on her daughter's arm, and Steph snapped out of her haze.

"Nothing." She looked away to hide her sudden tears. "Maybe I am a little tired."

Helen drew her away from the table. "Then leave this all for tomorrow. Lucena can take care of it— that's what we pay her for." She urged Steph toward the stairs. "Go take a nice hot shower and get some rest. You don't want bags under your eyes."

"But, Mom…" She nearly tripped as her mother hustled her along.

"Go on, baby." She stopped abruptly and cupped Steph's cheek, an almost manic look of love shining in her face. "As long as you live under this roof, you don't have to worry about a thing." The words were uttered in a low coo, but Steph felt something more behind them this time, as if her mother knew exactly what was wrong and would fix everything.

That's what she did. She fixed *everything*.

Helen shooed her up the stairs the same way she had throughout Steph's high school years. As fast as Steph climbed, though, she felt as though she were sinking deeper into the rut of her life. In the seven-hundred-square-foot suite that was her bedroom, she shut the door behind her and leaned against the door frame.

Cold winter light gleamed off all the surfaces. Her mom had filled the suite with mirrored furniture, saying how she loved the way it made her daughter look like a queen standing in her diamond palace. Steph had loved it, too, but right now she thought the room looked sterile, the light casting weird shadows across the walls and distorting her image in every reflection.

It used to be easy to simply go to her room and whittle away her worries with a manicure while watching a DVD, followed by a shopping trip into town. That's what she'd done since she was a teen.

But she wasn't a teen anymore. She was thirty… and still living at home with a closet full of designer clothes, the latest in home fashions and anything else she could ever want or ask for. She had a job to give her days meaning and show the world she wasn't just a princess waiting for her prince to sweep her away. She volunteered at the old folks' home and at many charity events her parents supported. She had a well-padded bank account, a pretty nice car, a loving family and not a care in the world.

But it wasn't enough.

Something had to change.

Now.

"I'M SEVENTEEN MINUTES AWAY," Aaron Caruthers declared over the hands-free cell phone, keeping the rumbling U-Haul truck at a steady forty-five miles per hour along the gray, slush-slickened road. His life's possessions rattled around the interior, and he winced every time he hit a pothole. He hoped he'd used enough bubble wrap.

"Oh, Aaron, you didn't need to call me to tell me that. I'd rather you have all your focus on the road." Georgette Caruthers's tone held a note of anxiety only her grandson could detect above her voice's buttery warmth.

"I didn't want you worrying. Traffic was heavier than expected out of Boston, and I stopped to help a lady change her tire just outside the city."

"Well, aren't you the superhero?" His grandmother chuckled, each word curling with the slight

English inflection she'd never shaken. "Was she pretty? Did you get a phone number?"

He laughed. "She was married and very pregnant. I actually stopped because her baby bump flagged me down."

"You're a good boy, Aaron. Thanks for calling. I'll have a nice cup of coffee and your favorite bran muffin waiting."

"You're the best, Gran. See you soon." He hung up and focused on driving, knuckles white as he gripped the steering wheel.

Even though the road here had been paved and widened, with additional barriers, signs and reflective markers delineating the solid cliff face rising up on the turn, Aaron always took this particular stretch slowly. He never took chances here— or anywhere, for that matter. He brought the truck down to thirty, leaned on his horn as he made the turn to alert any oncoming drivers, then sped up once more as he caromed around the corner.

His shoulders gradually slackened, the tension draining away as he moved past the spot where his parents had been killed in a car accident. He hated that stretch of the highway. He could've taken the long route to avoid it, but frankly, that road wasn't any safer. At least he knew exactly what to expect on this route to Everville and how to deal with any emergency that might crop up.

Fourteen minutes later, the truck rumbled past a new hand-painted sign that said Welcome to Everville: The Town That Endures. He slowed as down-town hove into view. The buildings were painted blue-gray by the early evening light, prettily framed between wrought iron latticework streetlamps and small piles of flecked snow. As he pulled onto Main Street, the pavement gave way to gray-brown mud and gravel that splashed and scattered beneath his tires. Bright orange pylons and construction signs jutted from the ground like oversize, mutated flow-ers in a post-apocalyptic small-town Americana landscape. His gran had said the town was undergo-ing a massive renovation as the old sewer mains and pipes were replaced. It was a good thing his grand-mother's bakery was on the road outside town; he couldn't imagine how this construction affected businesses in the area.

Change is good, he reminded himself. Even if it was a little scary.

Gran's house was just off Main Street. He pulled the truck onto the curb as Georgette opened the door to the bungalow. Warm light spilled into the street. He hopped out of the cab.

"It's so good to see you…and all in one piece." She opened her arms.

"You shouldn't be out in the cold in your condi-tion," he said, hugging her.

"Pshaw. I'm not *that* frail, Aaron. Come inside. There's plenty of time to unpack later. I asked some friends to come help."

"You didn't have to do that." Since Gran was in

no shape to carry anything heavier than a plate of biscuits, he was grateful for assistance, even if he wasn't wild about near-strangers poking into his personal belongings. Pretty soon, everyone would know he was back. It'd been a while since he'd been home. The fishbowl of small-town living was something he'd have to get used to all over again.

The bungalow Aaron had grown up in hadn't changed since he'd first moved in when he was barely eight years old. The immaculate carpets were still that odd shade of pink-gray, which went with the floral wallpaper and powder-white floral-themed light fixtures throughout the house. The place had always reminded him of a wedding cake. Gran still had the same furniture, too, meticulously kept despite those years of having a school-age boy living under the same roof. Then again, Aaron had always been a neat freak. He hated messes.

Georgette slipped off her shawl, and Aaron flinched. Gran had always been dancer thin, but seeing how her clothes hung off her now shocked him. And she moved so much more slowly. He followed her into the kitchen, insisting on getting his own coffee though she fussed over it. Nothing in here had changed, either, from the glass-fronted cabinets to the chintz-pattern china. The aroma of coffee and baking permeated the air.

Aaron made her sit while he took out the cream and sugar. Everything was exactly where it had been all those years ago. Muscle memory took control as he poured coffee into the mugs he'd always thought of as his and Gran's. The promised muffins were warming in the oven, and he put two on chipped saucers for each of them.

"How are you feeling?" he asked as he sat.

"Tired. I've got a headache most days. Nothing serious."

"Of course it's serious." He took her hands. "You've probably already heard this enough from everyone else, but I'm going to say it again. There's nothing minor about a minor stroke." She wouldn't quite meet his eye, which made him worry. "Are you having any loss of sensation still?"

"In my left hand." She flexed it, just barely, and he frowned. "The physical therapist will decide whether or not I need to work on it."

"Of course you need to work on it. I'll make sure they give you something."

She tucked her hand beneath the table. "Aaron, really, I'm fine. You didn't have to pick up your life and move back here."

"I wanted to. And I couldn't let you be on your own."

She waved a hand, but not as vigorously as her protest might have warranted. "I just don't want you worrying over me. You have a life in Boston."

"It was time for a change." He kissed her on the forehead. "Besides, it's worth coming home for your baking." He grinned as he broke the bran muffin and bit into the warm, moist pastry. People had laughed when at ten years old he'd declared bran muffins were his favorite thing Gran made. He hadn't been into sugary treats, which apparently was heresy for the grandson of a baker.

Gran had understood. Aaron was simply more practical when it came to his diet. He was practical when it came to everything, and moving home to take care of Georgette was the best and most practical solution to her long-term care. He would never abandon her to a facility full of strangers. She'd taken him in and raised him after his parents' deaths. He owed her, and he was happy to do whatever necessary to make her happy and comfortable.

For however long she had.

He washed the suddenly dry bite of muffin down with a sip of coffee. "So how's the bakery doing?" he asked, bracing for a fight. Gran had lived and breathed that bakery for years. She and Grandpa had opened it right after they'd married, and she'd kept it running since his death more than twenty-five years ago.

"The bakery's fine," Georgette replied. "I have help these days, and I'm delegating more responsibility. Otherwise, I'd be there right now."

Gran had always been a bit of a control freak and workaholic. For her to give up any part of the business was major. Aaron put down his mug and leaned forward. "Financially speaking, how are you doing?"

His grandmother's eyes flicked around the room

like a trapped bird searching for an escape. It was a moment before she responded. "We had a good Christmas season. Valentine's was a little slower this year, but…" She shrugged.

Aaron sighed. He would have to look at the books himself. Gran rarely shared her problems with him. He hadn't realized until high school how tight things had been, and then he'd done whatever he'd been able to help get the business out of the red. After he'd finished college he'd learned the reason for all that debt had been that his grandmother had been putting aside everything she could for tuition.

"Really, I am happy to see you." Georgette touched his arm. "But I feel terribly guilty for taking you away from your life. What are you going to do for a job in Everville? I'm not sure there's much call for real-estate lawyers here."

"Well, I did say I was ready for a change." Which wasn't far from the truth. He was good at what he did, and probably would've slaved away at his firm for the rest of his life had that phone call from the hospital not come. But the moment it had, he'd been prepared. Part of him had always been prepared with a plan B, an exit strategy.

Things happened all the time. You had to be ready for them. That was how he'd known what he would do the moment he had to return to Everville.

He set his coffee down. "I'm thinking of opening a bookstore."

Georgette blinked. "Really? Here?"

"I've always wanted to. A well-stocked book-shop is exactly what the town needs, and attaching it to the bakery will make it a destination. See, I was thinking of renovating the bakeshop's dining room. It hardly gets used, and it's such a big space. We could minimize the eating area with just a few café tables, then add a patio for the warmer months. Most of your eat-in business comes in during the summer anyhow."

"So...you're staying in Everville?"

"Of course I am. How will I take care of you otherwise?" He didn't see why Gran should be so astonished. "I've been thinking about this for years. Did all my research and everything." He had a binder in the truck with all the information he needed to put his plan into action. He'd started it the day he'd realized Gran was getting older. "I was just waiting for the right opportunity to jump in."

Georgette's eyes grew wet, and her smile crimped in at the edges. She squeezed his arm. "You didn't go to school so you could stay here. You always wanted to get away."

True. But that had only been for a handful of reasons, and those reasons were gone now. "Things change. I want to be *here*. With you." A sudden thought occurred to him. "I mean, if you want to keep the dining room at the bakery, I can work something else out, and I can get my own place if you want your privacy, but I can't take care of you if—"

"Nonsense. You'll stay here, of course. I wouldn't have it any other way." She leaned forward. "Now, about this bookshop."

He outlined his business plan for her, with his vision for the store itself. He had his own seed money, but he'd also be taking out a small loan to do the renovations. The more he talked about it, the more excited he became.

He was about to get the binder with his notes from the truck when the doorbell rang.

"That will be the moving team," Georgette said, rising slowly.

"Take it easy, Gran. I'll get it." He put on a smile for whoever had volunteered to help with his move, excited to also tell them about the bookstore and get some momentum going.

He opened the door.

And came face-to-face with the second-to-last person he wanted to see.

CHAPTER TWO

"HI, AARON." STEPHANIE'S voice sounded brighter than she'd intended. Aaron Caruthers had grown up quite a lot and... Well, wow. "Remember me?"

His expression shuttered so quickly, she swore she heard doors slamming. "You're still here." His tone was flat, almost angry.

That wasn't exactly the response she'd been expecting from a guy who used to have a crush on her. "Yup. Still here. And I brought friends." He stiffened as she introduced the burly men behind her. "This is Devon and Manny. Devon runs the computer shop on Main, and Manny—well, he does everything. They owe me and Georgette a few favors."

"But we came for the pie," Manny said, rubbing his hands.

"Is Georgette around?" Steph tried to peer past Aaron.

"I'm right here. Thank you so much for coming." The elderly woman stood in the kitchen entryway clutching the door frame.

Steph went straight to her, taking her hands.

"How are you feeling? Can I get you anything?" She started to lead her toward the sofa.

"No need to fuss around me in my own home, dear. Just tell me, how have things been at the bakery?"

"Everything's going smoothly. The new girl, Kira, is working out great."

"And you're handling the orders fine?"

"Piece of cake." She winked. "How are you?"

"Bored." She sighed. "And I miss all my grandchildren."

Steph smiled. Georgette called everyone under the age of forty her grandchildren. She'd been Everville's self-appointed grandmother since before Steph was born.

"She *works* for you?" Aaron's strident tone made Steph's hackles rise.

"Stephanie's been working at the bakery for... What has it been now?"

"Five years." She challenged him with the brightest grin she could manage. His face ticked—just like her girlfriends' had at Christmas. The corners of his mouth turned down.

"How about we start moving stuff in?" Devon suggested.

"Of course." The two frequent customers had been promised treats in exchange for their help, and in this chilly weather with darkness creeping in at barely five in the evening, she wanted to get this job done quickly, too.

The three men went out to the truck. Aaron unloaded boxes and directed Devon and Manny to carry them to their assigned rooms while Steph ensured no one tripped over anything. She was grateful to be inside, though Aaron's reception had been colder than the February weather. Not that she'd expected a hug or anything. She just didn't think he'd be so surprised to see her, considering how long she'd been working for his grandmother. She knew he visited at least once a year at Christmas. Georgette always talked about him and what he'd been up to. Had she not mentioned anything about her longtime employee to him?

Then again, why would she? It wasn't as if Aaron should care about her after all these years. They'd barely known each other back in high school.

She peeked out the window as the last of the boxes was hauled out. Aaron closed the truck's door, his long, lean form stretching to reveal a flat stomach and lean hips beneath his sweater. He was still kind of geeky-looking with his tousled brown hair and long limbs, but gone completely was the chubbiness of his high school days. He looked like a young professor, or maybe a grown-up Harry Potter in jeans and loafers. Mercifully, he didn't have those big wire-framed glasses anymore, though she'd noticed a pair tucked in his breast pocket. A certain type of girl might find that brainy look attractive, she decided.

The guys came in, and Steph helped Georgette set out the coffee and treats. Most of the boxes had been placed inside the empty guest bedroom, which she supposed had once been Aaron's. She wasn't sure why she was surprised not to find a trace of him there, though it made little sense for Georgette to keep his room intact after all these years. Packing up everything and leaving home for good was an alien concept to Steph. After she'd moved out just last month, Mom and Dad had promised to keep her room exactly as she'd left it so she wouldn't have to worry about finding storage space for what couldn't fit into her tiny apartment. They hadn't been happy about her leaving the nest, but she'd made it clear they couldn't stop her. And they hadn't.

After the coffee and spinach-and-goat-cheese pastries were laid out, Steph went into Aaron's room and started unpacking. She didn't feel as though she'd earned a treat yet, considering all she'd done was shuffle boxes around.

Three boxes into her digging, she discovered pretty much all Aaron owned was books. She exhumed the heavy law textbooks from the first box—the spines thoroughly bent and the pages marked with multicolored Post-it notes—and placed them on the bottom of the big brown bookshelves. The next box had an assortment of trade paperbacks, a lot of them with long titles about things she didn't know anything about. Peak oil, electric cars, global economics, science, history…

"What are you doing?" Aaron asked from the doorway.

"Just thought I'd help you shelve some of this stuff." She hefted one of the boxes, letting out an "oof!" It was a lot heavier than she'd thought.

Aaron rushed toward her. "Good God, you're going to break your back doing that."

"What, lifting this?" She bent her knees and jiggled the box. "Nah. I carry fifty-pound sacks of flour all the time." She'd always been at the bottom of cheer pyramids, too. Mom had never liked that other girls were standing on her, but she hadn't minded.

Georgette's grandson gave her a stern look. "Still." He gently slipped the box from her grasp and set it down with ease. "You don't need to do this."

"It's no problem." She flexed her aching fingers discreetly.

His eyes narrowed. "No, seriously. I'll do it myself."

"Really, it's no problem."

He frowned. "I'm particular about how I shelve my books."

The steel in his voice had her reconsidering. "Oookay." She took a step back, hands raised. "How about your clothes? I can fold them and put them—"

"Don't worry about it. I'll deal with everything later. Really."

Was there something he was hiding? Or did he simply not want her help? She hid her soreness at being dismissed by dusting her hands together as she left the room. "All right. You'll be at it all night, though."

He closed the bedroom door firmly behind him, and they rejoined the others in the kitchen.

"Not letting you help him unpack, is he?" Georgette chuckled when they entered. Devon and Manny were digging into their pastries with gusto. "Aaron's always been fussy about his things. He never even let me clean his room."

"That's because I can do it myself." Something about Aaron's tone irked Steph, as if he were implying she couldn't put things away *her*self. No. She shouldn't read into what other people said— Mom told her she got defensive sometimes without proving...provoke...*provocation*. It wasn't as if she had any reason to react so strongly to Aaron.

He shook hands with Manny and Devon. "I appreciate the help today, guys," he said.

"Anything for Georgette's spinach pies," Manny said, toasting him with his coffee.

"Oh, Aaron, you should talk to Devon about getting Wi-Fi installed at the bakery. I think he's done it for other businesses in town."

"Why do you need Wi-Fi?" Steph asked.

Georgette beamed. "Aaron's going to renovate the bakery's dining room and turn it into a bookstore."

Steph stared, her feet suddenly cold. She tried to hide her shock and simply look interested in what was being said, as she'd been taught, but she felt her whole future and everything she'd been working toward slipping from her grasp as readily as the smile from her face.

"But…where will the customers eat?" she managed to ask.

"I'll still keep a few tables in the main part of the bakery, but most of the business has always been takeout anyhow," Aaron explained. "Plus, I'm adding a patio for the warmer months."

What did he even know about what business was like at Georgette's? He hadn't worked there in the five years she'd been there. "When were you going to do all this?"

"As soon as possible. I'm meeting a few contractors on Monday. I want renovations done by the end of April so we can be open for patio weather."

And when, exactly, had they planned on telling her about these changes? After all she'd done for Georgette's, wasn't she owed at least an explanation?

Sure, Steph was only an employee, but she was a damned good one. She was the only person Georgette had trusted with her recipes, the only person capable of running things solo since Georgette's stroke a few weeks ago. She'd hoped the elderly baker would sell the business to her when she retired—clearly the eighty-two-year-old couldn't run it by herself anymore.

But now Aaron Caruthers was here, nosing in and ruining all her plans.

Her throat tightened and her tongue felt thick as objections tumbled one on top of the other. She was so frustrated she couldn't spit out a single word of protest.

They were still talking, but she couldn't understand what they were saying. She was drowning in words, all of them mashed into a messy jumble by her building anxiety. She wanted to tell them this wasn't what she wanted, that this wasn't what she'd planned, but she couldn't say it without sounding petulant.

"I'm hoping the two of you will work together," she heard Georgette say. "Steph knows everything about how the bakery runs. I don't mind change, you know, but I do want some parts of what your grandfather and I built to remain intact."

A lifeline. Steph smiled gratefully with the knowledge that Georgette had secured her place in the world.

"Of course, Gran." Aaron hugged her shoulders briefly. "I promise you'll be included in all the big decisions."

And just like that, Aaron had cut Steph out of the business, despite being ordered to work with her. He hadn't even *looked* at her. Her blood rushed through her veins, swift and hot, so that the sting of dismissal vibrated across her nerves. She'd been certain Georgette had been grooming her to take over one day. What did Aaron even know about baking?

She took a deep, calming breath. There was no sense in complaining and being indite...*indignant* about it now. She'd just have to show Georgette she was not only indispensable, but also the right person to take over the bakery.

AARON LISTENED WITH half an ear as the contractor led him through the estimate on the dining room renovations. He was already aware of some of the larger costs, knew where he could save money by doing the work himself. It was the woman behind the counter who was distracting him.

Stephanie Stephens. He couldn't believe she was still in Everville. She hadn't changed a bit, outwardly—she still had that perfect brass-blond hair that she kept tied in a high ponytail and that fantastic cheerleader's figure with curves and muscles in all the right places.

He shook himself. He wasn't that kid anymore, lusting after a football player's trophy girlfriend. Never again would he humiliate himself over Stephanie Stephens.

He silently listed all the reasons they weren't right for each other and never had been. Sure, he'd fantasized about tutoring her, about how lending her his notes might actually lead to something more meaningful. And he'd lent her pens whenever she hadn't had one, which was frequently. How many pens had she borrowed and never returned?

Twenty-three.

Yes, he'd counted. Nearly a whole box of his favorite roller balls that he'd never asked she return. Except that one time. He'd learned his lesson then not to trust anything with her—not even a pen.

And here she was, working at his grandmother's bakery, losing who knew how many pens' worth of income a day.

He refocused on the contractor's words as the man gave him estimated completion dates. The guy's rates were reasonable and he was friendly enough, but Aaron was interviewing one more contractor that afternoon. This was going to be his business, after all, and he had to get the best rates wherever he could. He was nothing if not thorough.

The part-timer, Kira, a lean high schooler with short dark hair and thick-framed glasses, was busy serving a customer while Steph blabbed away with a woman holding a baby. Two other people waited patiently behind them.

Aaron scowled. Did the woman have any sense? She should be working, not chatting with her friends.

"Excuse me a moment," he said to the contractor, then marched over to Steph. The woman she was chatting to handed her the baby, and Aaron was

taken aback a moment as she bounced the drooling, babbling bundle of joy and cooed at her.

"Um, Steph?"

"Oh, hey, Aaron." Her demeanor was a touch
cooler than it had been with her friend. She nodded. "Isabel, this is Aaron Caruthers, Georgette's
grandson. He's come back to...take care of things."

"Nice to meet you." They shook hands. "How's
Georgette doing?"

"Better, thanks for asking." He didn't want to be
rude, but customers were still waiting. He turned to
Steph. "Would you mind looking after those folks
there, Steph?"

She stared at him, her cheeks tinting darker and
darker. The baby patted her hair as if reminding her
to breathe. She handed the squirming child back to
Isabel. "Excuse me."

"I'd better get going." The mother paused. "I'm
sorry—I didn't mean to distract Stephanie."

"It's not your fault," he said, feeling bad now for
interrupting. Isabel was a customer, too, after all.
But time was money...

He glanced at Steph. She moved slowly, as if she
were picking flowers in a field rather than filling
orders. If that was her usual pace, he could imagine how much business the bakery lost on a daily
basis. And now, Steph was chatting up the next
person in line and—

Was she giving out free cookies?

Aaron didn't have time to ask, though, because

the contractor had come up and was telling him he had to leave on his next call. Aaron thanked him and saw him out the door, but not before Steph ducked out lickety-split from behind the counter and handed him a coffee and a brown bag. Why couldn't she move that fast to serve *paying* customers? Aaron thought irritably.

"Fresh doughnut and coffee for you," she told the man happily. "No one leaves Georgette's empty-handed."

The contractor's face brightened "Oh, I couldn't—"

"Of course you can." She pushed the treats at him. "It's cold out there. You need to keep warm, and this is just the thing to do it."

The man chuckled. "I hope I get this job if this is the daily take-home." He shook Aaron's hand. "Give me a call. We can play with some numbers if we have to."

He left. Aaron turned to tell Steph to stop handing out freebies, but her look froze his tongue. "Excuse me, I have customers."

He might have snapped back at her, but that would've been unprofessional. Still, Georgette's wouldn't survive if this was how business was conducted every day. Who knew how much Stephanie was costing his grandmother? He wasn't about to throw any accusations around, though. Not without evidence. After all, he was nothing if not thorough.

SWEAT DRIPPED OFF the tip of Steph's nose as she polished the countertops and fumed.

Aaron had always been a stick-in-the-mud, but now he'd become a grade-A prick. Embarrassing her in front of Isabel. Really! Where did he get off telling her what to do? He didn't own Georgette's. He wasn't her boss. He'd only arrived yesterday.

"I'm done here," Kira said, removing her apron. "Is it okay if I take off? I have a lot of homework."

"Sure thing." She put on a smile for Kira's benefit. The timid but eager girl didn't need to be exposed to her bad mood. "Thanks. You did great today."

"Hey, can I ask you a question?" Kira moved closer and glanced at the closed office door where Aaron counted the till. "Is Aaron taking over for Georgette?"

Steph sucked in her lower lip. "I don't know." *I hope not.* "He's got plans to open a bookstore where the dining room is. I'm not sure how that'll work with the bakery attached."

Kira wrinkled her nose. "If they do renos it's going to make a huge mess. How're you gonna bake?"

Steph hadn't thought of that, but Kira was right. They'd lose all kinds of business while Aaron worked on his precious bookshop, and Georgette's couldn't afford that. They were barely breaking even as it was.

She had no choice. She had to talk to Georgette. Aaron would ruin the business with these plans of his, and it was up to Stephanie to stop him.

CHAPTER THREE

"WHAT ARE YOU SAYING, exactly?" Georgette peered up at Aaron over her plate of spaghetti.

"I just want to know if you've ever noticed any discrepancies at the register." There was no way to broach the topic lightly. He was concerned by what he'd seen today. The till had been short nearly fifty dollars, and the ledgers for the past two months showed a steady decline in revenue. How was Gran keeping up with the bills?

"Nothing out of the ordinary," she said, cutting her noodles with her spoon. Aaron had noticed she had a little difficulty chewing—he'd have to ask the doctor about that at her next appointment.

"So you're always short at the till?" he prodded.

"Short, over, both. It all works out in the end." She shrugged. "I assume it's simply my old eyes counting wrong."

"Does Steph ever count the till?"

"Occasionally. She certainly would've while I've been away."

From what he'd seen, the same pattern had emerged, with tills under and over by some amount at closing time, but made up for the next day. The receipts roughly matched the takings by week's end, though, so at least they weren't dealing with sticky fingers…he hoped.

It wasn't as if Stephanie needed the money—her family was filthy stinking rich. If she was stealing, it had to be for the thrill of it. Somehow, that didn't strike him as Steph's style, but what did he know?

"How did your meetings with the contractors go?" Georgette asked, changing the subject.

"Good. I've decided to go with Ollie White. He gave the best rate, and he seems like an upstanding guy."

"Ollie's good," Georgette agreed. "But I do wish you'd considered hiring Jimmy Tremont."

"Gran, he's not a licensed contractor." She'd brought him up when Aaron had started talking renos. The guy had lost his job at a processing plant last month. "I'm not paying some random guy for a big job like this."

Georgette moved the food around her plate demurely. "He's hit hard times, Aaron. We try to help each other out around here."

"He's not even insured. And I'd end up paying him under the table."

"But you'd keep food on his family's table," she said, studiously eating her cut-up spaghetti.

Aaron sighed. Gran was a softie, taking in strays and playing patron saint to the hungry and down-on-their-luck. Not that he didn't appreciate her generous spirit—he'd been one of those poor lost souls once. "I'll see if there are any small jobs he can handle," he said. He'd already planned to do the painting himself: Jimmy could help him with that and a few other finishing touches.

"By the way, Stephanie called me. She was concerned about how the renovations would affect business. She's worried about the mess it would make."

"I've already consulted Ollie about this. He even talked to Ben, the health inspector in town. We can keep the bakery open. Everything's going to be isolated in the dining room. As long as we seal it off and keep a ventilation fan pointed outside, we should be fine. Knocking down the dividing wall and tearing up the flooring will take less than a day. It's the electrical and drywall and finishing touches that take time."

"It takes weeks for plaster dust to settle, Aaron. Don't get me wrong. I'm excited for this project of yours, and I wouldn't think of stopping you. But... I'm hoping you'll reassure Stephanie."

Aaron stuffed a forkful of noodles in his mouth and chewed to hide the tick in his cheek. "She's got nothing to worry about."

"She's a sensitive girl. She doesn't handle change easily."

Well, that's too bad. But he knew it was unfair to be so coldhearted. Gran liked her and had hired her, and that should be enough for him to at least give her a chance.

Privately, he admitted he'd been rude to her. Not because of what she'd done to him in high school, and not because he suspected she was costing his grandmother hundreds if not thousands of dollars. It was because her very presence upset his equilibrium. Made him lose focus. As far as he could tell, she was still the same girl she'd been in high school: flaky, flighty and so self-centered that she was oblivious to what was going on around her.

And he was still attracted to her. It made no sense. At all.

She wasn't his type—not anymore. He shouldn't be feeling anything for her. But the line between grudge and the burning regret that accompanied unrequited love was blurring rapidly. He hated that her reappearance in his life should give rise to such angst.

He was a grown man, dammit. And he had adult things to take care of.

"I'll talk to Stephanie," he said shortly.

"Good. It means a lot to me that you're both trying so hard to keep the bakery going. Your grandfather would be proud." She put her spoon down carefully. "I think I'm done here."

"You barely ate."

"I haven't had much appetite." She wrinkled her nose. "It's probably the medications."

He frowned. "When's your next appointment?

I'll go with you and we can ask the doctor to switch your prescription."

"Don't worry about it, dear. You need to focus on this book business."

"No, I need to focus on *you*. The bookstore is second. Anyhow, once the renos begin, I can't do much on-site. I'll be contacting publishers and ordering inventory, but I can do that from home." When Georgette looked as if she was going to argue, he said, "I'm your grandson. You took care of me. Let me take care of you, okay?"

She patted his arm with a rueful twist of the lips. "You're a good boy, Aaron."

Not good enough if he couldn't keep Gran happy and healthy and make sure the bakery survived.

"Aaron Caruthers…" Helen Stephens drew the name out over the phone later that week as if it were taffy. "No, I can't honestly say I remember him. Did he come to your graduation party?"

"It wasn't a *grad* party, it was an end-of-school party." Despite the fact that she hadn't graduated with the rest of her class, her parents had let her throw the bash anyhow, complete with a DJ, catering and decorations. They'd even bought the beer kegs. The football team and cheerleaders had had a wild night, vomiting everywhere but in the toilet and breaking one of Mom's favorite vases. Helen hadn't been that upset. She'd just wanted her only daughter to be happy. "Aaron *definitely* wasn't there."

"Are you sure? There were so many kids I couldn't keep their names straight."

"Trust me, Mom, he wasn't there." Back then, Steph wouldn't have been caught dead inviting someone like Aaron to her party. He'd been one of those nerdy, intense kids who nobody had understood whenever he'd opened his mouth. She was seriously regretting not being nicer to him now.

"In any case, it doesn't sound like he's doing anything unreasonable. He left his life behind to take care of his grandmother. That's quite a sacrifice for a man to make."

"But he's *taking over*," she said, an exasperated whine pitching her voice. She cut herself off ruthlessly, pressing a fist against her lips. At the moment she was a particular kind of frustrated— the kind that couldn't be placated with a few kind words—and she was having a hard time communicating that to her mother. "I've worked there five years. *I'm* the one who knows how everything works. *I'm* the one who knows all of Georgette's recipes. He's been there a week and he acts like he owns the place."

"He's entitled to it. Blood is thicker than batter, and he's Georgette's grandson. Why, we'll be lucky if the place doesn't shut down after she kicks the bucket."

"Mom!" Steph gasped.

"I don't mean that in a mean way, dear. I don't want to see her go any more than you do. Where else would we get our croissants?"

Stephanie set her teeth. Mom wasn't shallow, but she did have a habit of trivializing bad things to avoid thinking about them. "Georgette's not going to die. Not anytime soon." Not before Steph could convince her to sell the bakery to her, and not for a long time after, either. Steph would take care of Georgette herself if it came down to it. She loved her as if she were her own grandmother.

"Everyone dies, dear. All the more reason to find a special someone and give me some grandchildren as soon as possible."

Not this again. *"Mom."* A headache gathered between Steph's eyes. "I told you, I'm trying to find myself right now. I don't want to be involved with anyone until I figure out who *I* am." Thank God for daytime talk shows. One of the many *Stop Controlling My Life!* episodes had given her those words to practice.

"*I* know who you are." Helen's sweet voice was tinged with a sour bite. "You're my daughter. You're a sweet, beautiful, kind, lovely young woman."

"But I'm *more* than that. At least, I know I can be. I've spent too much time stuck in a rut. I want more."

"Like living on your own in a tiny little apartment when you could be comfortable here at home?" Whenever Helen was miffed she made a noise through her nose that sounded like a pig whistling through a teakettle, as she did now. "I understand that you want to spread your wings, but wouldn't it be better if you went away—on a trip? We could send you to Europe. Shake off your wanderlust before you decide to settle down. Maybe you'll even meet someone abroad."

Steph massaged her temples. Her mother had a one-track mind. "This isn't about wanderlust." They'd had this argument every time she'd called since moving out. After the reunion, she'd made it her mission to move on and up in life. Moving out of her parents' house had been the first big step. "And I can't settle down. Not right now."

"Listen to me, baby. I thought the same thing when I was twenty-five. Your father and I were still young and we thought we had all the time in the world. But when we were ready for kids, we tried and tried... We wanted four kids, you know that?"

She closed her eyes. "I know, Mom."

"It wasn't until very late in the game that we finally had you. But there were complications. I was sick for weeks afterward, and the doctor said I couldn't risk having any more children. I still thank God every day I have you, our perfect little angel."

Every time Helen told this story guilt pooled in Steph's gut. "That's sweet of you to say, Mom, but—"

"You're *thirty*, dear." She made it sound like a curse. "Don't you *want* to have kids?"

"Of course, but—"

"Then you need to think about that." Her words were precise, final, loaded with prim admonishment.

Stephanie mouthed a curse at the ceiling. This was exactly why she'd needed to move out. Living at home, she'd accepted her mother's wishes that she go forth and multiply as if that were her only purpose in life. And, for a while, she'd believed it. After Dale, she'd dated a lot, including men her parents had found for her, but no one had held her interest long enough to sound the wedding bells. Her Mom once had accused her of being picky, and they'd gotten into a big argument. That'd been around the same time Steph had started working for Georgette.

"You're coming next weekend, aren't you?" Helen asked, her tone switching back to honeysweet.

"For Dad's birthday party? Of course. Once all the morning baking's done, Kira should be able to handle the counter. And Aaron will be there, I guess." She grudgingly accepted that he'd take care of things at the bakery and make sure his grandmother got her rest. She'd almost canceled on her mom, but Georgette wouldn't hear of her missing Terrence Stephens's sixtieth birthday.

"Good. Because there's someone I'd like you to meet."

Steph suppressed a sigh. "You're not trying to set me up again, are you?"

"You'll like him," Helen insisted. "You really will. He's a rancher we met at the club last week—"

"I'll come to the party, but don't expect anything." Steph would be polite, but she made no promises. She was determined to become the best Stephanie Stephens she could be, and for now, that meant no dating.

AARON RUBBED THE crust from his eyes, cursing the cold, dark February morning. Six o'clock was way too early to be up and driving, but he'd wanted the contractors to get the dining room sealed before the bakery opened at seven.

Only one other car was in the lot—a rather nice Mercedes mini SUV. As he got out of his Gran's station wagon, his foot met a patch of ice. With a yelp, he snagged the door before he slid under the chassis, then regained his footing, cursing. The slick parking lot was a lawsuit waiting to happen. He'd have to take care of that.

Unlocking the door to Georgette's, his mood was temporarily dispelled by the sweet smell of baking.

He inhaled, thinking of happier times. Mom and Dad taking him to visit his grandmother; carefully choosing the one treat he'd take home with him in the car—it was almost always a bran muffin, though he'd sometimes choose an oatmeal cookie;

enjoying the long, winding drive out of Everville to see the fall colors...

His walk down memory lane came to an abrupt halt as he entered the kitchen and tripped on an open bag of flour. He managed to right it before it spilled onto the ground.

Steph glanced up from a mixing bowl. Her brassy hair was tied up in two pigtails, and a hair-net hung off them like a saggy black spiderweb. Her white apron was stained with smears of choc-olate and batter, and there was a dusting of flour on her cheek, but she glowed with sunny cheer. "Good morning," she greeted brightly. "Two cups of brown sugar." He was confused for a moment as she emptied a measuring cup into a large bowl. "Watch your step, there."

He grabbed the bag and dragged it out of his path. "What are you doing here so early?" he asked irately.

"Uh...baking? I've been here since four."

Duh. Of course. He *so* wasn't a morning person. "You didn't salt the parking lot."

Her smile faltered. "Huh?"

"The parking lot. It's covered in black ice. I slipped out there. Could've broken my tailbone."

The rays of happiness wreathing her face dis-appeared as if clouds had gathered around her. "A pound of butter," she muttered as she dumped the cubes into the mixing bowl. She stirred, her arm working hard. "Sorry to hear that," she said to him.

She wasn't. And she wasn't taking him seriously. Just another indication of how thoughtless and self-absorbed she was. She hadn't changed a bit. "I'd appreciate it if you could have taken a minute to make sure other people weren't getting hurt by your carelessness. If someone broke a leg out there—"

She slammed her spatula onto the worktable. "Look, if you're not going to be helpful, I need you to get out of my way. I have a lot to bake still and I have three cake orders to fill today. You do what you need to do, but I don't have time to deal with icy parking lots or whatever your problem is."

For a moment, Aaron was shocked by her flash of temper. More surprising was the shame he felt. Barging in and acting like a tyrant wasn't his style. He needed to get a grip.

"I'm sorry. I apologize. I didn't mean to snap at you. I…" He shook his head. "I need coffee."

With a glare, she pointed toward the door. "On the counter up front. A quarter teaspoon of salt." Her dismissal was clear, even if her instructions to herself were perplexing.

He pushed out of the kitchen, went to the carafe and filled a mug. His first big gulp scalded his tongue, bringing tears to his eyes. He deserved that. He'd been an asshat to Steph for no reason except that he was cranky and had slipped on some ice.

She clearly resented his presence at Georgette's. Maybe she'd thought *she* was going to inherit the bakery. He hadn't considered that before, but it would explain that hunted look she often bore, as if she were expecting him to kick her out any minute. He might not do that, but there was no way Aaron would allow Stephanie Stephens to run his grandmother's legacy into the ground, either. He may never have woken up at four in the morning to bake, but he knew how to run the business. Besides, he was family. His grandmother would never choose a former cheerleader over her own kin.

Family or no, Georgette would not be pleased to hear they'd already started off on the wrong foot. He needed to smooth things out with Steph.

He took a few minutes to scatter deicer and sand over the front steps, around the lot and along the walkway. When he got back inside, he was shivering, but the bracing cold had cleared his head a little. He took a deep breath and pushed back into the kitchen.

"Stephanie." She flicked him the briefest of glares, and he continued. "Look, I was out of line. It was rude of me to talk to you that way. I appreciate that you're busy. It can't be easy doing all the baking on your own."

The chill in her storm-blue eyes thawed some, but she didn't stop moving as she spooned batter into muffin tins. "It's not."

"What can I do to help?"

She gave him a pensive frown. "Aren't your contractors coming?"

"I already moved the tables and chairs and stuff

out of the dining room, so all I can do now is wait. Guess they're a bit behind." The recent snowfall had made the roads treacherous. "Did you prep the croissants yet?"

She blinked. "No. They're—"

"Ready-made in the freezer. Eight to a tray at 425 degrees, right?" He smiled lopsidedly. "I remember a few things from working with Gran."

The puzzled look on her face wasn't entirely hostile, so that was progress.

He got to work laying the frozen premade pastries onto baking sheets. Georgette always made large batches of croissants and froze them for use in the bakery, but people also ordered boxes of them frozen to bake at home. As he worked, he could hear Stephanie muttering to herself under her breath. At first he thought she was grumbling about him, but then he realized she was reciting the recipes she was working on. How odd.

He popped the trays into the oven as the contractors arrived. After a round of coffee, he worked with Ollie for the rest of the morning as they sealed the dining room with thick sheets of plastic taped across the entryway. They decided the workmen could access the area from a rarely used side entrance in the dining room. When they were done closing off the work space, the bakery felt a whole lot smaller.

The sun, a pale gold button against a silvery sky, peeked in through the shop's wide, lace-curtained windows. Stephanie came out and started loading trays of goodies into the display cases, then made a fresh pot of coffee. She frowned at the rippling translucent bubble of plastic as the door in the dining room was propped open. The cozy warmth was quickly sucked from the bakery.

"Is it going to be like this all month?" she asked, hastily pulling on a zip-up hoodie.

"I'll see about getting some space heaters in here." Aaron rubbed his arms.

She blew out a breath and mumbled something as she went back into the kitchen. Aaron followed her. "Listen, Steph. We need to talk. I realize I've kind of barged in here without any real warning. These renos must've come out of left field to you."

She gave him a flat look, confirming his suspicions. She wasn't displeased; she was *pissed*. "I promise, I'll do everything I can to keep things running smoothly, but we need to get this right the first time. I want to make this bookstore work for my grandmother's sake and make sure the bakery stays afloat."

She regarded him doubtfully. "That all sounds great, but I'm not sure you really *know* what's best."

He scowled. "Why do you say that?"

"You're starting a new business while Georgette's still recovering from a stroke." She propped a hand against her hip. "That's the opposite of being by her side and taking care of her. If it were me, I'd be with her 24/7."

His temperature spiked, and he clenched his fists. "If it were you—" He cut himself off. He didn't appreciate her criticism. She could hardly claim to know what was best… But he refused to argue about this. She was entitled to her opinions, even if they were damned wrong. Calmly, he said, "I have things under control. My grandmother wouldn't want me around her constantly, and I'd only make her feel worse if I hung around the house all day, watching her, waiting for something bad to happen. This bookstore is for the future, to make sure what she built endures."

"And it's your own pet project."

He pushed his glasses up his nose. "Of course it is. I can't give up my whole life for one person. In all honesty, yes, this is as much for me as it is for Gran. And it's my way of giving back to the town."

She looked away. It took her a moment to respond. "Right. Sorry. I shouldn't be criticizing you. I'm sure you love your grandmother very much and want to do what's best."

Mollified, he straightened. "I do. And I will." He firmly believed in his business plan, and so had the bank. Everville hadn't had a bookstore since Mr. Williamson's shop had closed when Aaron was fifteen. It'd been a major loss to Aaron personally. Reading had been his one great solace in the years following his parents' deaths. The library was all right, but the town hadn't had the money to keep it well stocked and up to date.

This bookshop was more than his fresh start. It was his way of making sure kids like him had a place to find and lose themselves. Being able to keep Gran's bakery going was icing on the cake.

"Don't worry, Stephanie," he said. "I promise I'll be a better boss."

Spite flashed in her eyes, hard and glittering. She didn't say anything as she marched back into the kitchen. The swinging door slapped the air behind her, and a chill seeped through his sweater and into his bones.

For crying out loud. What had he said now?

CHAPTER FOUR

STEPH'S PAYCHECK DIDN'T allow for extravagances like bottles of good French merlot, but today, she seriously needed to indulge.

Her friend Maya Hanes watched as she dumped the last three inches from the bottle into the bowl of her oversize wineglass. "Should you be drinking so much with your early start tomorrow?"

"I don't see how I *couldn't* be driven to drink considering the ignor...arro...*arrogance* of that man." Stumbling over the word in front of Maya only added to her frustration, but her friend kindly ignored it. She'd told Maya about how Aaron had made it clear where they stood: he was going to be her boss, and she had no say in the matter.

Maya reached for another one of Steph's chocolate-dipped macaroons. "Maybe this is a good thing. I mean, if he hadn't come back and something happened to Georgette—"

"Why does everyone keep thinking the worst? Georgette's fine. She's had a stroke, sure, but she's nowhere near..." She couldn't even bring herself to say it.

"All I'm saying is that Aaron means well, and he's doing what he thinks is best. It's not as if he's fired you."

"He might, though. I don't know what he has planned." She took a bracing gulp. "He could replace me."

"Hon, c'mon. I know you're upset, but I doubt Aaron would go that far. You're the only one apart from Georgette who knows her recipes."

"He doesn't like me. He's had it in for me since high school." She sat back and stared into her wine, brooding. "I wasn't very nice to him."

"That was a *long* time ago. I'd think—or at least I'd *hope*—you'd both have grown beyond that."

Maybe. Sometimes, everything about Steph's life felt stalled, as if she still had one foot stuck in high school. Aaron's return brought that home. It seemed fitting somehow that the past should come back to ruin her future.

"You need to give this time to work itself out," Maya said. "See how Aaron handles things. You said it yourself—he'll be busy with the bookstore side of the business. That probably means you'll be free to run the bakery by yourself."

"As an employee, maybe. But I want to *own* Georgette's and run it on *my* terms."

Maya tilted her chin. "Why's that so important to you?"

"*You* own your own business. I want the same things you have—to be my own boss and make my own hours." Steph didn't know how to explain that in her eyes, Georgette's was the epi…epistle… *epitome* of independence. Owning the bakery had been a longtime fantasy before the elderly baker had gotten sick, but now that dream was within her grasp. And she felt ashamed for thinking that way.

"I'm kinda surprised you haven't opened your own shop," Maya said, holding up a macaroon. "Your recipes are fantastic. I bet your folks would lend you the start-up money, too."

Steph shook her head emphatically. "Oh, hell, no. I don't want my parents to have a stake in any business of mine. Anyhow, I would never go into competition with Georgette. She taught me everything she knows. I can't stab her in the back."

Maya chuckled. "If you want to own a business, you have to be a little mercenary sometimes." Maya would know. She'd bought the consignment shop on Main Street for a song about nine months ago. She now specialized in vintage clothing and wore the most awesome outfits. She'd even helped dress all Helen's friends for a *Mad Men* party she had thrown. "Do you even know what it takes to keep the bakery going?" Maya asked, peering at Steph through her cat's-eye glasses.

"Of course I do," she said, then faltered. "I mean, I've worked there a long time…"

"Well, you baked and did all the front counter stuff, sure, but you didn't handle the background responsibilities. Making sure the shop complied with health regulations, filling out tax forms..."

"I can learn to do all that if Georgette gives me a chance. Or I can hire someone."

She knew Maya was only trying to make her see the reality of the situation. Even so, Steph couldn't help but feel affronted, as if Maya didn't think much of her abilities or ambitions. People were always waiting for Steph to make a mistake and give up.

"So what are you going to do?" Maya prodded. "Quit?"

"And do what? Go home a failure?" She gulped her wine and exhaled a heady cloud of vapor. "No way. Aaron can't scare me away. And neither can my parents or you, for that matter."

Maya grinned. "Good. I hate it when you play helpless little rich girl." She toasted her. "Sorry to act all mean, but I wanted to make sure you weren't..."

"Being a flake?" Steph supplied.

Maya's lips quirked. "Your words."

She knew she could rely on Maya for the honest truth. They hadn't been close in high school, but Steph appreciated her bluntness—and patience—now. She needed a regular dose of reality, something that had been lacking in her life, living at home with parents who gave her anything and everything she wanted. No one had ever criticized her, either, or if they had, it had never been to her face.

Or maybe she'd simply ignored it. She'd been frustrated by her grades, of course, but so many other parts of her life had been great, like her relationship with Dale, cheerleading and all the clubs she'd been in. Her parents hadn't minded the Cs and Ds on her report cards, though they had frowned at the handful of Fs she'd earned. In hindsight, she wished her parents had been a little tougher on her, but she knew her poor academic performance was all on her.

She understood now that if she really wanted something, she had to earn it, the way she had with her job and her apartment. Hard work and discipline had been the key to her independence, and now that she'd had a taste, she wasn't about to give up any of it. She had to win Georgette's favor if she was ever going to take over the bakery.

"So, what are you going to do about Aaron?" Maya prompted.

"I'd like to pour a bowl of batter over his head." That was the wine talking, of course. She heaved a sigh. "I'll stay on, I guess. What else can I do?"

"Well, if things get intolerable, quitting is always an option."

"Didn't you just say I *shouldn't* quit?"

"You shouldn't quit without really thinking about it, is what I meant. But I wouldn't want you staying there if you were miserable, either. No one would judge you for leaving if you were unhappy."

Steph didn't believe that for a moment, because

she'd judge herself. Working at Georgette's wasn't just a job to her. It represented everything she was working toward—financial independence, security, stability and professional pride. Maybe to some people her job looked like a way for a rich girl to pass time. But Georgette's Bakery was an institution. One that would fall apart in Aaron Caruthers's hands if she didn't make sure she was involved.

And to do that, she was going to have to play nice.

AARON ARRIVED AT Georgette's at quarter after nine. He would have been there when the bakery opened, but he'd wanted to go with his grandmother to her doctor's appointment and hear what the specialist had to say. Georgette would be visiting a physical therapist once a week to work on her mobility issues, and she would need to do daily exercises to get back the strength in her hands. The doctor assured them she was well on the road to recovery, but Aaron was going to keep a close eye on her.

He entered the bakery and found Steph chatting up a customer. She excused herself and brought him a steaming mug. "Fresh coffee?" She smiled brightly.

"Uh...thanks." He took the mug and headed to the office. Steph followed.

"Listen—" she lingered in the doorway "—I

want to say I'm sorry if I've acted nastily toward you. I think it's great that you're back for Georgette."

He blinked. She sounded like she meant it, but then he wasn't sure she'd ever given anyone a smile that wasn't carefully calculated to extrude the maximum result.

Oh, hey, Aaron, can I borrow a pen? Can I borrow your notes?

Can I borrow your heart so I can stomp all over it?

"Okay," he responded noncommittally. He'd apologized plenty for his poor behavior already. Still, it didn't feel right not to reciprocate. But with each second that passed, it got harder and harder to jump into that conversation. They lapsed into an awkward stalemate.

He picked up the binder of invoices his grandmother kept for supply orders and set up his laptop. He didn't realize until he looked up that Steph was still standing in the doorway watching him. "Something you want?" He cursed his curt tone. *Tell her you're sorry and that you appreciate her, too, idiot.*

She smiled faintly. "Just curious about what you're up to."

He patted the binder, glad for something else to talk about. "I'm looking at cutting some costs, getting quotes from other suppliers."

Steph gasped. "You can't do that."

"Why not?"

"You can't...*change* things." She gestured emptily, her movements shaky. "We have long, established relationships with our suppliers."

"If that's true, they should be offering you a better deal for what you order."

"They already do." Her voice rose, almost threateningly.

Aaron struggled to keep his tone even. "Not good enough. Not after nearly fifty years in business." Was she going to question and fight him on every decision? "Look, all I'm trying to do is make sure the bakery stays in the black, but it's dangerously close. We need to reduce our expenses."

Her eyes widened. "You're going to cut our hours?"

That wasn't what he'd said—her reaction was typically self-centered. He opened his mouth to reassure her that her job was safe, but realized he couldn't make any promises. Not until he'd gotten a real handle on the financial situation. "You should get back to the front," he said instead, glancing past the door and not feeling particularly sorry to end this conversation. "There are customers."

She looked as though she was going to say something else, but then whirled and made a quiet huffing noise.

Five minutes later, though, she was back. "I'm sorry...again. I'm used to doing things a certain way and...you're right," she admitted with effort.

She rubbed a palm up and down her hip and grudgingly added, "Cutting costs is good for business."

He studied her. She was really trying. To what end, he wasn't sure. But Gran had wanted him to work with her, so he had to make the effort, as well. "Sit down. I want to hear your thoughts. You must have some ideas on how to make things more efficient. You'd know where best to make cuts."

She sat gingerly, gripping her knees. "Well… I'm not really sure. We can't change the recipes."

"I wouldn't dream of it." He knew how proprietary Gran was of her recipes. She kept them in a binder in her safe at home. She wouldn't even type them up on the computer, afraid a hacker would somehow steal her life's work. He'd tried to explain that it didn't work that way since she didn't have internet access at home—something he'd soon change—but she was a bit of a Luddite.

Stephanie paused. "I've always thought it would save us a little work to prepackage some of the best-selling cookies during the summer months for the tourists, to help move them through more quickly."

"That's a good idea." He wrote it down.

"Labels for the bagged goodies would be nice, too. Like pretty stickers we could put on bags and tie with some gold ribbon."

That would cost money, and wouldn't necessarily translate into sales, but he noted it.

She rattled off a few more ideas—most of them were more about how the bakery looked rather than how it functioned, but he agreed the place could use a new coat of paint and maybe a change of curtains. "These are good ideas," he said.

"Thanks."

He put his pen down. Now that he had her attention, he needed to make an effort to be friendly. "So what happened to you after high school?" he asked. "We haven't really talked."

"You first," she insisted. "You went to college, right?"

"Harvard Law School," he confirmed, not without a little pride. He'd received a handsome scholarship and had worked part-time to feed and clothe himself. He'd been inching his way up the corporate ladder at the firm, but when Gran had gotten sick, he'd dropped everything. The truth was, he'd never really been into his job. He was an entrepreneur at heart.

Steph prodded, "No girlfriend?"

That was an awfully personal question. "Nope."

"No one? Not even someone you'd categorize as 'It's complicated'?"

"That sounds exhausting."

She rested her chin in a hand. "I take it that means no. How about a dog? Cat? Hamster?"

"I'm allergic to animal fur." Irked by her pitying frown, he added, "I'm not lonely. I date occasionally. I have friends." And then he felt stupid for getting defensive.

The truth was most of the women he'd been with

hadn't captured his attention. Not the way Steph did, perched on the edge of her chair, her focus on him. She'd always been like that, making you feel as if you were the only person in the world she wanted to talk to. But she'd been manipulative, too, knowing she could get what she wanted if she made you feel special enough.

It infuriated him that he should feel a twinge of attraction now.

"So, what about you?" he asked, turning the questioning back onto her. "Did you go to college?"

Her chin dipped. "No."

"Oh. I'd have thought you could study anywhere in the world."

"I didn't have the grades. Actually, I never finished high school."

Aaron sucked in a breath. He knew she hadn't graduated with the rest of their class, but he'd assumed an extra semester would have solved that problem. "How many credits did you have left?"

She picked at her apron strings. "Just one."

He caught his jaw before it dropped. "And all this time later, you still haven't completed it?"

"Why bother?" She scowled.

"Why—" He wiped a palm down his face. "You need a high school diploma. That's a basic requirement for any job."

"Says who?" She tipped her nose in the air. "I didn't need one to work here."

"But...basic math skills..." He bit his lip. He hadn't meant to say anything about that.

Steph's eyes narrowed. "What do you mean 'basic math skills'? You think I can't add or something?"

"I couldn't help but notice you've made some mistakes on the till, is all. I thought maybe..." Lord, he hadn't intended to bring this up now. He'd had some suspicions, but he hardly knew what to say. Unable to veer off this course, he asked, "You had a hard time in math, didn't you?"

"Really? We're going to compare report cards now?" She crossed her arms over her chest. "Since you're asking, I had a hard time in lots of things." She sniffed. "But I don't need a piece of paper to prove I can bake."

"You could at least have gotten your high school equivalency diploma. Don't you care what people think?"

"Are you *judging* me?"

"No, of course not." But he'd taken a second too long to answer, and now she pierced him with a dagger-eyed look.

"You think I'm dumb, don't you?" Her voice was dangerously low.

Uh-oh. "I never said that. Maybe you have... issues."

Her expression shifted from angry to stone cold. "What the hell do you mean by *issues*?"

He hastened to correct himself, not wanting to

go into that territory. Not now. "All I meant to say was that a diploma is important." He struggled to put into words why it was so important—to him at least—but instead he said, "It seems silly to me that you didn't finish your credits when you were so close."

"So now I'm silly *and* stupid."

He cringed. "What I meant—"

"I'm a good person, y'know. I have skills. Lots of people don't have diplomas and do fine, Mr. Harvard Law School."

"Of course you're a good person." He fought to keep his exasperation in check. "All I meant was that you could've gone to any school…" He took a deep breath. The fact that he'd had to work so hard to get what he wanted while she'd squandered her opportunities made him bitter and frustrated, but that didn't give him any right to judge her. "Education is important. Basic language and math skills, sciences, geography—"

"Stop explaining things to me like I'm a child!" She shot out of her chair. "I don't have any *issues*. I know what I want and I work hard. But you're never going to see that, are you? You're always going to look at me like I'm a dumb blonde cheerleader who dropped out of school and will never amount to anything."

She was being deliberately obtuse, hearing what she wanted to hear so she could be mad at him. He raked his hands through his hair. With a brittle, maddened laugh, he uttered, "One credit and we wouldn't even be having this conversation."

"That's right. One credit. And you're acting like it gives you the right to pick on me. Well, I hope your law degree taught you enough to run this place on your own—" she tore off her apron "—because I quit."

"What?" Aaron's heart stopped. He jumped out of his seat. "W-wait a minute—"

She threw her apron against his chest and stalked out of the office. He followed, calling her name. Two customers stared as she grabbed her purse and jacket and marched out.

"Steph, I didn't mean—"

Her one-fingered salute shut him up.

Aaron stood on the bakery steps as she threw herself into her mini SUV and peeled out of the parking lot, kicking up icy gravel in her wake. The cold air seeped through his clothes and into his skin, slowly freezing his blood.

Crap. What the hell was he supposed to do now?

CHAPTER FIVE

STEPHANIE CLENCHED HER JAW, sick to her stomach, heart pounding. As she drove away from Georgette's, she felt as if someone were digging spadefuls of hurt and bile straight out of her gut.

Twenty minutes later she pulled over, realizing she'd been driving aimlessly, blinded by her need to escape. What was it her old babysitter used to say? *Running away won't solve your problems, Stephanie.*

It was too soon to regret, she told herself. This wasn't her fault. Walking out was the only way to show Aaron she needed to be taken seriously. She wouldn't stand to be mocked and bellied... *belittled*.

That, at least, was what she'd tell herself until reality sank in.

She sat in the SUV, hands loose in her lap, the emergency blinkers on. She picked up her cell phone. Calling Maya was out of the question. After the pep talk they'd had, Steph didn't want to disappoint her. She didn't want to head back to her apartment yet, either. Stewing at her place alone would only bring the grief home quicker once she acknowledged she was out of a job.

There was only one place she could think of to go. She dialed, and after a brief conversation, turned her SUV back onto the road.

It was half an hour before she arrived. Mom and Dad lived in one of the big houses on the shores of Silver Lake. They had a great view of the water, and they owned a private strip of beach, which was why all the parties back in high school had been at the Stephenses'.

Though it was anything but, today the house looked low and small and sad against the gray-and-white world. The lawn was covered in thin patches of melting snow. Steph pulled into the long, paved driveway and parked in the four-car garage. Her mother met her in the interior doorway, beaming.

"I'm so glad you're home." Helen opened her arms in welcome. Steph leaned in for a brief hug, smelling cloves and Chanel No. 5 in her mother's hair. "I've got so much to do, and I could really use your help before your father's party."

Steph didn't reply. She hadn't mentioned it over the phone, but she had a feeling Mom already had heard about her falling-out with Aaron. Gossip was a professional sport in Everville, and Helen was one of its MVPs. "I've got a headache coming on," Steph said, not in the mood to be interrogated. Sometimes faking it was Steph's only way to ensure her mother left her alone. "Would you mind...?"

"Of course, baby. Go right up to your room. Lucena's already put fresh sheets on the bed and towels in your bathroom. Get some rest and I'll check on you later to see if you want dinner." She ushered her up the stairs.

Steph shut the bedroom door, and the cold, massive space closed around her. She waited three heartbeats to feel better, to feel safe, to feel that everything was going to be all right.

All she felt, though, was a leaden sense of failure.

"I'M SCREWED." ACTUALLY, *screwed* wasn't the word he was thinking of, but he was trying to shield Kira's delicate ears from saltier language. He didn't want to drive off his only other employee.

"Can't Georgette come and bake tomorrow's orders?" she asked hopefully.

Aaron gulped his black coffee and stared at the long list of standing orders. He hadn't realized how many local businesses they supplied with pastries and desserts. They'd lose a lot of cash if they had to cancel. "My grandmother's still recovering. I don't want to trouble her." He scanned what was left behind the counter. "Pack up what you can from the display case to fill these orders." He handed her the list. "We'll make what we have to once we see what we have on hand."

"What about stock for tomorrow?"

"I'll deal with it. I don't suppose you can come in for the rest of the week?"

She bit her lip. "I have classes…"

He waved a hand. "Don't worry about it, then. Come when you can, but don't you dare skip school." He paused. "Wait…it's barely noon. Why aren't you in school now?"

"I only go part-time."

He began to ask her why, but decided it wasn't his business. There were lots of reasons a young person might have for not going to school full-time, and right now having Kira here was a blessing.

He went back to the office and hesitantly picked up the phone. How was he going to explain this to Gran? She'd be furious, and then she'd insist on coming to fill the orders.

He put down the handset. No. He wasn't going to tell her. Not until he'd found a replacement. The doctor had said it was vital that Gran rest and keep her blood pressure down.

He took a deep breath to calm his own hammering heart. He'd spent his youth in the bakery working alongside Gran, though she hadn't let him in on her secrets. But he knew where everything was in the kitchen—at least he thought he did. All he needed were the recipes.

Which were in the safe at home. He drummed his fingers on the countertop. Georgette would know right away that something was wrong if he showed up at the house now. He would have to get the binder of recipes tonight after Gran had gone to bed. Well, no problem. He had his smartphone and a great data plan. He'd get some recipes off the internet and make those. They wouldn't be Gran's, but they'd be close enough, he was sure. A chocolate chip cookie was a chocolate chip cookie.

He glanced at his watch. If he started now, he could make a few batches. He rolled up his sleeves and headed to the kitchen. He could do this. Stephanie Stephens had, after all. How hard could it possibly be?

THE SATURDAY OF her father's birthday party, Steph was tasked with serving punch and cake, even though Helen had hired wait staff for the day. Steph suspected her mom had put her behind the big crystal punch bowl by the window to make sure she was seen by all the guests, including those who knew some eligible bachelors.

She smiled wanly as Helen, dressed in a salmon-colored two-piece suit, picked up a glass of punch. "I still don't see why you couldn't have made Georgette's coconut cake," she murmured. "It's for your father, after all. You know he loves her coconut cake."

"I've told you, I don't make Georgette's desserts for anyone unless they pay for them."

"If this was about money, I would've paid you." Helen sniffed.

"And if you'd wanted the cake, you should've ordered it from the bakery *before* I quit. It's *her* recipe, and I don't work for Georgette anymore, so

I can't use it." She didn't know why her mother argued with her about this all the time. Helen knew very well Steph had signed a nondisclosure agreement that kept her from sharing her employer's recipes. In one of her more melodramatic moods, Helen had once claimed her own daughter wouldn't give her Georgette's recipes to save her life. To her mother's everlasting shock, Steph had agreed.

Leaving their argument dangling, Helen trotted away to greet some guests. Steph stifled a yawn. She'd woken up before the crack of dawn, still attuned to her baking schedule. She'd never slept much, but now that her internal clock was thrown off she had a hard time coping.

Truthfully, she worried about what was happening at Georgette's. She'd stormed out before she'd gotten any of the next day's baking done. But she snuffed out the impulse to call, because the next thing she knew, she'd be driving there to put a pan of date squares together. She firmly reminded herself that the bakery was no longer her concern. Aaron would have to figure things out himself.

Damn that stupid, stupid man. Calling her on poor math skills? Hitting her where it hurt? What kind of guy did that? He knew she'd struggled through school. Everyone knew. Telling her she had *issues*…

Well, she didn't. She'd asked her parents about it once, and they'd assured her absolutely nothing was wrong. She'd simply been a little slower on the uptake.

Slow. As if she really wanted a reminder of how people saw her. Stupid and useless. But not to everyone: Georgette had seen what she could do.

Steph shifted restlessly. She hadn't called her yet to explain why she'd left. The truth was she was too cowardly. Disappointing Georgette was worse than disappointing anyone else she knew. And she'd done it anyway.

"Pardon me." A tall man grinned down at her, interrupting her brooding. The sun made his grass-green eyes shine and caught in his gold-brown hair, distilling it to bourbon in its roots. "I'm looking for Helen and Terrence Stephens."

Steph smiled back. "They should be around here somewhere. I'm their daughter, Stephanie."

"I was hoping you'd say that." He held out a big, weathered hand. "Wyatt Brown. Your folks were kind enough to invite me over to meet the neighbors." He had the slightest accent, one she couldn't place.

"Wyatt." Helen hurried over. "So glad you could come. I see you've met my lovely daughter, Stephanie. You can call her Steph."

Ah. Now Steph understood. This must be the rancher her mother had mentioned.

She gave him a once-over and decided her mother's taste wasn't terrible. In a pair of khakis, a green Ralph Lauren sweater and mud-stained loafers, he looked like a model out of a magazine. More Sears catalog than *GQ*, though. He was one of those big guys whose bodies were built for hard work. Thick muscles bulged as he shifted, stretching his clothes in interesting ways. Compared to the rancher, Aaron was a stick. Not that she was comparing the two.

Helen handed the rancher a glass of punch. "Stephanie, come out from behind there and show Wyatt around the house, won't you? I'll go get your father." With that, she flitted off.

Real subtle, Mom. "Sorry about that. She can get overly enthusiastic at times."

"I don't mind." His relaxed air put her at ease. He didn't push, which was nice, but he wasn't backing off, either. "Your mother's talked a lot about you. Good things only, I promise."

She was sure her mom hadn't ever had a bad thing to say about her daughter to anyone.

She led Wyatt on a tour of the house with its many guest rooms, offices and her mother's craft room. It had always seemed too big for the three of them, but they had friends stay over frequently. She and Wyatt chatted as they made their way back to the party. "My mom mentioned you're a rancher and that you just moved here."

"My folks have an operation in Australia, but we're from Montana originally. I wanted to branch out, so I bought a nice piece of land not too far from here. We're getting our first heads of cattle next week."

"That sounds interesting."

He chuckled. "You don't have to be polite. Most people glaze over the moment I start talking shop."

She stifled a laugh. Mom had always told her to look interested even if she had no idea what a person was saying, but she was glad she didn't have to pretend too hard. Wyatt went on, "You're a baker, right?"

"Well...I was." She looked down.

"What happened?"

"I kind of...quit." Ugh. She sounded like a total flake.

"What made you leave?"

"It's a long story."

The corner of his mouth hitched up, revealing a dimple. "I've got time."

She shuffled her feet, embarrassed she'd even brought it up. "Well, it's this guy...my boss, I guess you could say. He's taking over Georgette's Bakery—"

His eyes lit up. "That's the place everyone keeps telling me to visit."

"Oh, yeah. Bar none, the best baked goods in a hundred miles. People come in droves on the week-end and—" She stopped suddenly. This was the first weekend she hadn't worked in months. Years, even. At this time of day, she'd be baking for Sunday. Regret gnawed at her and she worried her lower lip. "Anyhow, we don't agree on some things."

"About the business?"

"Well, that, and he thinks I'm stupid."

His face darkened. "He *said* that?"

She winced, drawing out her response. "Not *exactly*." She hugged her elbows. "But I know he thinks it. We went to high school together and he used to have a crush on me..." Good Lord, why was she even telling him this?

Wyatt's crooked smile was knowing. "I take it you didn't return the feeling?"

"I had a boyfriend at the time. Aaron was nice and all, but he was..." The word that automatically came to mind was *pathetic*. Dale had called him that a lot—a pathetic loser. Aaron had always been kind of intense around her, breathing down her neck to make sure she copied and returned his notes instead of letting her take them home, and looming over her to return those pens that one day. "Well, he wasn't my type."

Wyatt smirked. "So you think he's getting back at you now?"

"Maybe." She released another huff. "No. I don't think he's being mean intentionally. I think he thinks because I didn't graduate and I'm still here in Everville and never went to college..." She was babbling. Mom had always warned her about boring people. She tossed her hair and gave a weak laugh. "I'm overthinking it. I'm sure it must sound silly to you."

"It's not silly to want to do something with your life that makes you happy," he said seriously. "And from what I gather, this job made you happy."

"It did." Her shoulders slumped. "I screwed that up."

"You're being too hard on yourself." He gave her hand a gentle squeeze. "If you love something enough, you'll find a way to make it happen."

She dipped her head self-consciously. Wyatt was only being nice, she told herself, though awfully touchy-feely considering they'd just met. "Thanks. I guess I need time to process it."

"Oh, look at you two!" Helen bustled up, face radiant. "I'm so glad you're hitting it off. Didn't I say she'd like you, Wyatt? You two are perfect for each other!"

Steph dropped the rancher's hand as if it were a live grenade, blushing furiously. She wasn't feeling anything beyond the beginnings of a friendship with Wyatt. He was a nice guy who'd been patient enough to listen to her ramble. That was all.

"Leave those two alone, Helen. You'll scare the poor man off." Steph's father strode up and vigorously shook Wyatt's hand in greeting. Steph had inherited his sturdy height and kind eyes, as well as his brass-blond hair, though his was going a distinguished silver at the temples. A splash of barbecue sauce glistened on his white shirt collar. When

Helen spotted it, she exclaimed loudly and attacked him with a napkin.

"Happy birthday, Terrence," the rancher said above Helen's head. "You have a lovely home and a wonderful family. You're a lucky man."

"It's true." He gently extricated himself from his wife's fussing. "Come on, I want you to meet some people." He led him off, leaving Steph with her mother.

Helen crushed her fingers in her grip. "He's nice, right? Didn't I say he was?"

Steph shook her off. "He's fine. But stop pushing for something that's not going to happen."

"Why not? Didn't he tell you about his ranch? The man owns three hundred acres south of Everville, prime real estate. He's worth upwards of a hundred million, you know."

"Mom!" Steph was appalled. Her mother wasn't usually this shallow. "How can you talk about him like some kind of...gold digger?"

Helen gave her a pooh-pooh look. "Nice is nice, but honey sweetens the pot. I'm simply looking out for you, baby."

Steph glared. She grabbed her mother's arm and tugged her into the empty den, temper reaching the boiling point. "I've told you, I'm not ready for a serious relationship."

Her mother folded her arms. "I don't see why not. You've quit your job. How else are you going to fill your time?"

Steph stared, so exasperated her mind had gone totally blank. She counted backward from five before she settled both trembling hands on her mother's shoulders. "Mom. I'm an adult. I know you mean well, but you need to stay out of my personal life."

Her mother inhaled sharply. She drew herself up and lifted her soft chin high. "I'd think you'd be more grateful for all the opportunities we've given you."

Steph took two steps back, fingers curling. There was that tone again, the one everyone used to imply she was obligated to live up to *their* standards. She wanted to yell at her mother, but it was her father's birthday, and she didn't want to make a scene.

"I can't talk to you right now." Before she could say anything she'd regret, she hastened out onto the back deck and dug her nails into the wood railing, suppressing the scream climbing up her throat.

Gradually, her fury drained out of her as a damp gust of wind penetrated her dress and sapped away the heat of her anger. The lake glistened cold and silver beneath the pale orb of the sun. Its struggle to shine through the cloud cover was a flickering promise of warmer spring days ahead, but at the moment all she could see were the dirty, desolate snow drifts and ice-crusted puddles of mud.

The door closed quietly behind her. "Everything all right?" It was Wyatt. She didn't really want to talk to him right now, not while her mother was pushing him at her. Any indication of interest—of which she could honestly say she had little—would only encourage Helen to drag out the pageant. They'd invite him over for dinner, then force him to spend time alone with her under some pretense. It'd happened before.

"I needed some fresh air." She tried to keep her tone cool without being rude. He didn't need to know about her argument with Mom. But either Wyatt didn't get her message or was too gentlemanly to leave her alone. He pulled his sweater over his head and—good Lord, he was all muscles beneath his shirt—draped it across her shoulders. It smelled like leather and lemons.

"Thanks." It seemed rude to refuse it.

Wyatt leaned against the railing. "Look, I want to apologize."

"For what?"

"I think I came on too strong. To your parents."

Steph blinked. "I don't understand."

He rubbed his chin and chuckled ruefully. "This…this is going to sound crazy." He sucked in a breath as if steeling himself. "I've spent my whole life helping my folks on their ranch to the exclusion of everything else, which is how I found myself at age forty-two single and childless. I don't mean to sound like a sad and lonely cowboy…but I haven't gone on a lot of dates." He peeked over at her. "This is the part where you start to get suspicious."

A handsome, rich cowboy like Wyatt didn't date? "Suspicious, no. Surprised, yes."

"There've been women. Just not women I was really all that into, or who were more into my family's money than they were into me." He scratched the side of his nose. "When I met your parents at the country club and got to know them, they seemed like really great people. They mentioned you a lot. They didn't know I was single at the time…but after a bit, I told them I wanted to meet you."

A prickly feeling climbed up her arms, as if the sweater were creeping over her skin. She furtively shrugged it off her shoulders so it clung loosely to her elbows. "Um. Okay."

"Look, I don't want to sound weird. We've just met, but…I like you."

"That's…" Clumsy words weighed down her tongue. Too many confusing thoughts assailed her, first and foremost being that this was not something she wanted to hear right now. But instead of saying so, she said, "Thank you. I like you, too."

Smile lines carved pleasant valleys into his sun-weathered face. "I'd like for us to get to know each other better."

"Oh. Well…" Her pointed words of warning to back off wouldn't come as easily with Wyatt as they had with her mother. She knew she should tell him she wasn't interested, but the guy was too damned *nice*. The worst part was that despite his other attractive qualities, *nice* was the only word that kept coming to mind.

"I know I'm moving too fast." He took a step back, hands raised. "But I'll admit I like what I see and hear. And frankly, I'm not the kind of man who has the time or patience to play games." He shoved his hands into his pockets. "Might as well go for broke." He blew out a breath and looked her full in the face. "My parents are getting older. I'm looking for someone to settle down with, and I mean to start my family as soon as possible."

Steph choked on a breath she tried to inhale and swallow at the same time. She supposed she should appreciate how up-front he was being, but alarm bells sounded a warning in the back of her mind. Maybe at some other point in her life, she would have loved hearing those words, but not now and not from Wyatt.

She coughed and cleared her throat. "Look, Wyatt…you seem like a great guy. Really." The corners of her mouth strained as she tried to lift her lips. "But I've told my mother the same thing I'm going to tell you. I'm still trying to find myself. And I don't think I can do that if I'm with another person right now."

"I'm not hearing an absolute no."

She gave him a tight smile. "I need time to figure things out for me."

He tilted his chin down, thinking. "All right. I'll give you time." He pushed off the railing and touched his forelock as if he were wearing a broad-brimmed cowboy hat. "If you wouldn't mind some advice...?"

Warily, she said, "Go on."

"They say do what you love, the rest will follow. But if that were true, I'd be sleeping and eating Wagyu beefsteaks at all hours of the day." He chuckled. "If you want to be a success, you gotta do what you *have* to do before you get to do what you love. Pay your dues, as it were. It isn't always pretty or fun, but it'll make what you love all that much sweeter in the end."

He was talking about her job. It was almost a relief to hear after their intense relationship talk. He wasn't even being condo...*condescending*. And his advice made sense.

A little salt to bring out the sweetness—that was something Georgette had taught her early on when it came to baking. "Thanks. That's helpful, actually."

"I'm glad. I'll let you think about that," he said, then flashed a grin. "But I suspect you'll see more of me soon."

He went back indoors, leaving her alone on the deck once more. Steph's chills deepened. She started to pull the sweater around her, but then stopped herself. She took it off and headed back into the party.

The rancher was right. She had to make things happen for herself. She wasn't going to get what she wanted by wishing for it. Everything came at a price, and she had to be willing to pay it. It looked as though she was going to have to eat crow if she was ever going to own Georgette's.

CHAPTER SIX

"MRS. LAWLER CALLED and said the chocolate chip cookies she ordered on Friday weren't the ones we usually sell." Georgette's tone over the phone had all the pointedness of an awl gouging into Aaron's good intentions.

He broke out in a sweat, pressing himself into the office chair as if he could disappear in the crumb-filled seams of the vinyl upholstery. He'd tried to keep this conversation from happening since Stephanie had left two days ago, but his time and luck had run out. "I know. I used a different recipe."

"Why on earth would you do that?" Gran asked sharply.

"We were out of cookies. I had to whip up something I could make—"

"But those aren't *Georgette's* cookies. People don't come to the bakery to get something they can make from an online recipe."

"I know, I know." He hadn't thought his cookies had turned out *that* bad, even if they were a little hard and lacked the smooth, melt-in-your-mouth texture his grandmother's were famous for.

He hadn't had time to make another batch, though. All day Friday and well into the evening he'd thrown together recipes from the internet to fill the standing orders while Kira took care of the customers out front. By Saturday, all the premade pastries and batters had been used up and he found himself saying, "Sorry, we're sold out" more often than "Thank you. Come again."

Worse yet, he hadn't been able to get the recipe binder from the safe—Gran had changed the code, and he couldn't ask her for it without telling her why. Now they were almost completely out of stock, and he was scrambling to prep inventory for Monday. Flour dusted his running shoes and batter was caked on his jeans. He ached head to toe, and the lack of sleep after only two days was taking its toll.

"I don't understand why you didn't ask Stephanie to make more cookies." Georgette waited for his explanation, and Aaron finally relented with a sigh.

"Stephanie quit on Friday."

"Yes. *I know.*"

He sank deeper into the chair. He hadn't really expected to keep such a huge secret in small-town Everville, but he'd hoped… "So you heard."

"Betty told me when she came for tea yesterday. She said Stephanie stormed out in quite a mood. I thought I'd wait to hear the truth from you." Every word lashed him with razor-sharp reproof. "How long were you planning to keep it from me?"

"I didn't think you needed to know. I can handle it. You should be resting and recovering."

"Don't give me that," she snapped. "That is *my* business, Aaron. I'm grateful that you want to take care of things. I put a lot of faith in you, waiting as long as I have to see how you'd solve this problem. But I told you from the start, didn't I? You *need* Stephanie. You were supposed to work *together*."

"Things didn't work out."

His grandmother's stony silence on the other end of the line told him that was not a satisfactory explanation.

"And what, exactly, are you going to do for inventory?" she asked.

"Well, since renos are happening anyhow, we could close up for a week or two. It'll give me time to interview for a replacement baker."

"A replacement?" She said it as if he'd proposed they grind bones for flour. "Absolutely not!"

"Gran, be reasonable."

"You don't understand. *I* trained Stephanie. *I* trusted her with my secrets. I'm not going to hand over my recipes willy-nilly to some stranger. We've no guarantee they won't take everything they've learned and start their own bakeshop in town."

"You didn't have that guarantee with Stephanie," he pointed out.

He could almost feel her imperious glare through the handset. "Loyalty isn't something you can teach, Aaron. It's bred into you. Stephanie would've stayed if I'd asked her to."

Would she have? Aaron wasn't so sure. He'd been rude and downright patronizing toward her. He hadn't meant to insult her. He simply couldn't stand it when things were left unfinished.

One credit. That was all she'd needed. And he'd made a huge deal of it instead of dropping it and appreciating what she *could* do. Like keep the bakery in business.

Boy, had he ever screwed this up. He never would have anticipated Steph quitting over his stupid comments. He wanted to blame her for being overly sensitive and taking his words too personally. He'd only meant to be helpful, after all. Making suggestions that would increase efficiency and cut costs had served him well in his old job, but that tactic didn't work here. Steph was a person, not a business. She'd taken his criticism personally because it *was* personal. And he'd completely disregarded her pride.

He heard something thump on the other end of the line. "I'll have to come in tomorrow morning to fill the orders."

"Gran, you should be resting."

"I can't relax knowing my bakery is falling apart and my customers aren't happy. I'm likely to have another stroke worrying and not doing anything about it."

"Your blood pressure's still too high. What if you

fall or hurt yourself? You can't lift all those heavy bowls and sacks of flour on your own."

"And you can't bake to save your life," she shot back. "Listen to this. You hear it?" There was a loud tapping noise on the other end of the line. "Those are the cookies you sold Mrs. Lawler. God forbid I let you fill Monday's orders. I may be old and my brain might be weary, but I still remember I'll need to make three pies for Bartlett's, two cakes for Sealy's Bistro, and a flan for Mrs. Hendrick's birthday. Do *you* know how to make flan?"

Aaron conceded that he did not.

"I'm going to bed now," Georgette said waspishly. "I've an early start tomorrow, and you're going to drive me to work." She hung up, her anger and disappointment echoing in his ears.

He rested his head in his hands. He was supposed to be making Gran's life easier, but instead he'd made a mess.

Kira appeared at his office door. "Hey, Aaron?"

"What's up?"

Her fingers curled around the door frame. "Something's come up. Would it be okay if I left early?"

He frowned. "I really need you here, Kira. What's so important that you have to leave right now?"

"Family emergency." She glanced at her toes. "Please, I really have to go. I'm sorry."

The anxious look on her face said she wasn't

kidding around, so he waved her off. They were closing soon and no one was coming in anyhow. She thanked him and dashed out, backpack slung over one shoulder, her hairnet still clinging to her head.

He rubbed his temples. If Gran wasn't going to trust her recipes to a replacement baker, he didn't have any choice. He needed to get Stephanie back. He had a feeling it would cost him more than his ego, though.

AFTER HER FATHER'S birthday party, Stephanie returned to her apartment. She'd had enough coddling from her mother and was eager to be back in her own space. She was going to suck it up and get back her job at Georgette's.

First things first: she had to organize herself. Making to-do lists would line up all her priorities. When she was a kid her babysitter, Kitty, had been all about lists, and she'd gotten her into the habit. She took out her phone and started typing, saying the words out loud as if it would commit her to the cause.

"One. Buy school supplies." She'd left most of her old notebooks and the like back at her parents' place. She might be able to dig them up, but she'd be more motivated to work if she had all new stuff. It was like working out in new gym clothes. Besides, it was an easy task, and Kitty had always said accomplishing small things would help get the ball rolling on bigger projects. She could get the basics downstairs at the pharmacy…or maybe she'd drive to a big-box store and get some new jeans while she was there.

She typed in her second goal: "Two. Buy jeans." It was important that she treat herself now and again, after all, and she'd had a rough couple of days.

Number three on her list was a little more complicated. "Get high school diploma." She typed it slowly and stared at the item.

Simple. Yeah. She wouldn't even have to finish that one credit Aaron had harped on about. She could do a high school equivalency test and shove that piece of paper in his face.

She sucked a breath between her teeth. No, she was going to be mature about this. Getting her diploma wasn't about Aaron. It wasn't. And he hadn't forced her out of Georgette's, either. She'd walked out on her own. If she really wanted her job back, she was going to have to be honest with herself and her employer about it.

That was number four. She typed it out as she declared it to the empty room. "Get…job…back."

Right. She looked at her list and decided now was as good a time as any to get things done. Carpet denim, or whatever that saying was.

She drove to the Target in the next town, picked up a package of lined paper, a couple of binders, a pretty notebook, some gel pens, pencils, erasers and a stylish pencil case, along with a sharp new teal-blue backpack. Oh, she'd missed back-to-school shopping.

She spent some time picking out a pair of jeans, and then added a couple of new spring tops and a pair of espadrilles.

She walked out of the store and started the drive home. Two out of four things done on her list. Pretty productive, if she did say so herself.

Before heading back to her apartment, Steph stopped at Maya's consignment shop. She'd told her briefly about meeting Wyatt, but still hadn't said anything about quitting Georgette's. She hoped to get her job back before Maya found out.

The bell above the door jangled. The familiar mixed scents of old leather, patchouli and moth-balls were strangely comforting.

Steph made a beeline for the back room, where she found Maya steam-ironing a silk blouse. "Hey, you." The shopkeeper hung up the steam wand. "I thought you'd be at work."

"I took a day off to get some errands done." The lie came too easily, pricking Steph's conscience. "Actually, I came to ask you a favor. I want to get my diploma—my GED or whatever it's called now. But I'm not sure how to do it."

"That's great." Maya's tentative smile should've made Steph feel indignant rather than sad. It'd always galled her when people told her what she could and couldn't do. But Maya had witnessed her give up on a lot of projects: learning to play the guitar, rock-climbing lessons and knitting classes, to name a few. She had a right to be cautiously optimistic. "I'm sure you can find lots of study guides and stuff online."

"I haven't looked yet. I only made the decision today. What I meant was…"

"You need someone to help you study."

Steph ducked her chin down. "I know you're busy, but this is something I really want."

"Of course I'll help." Maya squeezed her friend's shoulders. "You should totally go for your diploma. To be honest, though, I'm not sure how much help I can be. I wasn't exactly a straight-A student."

"But you know how to get things done, and I need that more than anything." Steph knew she lost focus easily and would give up in frustration when things got too hard. "I need you to breathe down my neck and make sure I do my homework. It'll only be one night a week to make sure I stay on track. I promise to keep you in cookies and pies until I pass."

Maya gave a snort of laughter. "Wow, my hips won't thank you for that. But if you promise to stick with it, then you can count on me to scream at you like a drill sergeant."

"Thank you." She hugged her tight. "I really appreciate it."

"Don't thank me yet. You know I can be a taskmaster." She held her away. "Topic change. You owe me some gossip. Has this Wyatt guy called you yet?" Maya prodded slyly.

"It's only been, like, two days. Don't guys usually wait at least three?"

"From what you told me, it sounded like he was raring to go." Maya snickered. "I bet he'll ask you out sometime this week."

Steph shrugged. "Well, he's nice, but…"

"*Nice butt* is all I need to hear." Maya slipped on her cat's-eye glasses as she hung the blouse on a rack. "Tell me honestly—is he hideous or something?"

"No, he's pretty good-looking. Great body. Kinda like if Bradley Cooper and Hugh Jackman had a love child."

Maya gaped and fluttered her lashes. "You're sure you don't want to date him? 'Cause if you don't, I will."

"You're welcome to him. Honestly, I've got other things on my mind."

Maya peered closely at her. "Like getting your diploma? Does this have something to do with Aaron Caruthers?"

Steph flinched. "No."

Maya waited, crossing her arms over her chest. Steph exhaled gruffly.

"Okay, maybe. I want him to stop thinking I'm stupid."

Her friend frowned severely. "You're not stupid, Steph. You have to stop saying that about yourself."

Steph grimaced. The truth was there *were* times she felt dumb. Sometimes she had trouble understanding what people were saying. She'd think she was listening only to realize that she wasn't, and was too embarrassed to ask for clarification. In her freshman year of high school, she'd asked her geography teacher, Mr. Wiltshire, to repeat something she hadn't understood. He'd called her a "bimbo" and an "airhead" who should stick to cheerleading.

She got that some people, teachers included, had a hate-on for the "popular kids," the ones who got special treatment because of their status on sports teams. But Mr. Wiltshire had been exceptionally judgmental. For a moment there, Aaron had reminded her of him, with his disapproving looks and buttoned-up facade. He'd made her remember the difference between her and the other kids in school.

Maybe that was why she'd left Georgette's, even after she'd told herself she wouldn't. She'd thought he was making fun of her, so she'd bolted. It'd always been easier to give up than risk failure and utter humiliation.

Steph rubbed her jaw. "What Aaron thinks is only half of it. I want my diploma so I can show my parents I'm more than a walking, talking uterus that can make grandkids for them." She stuck out her tongue. "I don't know what makes either of them think I'm ready or willing to have kids."

"Your mom's probably feeling like an empty

nester. Maybe you should get her a cat or something," Maya mused.

"I would, but she hates dirt, and animals are all poo and fur to her. Even with Lucena around, nothing can ever be clean enough. Makes me wonder how she dealt with me when I was a baby."

"Parenthood can change a person," Maya said. "She's been your mom for thirty-plus years now. You can't blame her for caring."

"I know. You're right."

They chatted a bit more, making plans to meet for dinner later that week. Steph promised to get in touch with Maya when she figured out how to do the high school equivalency exam. After a good amount of stalling, she headed for Georgette's house to beg for her job back.

Her insides quivered. It'd felt disloyal and dishonest to quit the way she had, especially when she knew she was needed. She'd been unprofessional, emotional and implus...*impulsive*. She couldn't think of any reason why they *would* hire her back. Maybe she should just turn around and drive away.

No. She had to do this. She'd put herself in this position. If they yelled at her for daring to show her face, there was nothing she could do about it. But not even trying to get her job back would be a *real* failure.

At the very least, she could apologize. Her throat grew raw at the thought that she'd thrown away the one thing that had ever made her feel worthwhile because of something Aaron had not said or maybe thought at all. Her self-doubt grew the closer she got to the Caruthers' home.

She parked in front of the bungalow off Main Street and tidied herself in the rearview mirror, breathing deeply as she exited the car. *I can do this*, she told herself.

She rang the doorbell. The door flew open almost instantly. She'd hoped it would be Georgette who answered, but it wasn't.

CHAPTER SEVEN

"STEPH." THE BREATHLESS quality in Aaron's voice snagged something in Steph's chest.

"I—I came to talk to Georgette. Is she around?" She jammed her trembling hands in her back pockets.

"She is. But listen, I want to talk to you first." He closed the door behind him, and they faced off on the porch in the damp chill. "I want to apologize... again. I'm sorry if I made you feel anything less than vital to the bakery. I've learned over the past few days how hard your job is, and how much you put into it."

Steph was brought up short. She'd had a whole speech prepared that would lead up to asking for her job back, but those words fled.

"I accept your apology," she said, and then decided humility and honesty were the best approach. "I'm sorry for walking out on you. It was unprofessional. I behaved...irra...irritate..." She screwed up her face and blew out a breath. "Irrationally."

"I was actually about to track you down," he

said, holding up a small package. "I wanted to give you this."

It was no bigger than a necklace box, and wrapped in brown paper, which she gently tore off. A pair of haunting eyes gazed up at her from a blue book cover she vaguely recognized. "*The Great Gatsby*?"

"You've read it, haven't you?"

She shook her head. She hadn't even seen the film, though she adored Leonardo DiCaprio.

His face lit up. "This was one of my favorite books in school. I've kept this copy with me all through college. I want you to have it."

"Why?" It wasn't even brand-new. The corners were soft and round, the spine worn, and it smelled a bit like Maya's shop.

He pressed his palms together in front of him as he struggled to explain. "Because it's important to me. This is going to sound weird, but when I want someone to understand what they mean to me, I give them one of my books." His Adam's apple bobbed. "This was a book that opened my eyes to a lot of things. I want you to have it so you can understand that my eyes have been opened."

The hopeful longing in his face told her Aaron was being sincere. Giving her this book really did mean something to him—even if she didn't get it. "Thank you," she said finally. "This is sweet of you."

He shook his head, as if insisting it were anything but. "I screwed up, Steph. We need you back at Georgette's. *I* need you."

A strange thrill zipped through her. No one had ever told her they *needed* her.

He went on, forking his fingers through his hair until it stood straight up. "We can't run the place without you. Gran came in this morning and nearly killed herself baking. I'd forgotten what she's like in the kitchen."

She gasped. "You let her go back to work?"

"I didn't have a choice. We ran out of stuff to sell on Saturday. I tried to bake what I could but..."

Steph bit her lip. Georgette was supposed to be recovering. Her own impul...*impulsive* departure had forced the woman to leave her sickbed. What if she'd hurt herself? What if she'd had another stroke? It would've been Steph's fault.

She was nearly gnashing her teeth when Aaron said, "I know I've been a jerk, but I promise I'll make it up to you. I've been thinking a lot about this. I'm going to make you assistant manager so that we can work together to figure things out the way Gran wanted."

Assistant manager. It was a shiny title, but did it mean anything?

"I'd like to offer you a raise, as well," Aaron added. "You'll still get the same hours. I won't make you do any overtime that you aren't already used to doing."

He was bargaining with her, she knew, but he

was throwing terms at her so quickly, her head spun. She noticed he still spoke as if he would be her boss.

She took a deep breath. She wasn't going to be tricked or bullied or forced to go back to work. She was going to make a deal that benefited *her*, even if she was ready to throw herself back into the kitchen to keep Georgette out of it.

"If you really want me back, then I want to have a say in everything you plan on changing. New recipes, new vendors, new clients…and the bookshop." She added the last as her bargaining chip. She didn't have much interest in running Aaron's bookstore, but his response would allow her to gauge his desperation.

Aaron's lips pursed, drawing her attention to their shape, along with his strong cleft chin and sharp cheekbones. He'd lost a lot of weight since high school, shucking all the baby fat that had put him on the doughier side of the hunk spectrum. Not that he was in any way hunky.

"What do you know about bookselling?" he asked. His skepticism wasn't unwarranted.

"Not much," she admitted. "But if you're opening a business attached to Georgette's name, we need to work together to make sure the bakery doesn't get pushed out of its space."

"I'd never do anything to jeopardize my grandmother's bakery."

So he said. "I still want Monday and Wednesday

afternoons off," she said. "I volunteer at the Everville retirement home and I won't give that up."

He nodded. "You've got it."

"And I want to make sure Kira doesn't lose any of her hours. In fact, she could use more if she can handle them."

"I'll look into it. As long as we can pay her, that will probably be good for everyone."

That left her just one major demand. "I want control of the kitchen. I can't run things without total control."

He shook his head. "I can't let you have that. My goal is to cut costs and make the business run more efficiently."

She got that. And she might have argued for it, but she was getting cold standing on the porch. She wondered if he'd trapped her outside on purpose so that she'd agree to his terms more quickly. "What's Georgette's stake in the business?"

"She still owns the whole shebang. I'm basically acting as her business manager."

"So only she can fire me."

He opened his mouth to form an objection, but then he closed it and pulled his shoulders back. "Yes. As the owner, she is your—*our* boss."

She bit back a smirk. It must kill him that he didn't have seniority over her. If anything, *she* should have seniority over *him*. For now, though, this was enough.

"All right." She held out her hand. "Consider me your new assistant manager."

Relief flooded his stormy eyes. As he squeezed and pumped her hand, a pulse of something thick and hot blew through her.

Oh, no. *Hell*, no. She was *not* attracted to Aaron Caruthers. They weren't just out of each other's leagues; they were playing different sports.

Well, she knew one way to level the playing field. She had her job back—check! All she needed now was her high school diploma.

THANK GOD STEPHANIE was coming back to the bakery. Aaron would've fallen to his knees if it meant she'd accept, but she'd made things easy for him. Maybe she hadn't really been ready to quit. Maybe she'd simply been trying to make a point.

He invited her inside, glad to come in from the cold. His grandmother sat in the kitchen, listlessly stirring a cup of tea. She was exhausted from her morning of baking. When Steph entered, Georgette perked right up.

"Please tell me you're coming back to work." Her plea stabbed Aaron through the heart.

"Yes, of course I will. We just had a…misunderstanding. I'll be back tomorrow."

"Thank goodness. I'm not sure I can survive another *misunderstanding*." She released a heavy sigh. "I can't run the place on my own anymore," she admitted. "Not until I'm better, anyhow. I need each of you to do your part."

"Of course, Gran." Aaron squeezed her shoulder, still feeling bad for putting them in that situation to start with. He met Steph's eye and was surprised to see remorse reflected in her somber expression. A silent agreement was forged in that moment. They'd do whatever it took.

"We'll figure things out," Steph said. Georgette shook her head.

"I'd feel better knowing we had a little redundancy. Stephanie, I want you to train Kira to do a few simple kitchen tasks. Some of the ready-made baking, and maybe one or two of the cookie recipes. I'll pass along the nondisclosure agreement for her to sign. Make sure she understands how important it is to keep my recipes a secret."

Aaron didn't think that was a long-term solution—a part-time high school student couldn't be expected to stay on forever.

"I'll look into hiring more staff," he said. "We can train them to bake in case—"

"You will not," Georgette snapped. "We've already had this conversation, Aaron. Kira will do fine. I trust her."

That effectively ended the discussion. Aaron knew arguing wouldn't accomplish anything, but he caught Steph's eye as he escorted her to the door.

"Gran's right, of course. We can't afford to hire more people right now anyhow. Still, I wish she'd see we need more than Band-Aid solutions to this staffing problem."

"I don't generally argue with Georgette," Steph said quietly, "but I do need help in the kitchen. I can't bake and run the front by myself if Kira calls in sick or something."

Ironic, he thought, that Steph had been the one to expose all these problems when she'd walked out. "I've been thinking...maybe you could teach me how to bake."

She arched an eyebrow. "You?"

"If you could teach me Gran's top three sellers, then at least we'd have those available. Besides, my grandmother can't argue that she doesn't trust *me*."

She gave him a thoughtful look. "That's not a bad idea. I mean, Georgette might object—you know how she can be about her recipes." He nodded. "But if it's for the good of the bakery..."

"It is," he insisted. He was more convinced than ever he could do this. Baking wasn't that hard. He simply needed to learn Gran's recipes.

"All right." She gave a decisive nod. "I'll teach you what I can. But it'll be our little secret." Her wink sent sparks along Aaron's skin.

After she drove off, he went back inside. His grandmother's critical gaze bored into him. "What?"

"Don't think I've forgotten how besotted you were with Stephanie when you were a teen."

He busied himself collecting the dishes from the

coffee table. "That was the past. The *distant* past. I don't feel anything for her except...well, nothing. And I wasn't *besotted*."

"You were never good at lying, either. She's bringing back all kinds of bad memories, and you've been reacting to them. You've always been the type to hold a grudge, Aaron, and I'm telling you now, if this partnership is going to work, you need to get over yourself."

Aaron hated that she might be right. His animosity toward Steph hadn't exactly been subtle. "I'm going to try harder with her."

"I don't want you to try harder. I want you to wipe the slate clean. It's been years. You've both changed and grown. Get to know her." It was a command, not a request. "Talk to her. You still see her as the girlfriend of that boy, but she's more than that. She's not even dating anyone right now."

He sucked in a sharp breath and battered down the hope expanding his chest. He was *so* over Stephanie Stephens. He'd been over her since the end of high school.

Which meant he had no excuse to avoid her. He would get to know this supposedly new and improved Steph. For Gran's sake.

STEPH ARRIVED AT the bakery early the next morning, excited for the days ahead. She still couldn't believe how easy it'd been to get her job back, though she wasn't about to take that for granted.

Tackling her high school diploma was going to be a lot harder, no doubt.

After she'd left Georgette's, she'd spent the evening reading up on the HSE, or high school equivalency exam, and perusing the practice tests and study guides online until way past her bedtime. Even those tests, though, had her breaking out in a sweat. Maybe they'd be less daunting once she actually sat down to do them. She wasn't about to let a few webpages scare her away from achieving her goal.

She unlocked the bakery door, yawning as she entered, and gasped as she took in the scene in front of her.

What the— She smacked her lips, and a chalky feeling settled against her skin. She hurried into the kitchen, flipping on lights all the way through.

The kitchen was a mess. The long stainless-steel worktable sported a gritty layer of dirt, as if someone had sifted fine sand all over the place. The renos in the dining room must've stirred up all the crud in the ceiling and on the walls. On top of that, all the dishes and utensils were in the wrong places. Various jars and ingredients had been moved, as well. Her anxiety ratcheted up as she stared around. Her setup was completely ruined.

A scream of frustration climbed up her throat, but instead of letting it out, she counted backward from ten. *Calm down*, she told herself in Kitty's stern voice. This was not something to freak out over. She'd clean up and put everything back where it belonged. Simple as that.

She dropped her purse and coat in her locker, put on a hairnet and apron and got to work, first wiping down and sterilizing all the surfaces. It felt hopeless, though. Every time she moved something, more dust and dirt rained down. She had to put everything on the floor, wipe the counters, then wipe down every item before putting it away.

It was nearly five thirty before she could start actually baking, and by then her nerves were shot. She didn't like it when her routine was thrown off.

She was putting a pair of cakes into the oven when Aaron arrived. He stuck his head into the kitchen. "You didn't make any coffee." He held the empty coffeepot aloft in one hand.

"I didn't make any coffee because I was busy cleaning crap off the counters. Oh, and good morning." She slammed the oven shut. The man had zero manners. It was as if all he could ever do was find fault with her.

"Sorry. Right. Good morning." He meekly retreated. Shortly, the heavenly scent of coffee filled the air, and she felt bad. She'd done exactly what Aaron had. She'd let her bad mood get the better of her. She didn't know why she and Aaron couldn't get along. It seemed as if they were always snapping at each other.

He walked in a minute later with two steaming mugs and placed one on the tabletop. "Peace offering," he said. "It was rude of me to expect you to have coffee ready."

She pushed a wayward strand of hair off her face. "I usually do, but…" She trailed off. She gestured around her helplessly. "It's disgusting in here."

"Sorry about that. Ollie assured me the kitchen would be safe from renos, but I guess he was wrong. Maybe we can lay down some tarps or plastic sheeting at the end of the day to keep the dust off the counters and store everything we use in covered containers until the renos are done."

She hated that her routine would be thrown off even more, but Aaron was right. She'd have to make sure she put everything away herself, too, otherwise she'd go nuts trying to find things. Just what she needed. More work.

She sipped her coffee and was pleasantly surprised that it was…well, perfect. "Did you put sweetener in this?"

"Yes."

"How did you know I take my coffee with sweetener instead of sugar?"

"I remember from high school. You ordered it at the cafeteria during exam time in our second year." He turned away stiffly. "You put in cream and two packets of sweetener."

"You *remember* all that?"

"I've got a good memory," he said over his shoulder as he headed toward the front. The kitchen door flapped on its hinges as he went to greet the first customers of the day.

Steph stared. Dale had barely been able to keep her birthday straight. Who the hell remembered a detail like how she took her coffee?

Right, the guy who'd had a crush on her all through high school. It might've been creepy coming from anyone else, but she found herself smiling as she got back to work.

She'd have to find out how he liked his coffee.

THE CONSTRUCTION CREW arrived less than an hour later. Soon, the sound of hammering and the buzz of power tools mingled with the scents of sawdust and cinnamon. When the morning coffee rush was over, Aaron returned to the kitchen.

"Kira's here, so I guess now's as good a time as any for you to give me my first baking lesson." He swung his fists restlessly, his expression somewhere between humble and hopeful.

"You realize that by doing this I'm going against the confidentiality agreement your grandmother made me sign, right?" she asked.

"I know. But I have no intention of telling her what we're up to. I love Gran, but sometimes she doesn't know she needs help."

"Agreed." Steph nodded with a chuckle. "As long as you don't say anything, I won't, either."

"I could always claim I picked it up in my youth. I spent a lot of time here helping out when I was a kid, doing dishes and pouring batter, that kind of thing. But I wasn't allowed to mix ingredients together."

Steph laughed. "That's Georgette. When I first started, she wouldn't even let me in the kitchen." She gestured. "Grab an apron and a hairnet. We'll start with chocolate chip cookies."

"They're still the top seller, I take it?"

"Second only to the croissants, but I'm not teaching you those till you're good and ready. Flaky pastries take a little more work." She started to grab ingredients, but discovered most of them had been moved. Normally, she tried to keep all the ingredients needed for one recipe together, but someone had messed up her groupings. She stared at the two containers marked Baking Powder and Baking Soda, forgetting which one she normally used.

"Something wrong?"

"Nothing." She grabbed the baking soda. This had to be the right jar. It had the worn old fruit sticker on the side she recognized.

"I noticed there were, like, seven separate jars of flour all over the kitchen." He nodded at the shelf. "Wouldn't it be more efficient if you kept your flours all together on one shelf, your sugars together on another…"

She stared at him. "But this makes more sense, see? We keep the ingredients for the recipes we do all the time together so we don't go running all over the kitchen for them. Also, they're not all the same flour. There's pastry flour, cake flour, whole wheat…"

"I know *that*." His drawl had that distinct *duh* tone to it that made her set her teeth. "I'm talking about seven jars of all-purpose flour in different places."

"So?"

"So, if you're doing that, how do you know if you're running out? Or when?"

Her fingers curled around the edge of the work-table. "I was wondering why I was missing so many jars this morning. Please, don't move my things around, okay?"

"But—"

"Please." This was why she'd wanted total control of the kitchen. She couldn't explain why her way was the right way. She didn't think she had to. She just wanted Aaron to agree with her on *something*. The kitchen was her domain, after all. She wasn't going to change things for him. As assistant manager, she was entitled to his trust and respect.

She hoped she was, anyhow.

"Okay," he said without further argument. She jerked in surprise. She'd been gearing up for a fight.

Maybe they were finally moving forward.

CHAPTER EIGHT

AARON LISTENED AS Steph led him through the recipe, but he was still hung up on the insane way she'd organized the kitchen. He'd been confused when he'd found four commercial-size bottles of vanilla extract and eight containers of white granulated sugar in different places. No wonder it was so cluttered. He'd tried amalgamating some of the ingredients, but there hadn't been time to reorganize everything over the weekend.

Now that he knew how important it was to Steph, though, he had to let her have her way...for now. Maybe he could convince her otherwise when they knew each other a little better.

She recited the recipe item by item, putting each ingredient in front of him. As he reached into the bag of flour with a measuring cup, his shirtsleeve came away white, and he grimaced. He hadn't gone to work without a shirt and tie for over five years. He supposed that would have to change if he was going to be baking.

He undid his tie, unbuttoned his shirt and shucked it off, leaving him in a clean white T-shirt. Steph stared at him as he reached into the bag once more. Was she checking him out?

"No, not like that," she said, taking the measuring cup from him. His ego deflated. "Don't pack the flour in or use it like a scoop. Spoon the flour in." She took a tablespoon and swept a large amount into the cup. "Fill it up, then get a knife to flatten it out." She scraped the back edge of a butter knife across the lip of the cup and leveled the flour. "See? That's one. Now do two more like that."

"I don't understand," he said, perplexed. "It's still a cup of flour."

"It's not the same. Trust me."

It seemed like an inefficient way to do something so banal, but he let it go. "How many cookies are you going to end up making with this batch anyhow?" he asked instead.

"About thirty."

He knew Gran made way more than that. "Why don't we double the ingredients and get it all done at once?"

Her eyelids fluttered as if she might pass out processing the thought. "It doesn't work that way," she said with a shake of her head.

"Why not?"

"It just doesn't. I'm sure there's a scientific reason, but I can't remember what it is." She tossed her head. "Your grandmother's recipes require you to be precise. It's chemistry."

"And chemistry is about math. Double the amount

and you get double the cookies and save time and energy." Surely other bakeries—especially the mass-produced brands—had figured this out.

Steph put her hands on her hips and let out a short huff. "If you want to try that, go ahead. But if you make a mistake, you end up wasting all that effort and the ingredients. Now, are you going to keep arguing, or do you want to find out what's next?"

Aaron lifted his chin. He couldn't be wrong on this. It was pure mathematical logic. Flour was flour, and doubling the ingredients couldn't possibly mean anything different.

His job, after all, was to find ways to make the bakery more efficient.

"I want to try doubling the recipe," he declared.

Steph looked as if she was trying to swallow a small lemon whole. "We have a rule here." The way she pointed at him reminded him of Gran instantly. "We don't waste butter. So if you make a mistake, you have to eat it. That's sixty rock-hard cookies going straight to your hips."

His gaze automatically slid down to the curve of her hips. Then he realized he was being inappropriate and fixed his eye on the bowl. "Maybe I should triple the recipe," he mused.

She scoffed. "You're insane. But if you want, go ahead." She flipped her hand at him as if swatting a fly.

"Could you write the instructions down for me?" He might as well keep a copy on hand.

"Nope. Georgette made me memorize them for a reason. She won't risk someone stealing them."

Of course. He was impressed by how loyal Steph was to his grandmother, even if teaching him her secrets was bending that rule to its snapping point. It almost made him feel guilty for what he was about to do. Almost.

He tripled the ingredients he'd already added to the bowl and quickly discovered it was too small to hold everything.

"Wet to dry, wet to dry!" Steph exclaimed as he dumped the flour into the egg, butter and sugar mixture.

"It's all still dough." There was probably a reason for the order, but he couldn't suppress that spark of rebellion that made him ignore Steph's directives.

She gave him a look of pure venom—as much as her pigtails and pink T-shirt afforded, anyhow—and started on her second batch of cookie dough, mumbling the recipe all the way. Aaron mixed his triple batch. He could have used the large stand mixer, he supposed, but it was an old machine Gran never used. Besides, Steph wasn't using it. Not wanting to be bested by what felt like twenty pounds of flour, sugar and butter, he applied himself, biceps burning. The handle of his wooden spoon suddenly snapped off. He stared at the jagged end protruding from the mixture like a broken Excalibur.

"Bad spoon." He extracted the rest of the utensil from the pulpy blob of cookie dough. Steph snickered quietly, and he felt a little jolt of pleasure. Back in high school, earning a laugh from her, even at his own expense, had always made him feel like he'd won the lottery.

A Pavlovian response, he thought with a touch of self-loathing. He used a large plastic spatula to work the dough. It took a while, and his arms felt like rubber by the time it had formed a homogenous glob.

He added the chocolate chips last, worked them in and wiped the sweat from his brow. He surreptitiously flexed his fingers, wrists aching. "There. Done."

"Are you planning on baking those right away?" she asked.

"I know Gran chills them for an hour. But—" he poked at his dough "—this seems stiff enough to hold its shape."

Her lips pouted into a little beak of a mouth he thought she might use to peck him to death. In the dining room, someone was hammering away, the concussive force of the strikes resonating through the mostly stainless-steel kitchen like a gong. "If you say so," she sang.

Uneasiness crept through him. He'd expected her to fight him harder on this, tell him all the ways he was wrong. But she went on with her work, whispering to herself as she recited the ingredients going into her bowl. He took out the baking sheets and lined them with parchment paper—that was the one thing he didn't skimp on, although he did wonder if investing in reusable silicon mats would be more cost-effective. He took a measuring spoon and started portioning dough on the sheet, but quickly decided he'd be better off using his hands. He put on a pair of latex gloves, pinched off hunks of dough and rolled them into balls.

Steph's lashes flickered, and he could've sworn he heard her make a high-pitched screaming noise in the back of her throat. "Something wrong?" he asked.

"Nothing." And then, under her breath, he heard, "Don't waste butter."

He thought about the cookies he'd baked for Betty Lawler and how displeased Gran had been with them. Maybe he was being bullish about all this, wanting to prove a point to Steph. Maybe he *was* wasting butter. But in the end, they'd still have cookies, wouldn't they? Maybe they wouldn't turn out exactly like Gran's, but it was her recipe. How wrong could they go?

It took him a while to roll out all the balls, but when he was finally done, he stood back and surveyed the trays ready to be put into the oven. Steph was only now starting her third batch of dough. Ha! His method was clearly the more efficient one.

"Oven at 375 degrees," she instructed. "Twelve minutes."

He filled the commercial convection oven. With

all those shelves, they'd be done in no time. Meanwhile, Steph's cookies were still chilling. Feeling smug, he washed up, taking all the dishes to the sink.

Twelve minutes later, the bakery smelled like heaven. He pulled the trays from the oven and put them on the cooling rack, gently lifting one cookie on each tray to check the underside. Not a single one burned. He picked one up, hissing as it flopped over and left scalding-hot melted chocolate on his fingertips, and popped it into his mouth. The chocolate scorched his tongue. He gaped like a fish, huffing hot air until he could chew.

Ha! They weren't bad at all. Soft and melty, but also kind of...doughy? And why did they taste as though they'd been in the fridge for a while?

"Pretty good," he said, chewing more slowly. Except for the fridge-y flavor and the first-degree burns on his lips, they were pretty close to Gran's.

He was standing there a full minute before he realized he was waiting for Steph to tell him what a good job he'd done.

"When the cookies cool, test them again," she said without looking up. "For now, though, take a break."

"Take a...?" He felt as if he'd been put in a corner. "There must be something that needs doing."

"Of course there is," she replied, her tone carefully measured with equal parts patience and dismissal. "But I don't want you to overdo it today. Make sure to drink lots of water. It's easy to get dehydrated in here. You should go to your office. Do some paperwork or something."

The grinding squeal of a circular saw accentuated Aaron's annoyance. He wasn't some weakling who couldn't take the heat. "If you don't mind, I'll stand by and watch you while you work."

Her brow furrowed. Okay, so waiting for cookies to cool probably wasn't the best use of his time. He probably looked like he was micromanaging, monitoring her productivity. "I want to get a feel for how things work around here," he explained. "We can talk about suppliers in the meantime."

She flicked him a dry look. "I can't get anything done with you breathing down my neck."

"I'll stand over here. I promise I won't get in your way."

"Hmm." She was taking more ingredients off a shelf—flour, sugar, an assortment of smaller jars, and eggs, cream and butter from the fridge, all different from the ones she'd just used—and arranging a new set of bowls and spoons. A couple of times, he wanted to ask her why she did things the way she did, but decided not to antagonize her further today. She'd been defensive about her setup. And yet, despite the chaos he perceived all around him, she moved fluidly and precisely, almost dancing as she put the recipe together. She reminded him of a witch casting a spell, whispering incantations as she added eye of newt to her brew. What was she making anyhow?

"Angel food cake for Mrs. Watterson," she replied when he asked. "It's for her tea party with her knitting club. They get together every Thursday night and rotate their snack duties. Mrs. Watterson always gets angel food cake."

He was surprised she could remember all that. He had a hard enough time with names and faces, and he'd grown up in Everville.

"About the suppliers—"

"Have you talked to Georgette about them?"

"I did some research. I thought I'd make a phone call and see what kind of discounts we could get for a larger order, since we're so far out of their delivery area. I don't want to go to Gran before I have all the information."

Her lips twisted. "I know you mean well, but I don't think it's worth burning bridges with our current suppliers to save a few bucks."

"We'd be saving more than a few bucks. Anyhow, it's not personal. If they want to keep our business, they have to be competitive."

"But Georgette's used the same suppliers for years. Aren't those relationships worth keeping?"

Alarm pitched her tone higher. It seemed to him that Steph was overreacting to what she saw as huge changes to her world. "Nothing's been decided yet. I promised to talk to my grandmother and to you about any changes we'd make to the business, and I will."

She looked skeptical. He wasn't sure why he was so dismayed by her doubt in his promises. "Your cookies should be cool now," she said.

He went to the cooling rack, lifted one up and bit into it.

Rock. Hard.

Maybe it was a dud. He picked up another and tried to break it in half. His muscles strained, and then it exploded in a shower of crumbs. He dusted cookie bits from his shirt. "I don't understand…"

Steph's expression remained aloof. "I told you to scoop the flour into the cup. I told you to mix wet to dry. I told you not to triple the recipe. I told you to follow my instructions, but you *didn't*." She crossed her arms and leaned her hip against the worktable. "*That's* why they're rocks."

"But…what did I do *wrong*?" He stared at the ninety-plus cookies as his gut slid into his shoes—a good two hours of work and all that butter, wasted.

"A recipe isn't just the ingredients that go into the product," she said as if he were as dense as the cookies. "It's about the way it's done. I thought you would've known that."

"But…chemistry," he grumbled. And then remembered that chemistry wasn't only about the molecules and electrons. He'd been good at all those things—he had a knack for numbers—and when it came to the labs, he'd followed the instructions to the letter.

So why hadn't he done so here? Because he'd been hell-bent on showing Steph he was superior in this realm, too?

Well, he'd proved something, all right. He'd proved he was a stubborn idiot. Ninety inedible cookies' worth of stubborn idiot.

"You're right," he said morosely. "I should've listened to you."

She pumped a fist in the air and pointed at him. "Boom! That's what I wanted to hear. Apology accepted." She laughed then, as if this had all been a great joke.

A weird sense of relief rushed through him. "Why didn't you stop me?" he asked, chuckling as the ridiculousness of the whole episode struck him.

"As if you'd let me. Obviously, I had to let you make your own mistakes." The prim explanation made her sound just like Gran at her smuggest. "I couldn't have stopped you even if I'd tackled you."

The thought of Stephanie Stephens's arms wrapped around his waist while she bowled him over and pinned him to the ground was a lot more intriguing than it should've been.

"Do I really have to eat all these?" he moaned, nauseated at the thought.

She snickered. "You would, wouldn't you?"

His jaw ached at the thought of biting through those dental nightmares. "Maybe I could grind them up and turn them into a drinkable shake or something."

Steph's head popped up. "I have an idea. Grab the food processor off that shelf, will you?" She went to the freezer and rummaged through it. "I know Georgette had a pint of… Aha!" She pulled out a tub. "On Labor Day, we sold homemade ice cream sandwiches." She opened the tub and took a sniff. "Hmm. Not so fresh anymore, but it'll do for a trial."

"What're you doing?" He set the food processor on the table and plugged it in. Steph popped four of Aaron's cookies into the machine, then hit the button. The cookies jumped and spun and were soon pulverized into gritty crumbs. She emptied the mixture into the half-empty tub of ice cream and handed him a spoon. "Use those muscles and mix that up, will you?"

He silently obeyed, ridiculously pleased she'd noticed his muscles. The ice cream was a little hard to manipulate at first, but the kitchen was so warm it soon softened. He folded the cookie crumbs into the rich vanilla ice cream—the real stuff from one of the local dairies—and presented it to Steph. She grabbed two spoons and held one out to him.

"The best part of recipe testing," she said and dug her spoon into the container. Aaron did likewise and considered the mess before putting it into his mouth.

The cookie crumbs had softened slightly, but

gave the ice cream a delightful, almost nutty texture. He chewed through it, finding softer chunks of chocolate mixed in with crunchy cookie ones.

"Oooomigod," Steph said, slumping against the counter. "This is good. I mean, really good."

"Sellable good?" he asked hopefully.

"Let's not go crazy." She tapped the spoon against the edge of the tub. "But we could give it away. No one leaves Georgette's empty-handed, but I wouldn't send them home with those." She gestured at the trays on the cooling rack. "This, however—" she pointed her spoon at the ice cream "—we can work with. We'll grind the rest of your cookies down and bag the crumbs. Give away free samples with purchase, or sell it as—"

"Ice cream topping," Aaron said, catching on.

"Better yet, call it something cute." Steph snapped her fingers. "Unicorn bait. Slap on a label and there you go. Parents love that kind of thing."

He blinked in amazement. "You think it'll go over as something other than a mistake?"

"If it does, this could be a good way to get rid of leftovers." She grinned.

He was impressed by Steph's ingenuity. Not only had it saved him from wasting all those cookies, but she'd managed to turn his mistake into something useful.

"Way to go, team!" She held her hand up for a high-five, and Aaron obliged. They clasped hands for a moment—just a moment. But in that brief hold, something inside Aaron clicked and revved, like a free-spinning gear that had finally met cogs with another gear already in motion.

Their eyes met, locked. Something in his chest went *ka-chunk*! And in that instant, Aaron knew he'd fallen for Stephanie Stephens all over again.

CHAPTER NINE

AARON WAS SURPRISED by how quickly the day whipped by while he was in the kitchen. When he looked up at the clock, he was shocked to find it was closing time.

"If you can recite your grandmother's chocolate chip cookie recipe tomorrow, I'll teach you how to make her brownies," Steph said.

"Sounds great." Despite the cookie debacle, he was excited to be working alongside Steph again, even if it wasn't the smartest thing to do on a personal level. He emerged from the kitchen as the workmen were packing up for the day. The contractor, Ollie White, showed him everything they'd done so far—it was a mess, but at least there wasn't any mold or asbestos in the walls. The electrician would have to come before anything else was done. He'd be wiring for all the light fixtures. After that, the crew would install insulation in the exterior walls and then the drywall would go up.

As he saw the workmen out, sending them each home with a bag of "Unicorn Bait," a big white pickup truck pulled into the lot.

"You made it just in time," he said to the tall man in cowboy boots who got out of the driver's side. He wore a shearling coat and pulled a cowboy hat from the cab. Aaron smiled to himself. There were lots of farms and ranches in the area, but the owners generally didn't try as hard as this guy did to look the part.

The man put on his hat and tipped it up in greeting. "I just moved into the area. I've been hearing a lot about this place, and I finally managed to get away to see it for myself." He stuck out his big, calloused hand as he advanced up the stairs. "Wyatt Brown," he said by way of introduction. Aaron shook it. Wyatt was a good four inches taller than Aaron's six feet, with shoulders as broad as his smile. The guy was built like a linebacker, but he didn't radiate with menace like some guys Aaron knew.

"Wyatt." Steph's head popped up from behind the counter. Kira peeked up, as well. As if they'd rehearsed it, they both removed their hairnets and smoothed their hair back in synch. "What are you doing here?" Steph asked.

"I wanted to pick up some goodies for the guys. We're having a bonfire at the ranch tonight." He perused what was left in the showcase: an assortment of chocolate chip and oatmeal cookies, cinnamon snaps, gingerbread men and several types of bars, about three dozen in all. "Those look good. I'll take the whole lot."

Steph and Kira each grabbed a box and started loading them up. Aaron studied the man a little more closely, wondering what his angle was and how Steph knew him. "When did you move here?" he asked Wyatt casually.

"About two months ago. I bought the Gerritsens' and Couchs' tracts and livestock, kept their staff on to help manage the herds. Got a few horses for breeding, too."

"Sounds ambitious."

"You've got something interesting going on here, I see." Wyatt nodded toward the sealed off dining room.

"Aaron's opening a bookstore," Steph said from behind the counter.

"Ah."

Aaron tried to detect any hint of condescension or skepticism from the rancher. He didn't hear it. "How do you two know each other?" he asked instead.

"Terrence Stephens's birthday party," Wyatt replied. "I was there last weekend."

Of course. The Stephens had an enormous property out by Silver Lake. Aaron had never been there, but he'd heard the stories about the parties Steph had thrown back in high school. Not that he'd ever been invited, or had wanted to go, for that matter. Not really.

Steph and Kira finished boxing up the cookies, and Wyatt handed over a hundred-dollar bill and a handful of change. "Sorry. I don't have anything smaller."

"That's okay. Um..." She stared at the cash in hand, and Aaron watched while she pulled out the change. Slowly. And incorrectly.

He didn't stop her—she was off by about ten dollars—but it confirmed his suspicions about where the cash register discrepancies were coming from. Even though he'd brought it up previously, she still wasn't being very careful. *Issues*, he'd called them, and she'd dismissed them as easily as last year's fashions. It troubled him. Steph had worked here for five years. If, as Gran had said, the till had been under and over each day, how was the difference being made up?

"Oops. Miscount." The rancher dropped the excess on the counter. Steph gratefully scooped it up and put it back into the register. Her eyes flicked to Aaron's briefly before she cast them down again.

"Listen, if you're done work for the day, how about you come with me and see the ranch?" Wyatt gestured to Aaron. "All of you can come, of course. Plenty of firelight and open sky to go around."

A plea flashed across Steph's face as she looked to Aaron. He felt a pinch of jealousy. Of course she wanted to leave with the handsome cowboy.

"You go ahead, Steph," he said. "I'm a little tired, and I've got an early start tomorrow. I have to take Gran to the doctor."

Steph's spine jolted. "Oh, well, if that's the case, maybe I should—"

"It's okay. Take off. I'll close up shop. Have some fun." He could feel a tick starting in his jaw and smiled to hide it. "You earned it today."

"How about you, little lady?" Wyatt directed at Kira. The teenager looked shocked to be addressed at all.

"I…I… No, I have to get home." She rubbed her arms as if she were cold. "Thank you."

"Next time, then." Wyatt nodded to Steph. "Ready to go?"

Her gaze bounced between Aaron and the cowboy. "If you're sure…"

"Never question the boss when he says it's quitting time," Wyatt declared as he grabbed the bags of treats. "Come on. You can follow me in your car."

Steph took off her apron and hurried to get her things. With a backward glance, she followed Wyatt out. Aaron watched them go. His stomach felt as though it were a rock tumbler full of cookie bits.

"Holy cow," Kira breathed. "That guy was *hot*."

Aaron must've glared at her, because the teen ducked her head and scurried into the kitchen.

He let out a long breath. Who Steph went out with was not his business. In fact, it was a good thing she dated other guys. He had more important things to focus on—specifically, he had some suspicions he needed to look into. What he found out might answer a lot of questions about Stephanie Stephens.

THE FOLLOWING MORNING, Stephanie rubbed her eyes, grumbling as a bit of flour dusted her cheek and made her itchier. The bonfire at Wyatt's had been fun, but she'd stayed out way too late, and the smell of wood smoke still clung to her hair and clothes, irritating her sinuses.

Wyatt had given her a grand tour of the B Bar Ranch, including the sprawling ranch house. Eight bedrooms for a single guy seemed excessive, but he'd made it clear his hopes were to fill that mansion with a family.

"I just have to settle down with the right gal first," he'd said with a loaded look.

Steph hadn't been able to think of a response. Frankly, she had been embarrassed that he'd focused his attentions on her when he could have any woman he wanted. He'd proposed they go out for a horseback ride on her next day off. She couldn't say no. She loved horses, and it had been ages since she'd gone riding.

Priorities, she reminded herself. Kitty had always said she should focus on what was important in her life. The bakery came first. Getting her high school diploma was second.

Her "study schedule" was taped to her living-room wall. In big bold black letters on a sheet of red construction paper, she'd written STUDY FOR TWO HOURS: No Putting It Off. When she'd returned to her apartment after the bonfire, she'd spotted that sign and had groaned out loud. Refusing to break her pledge, she'd turned on her laptop and sat down to read the study guides. Exactly two hours later, she'd tumbled into bed, exhausted.

She hadn't slept well. Her whole nighttime routine had been thrown off, and she shouldn't have had that late-night hot cocoa. It felt as if she'd only gotten a couple of hours' sleep before her alarm went off.

She stared at the bowl of ingredients for a banana loaf in front of her. Had she already put in the baking powder? She couldn't recall. Usually, she recited the recipe out loud, but her throat was raw from the smoke. Unable to remember, she tossed out the dry ingredients. At least she hadn't wasted any butter.

She needed a break. She went to the front and poured herself a cup of coffee, then sat at one of the café tables. She took a few deep, cleansing breaths, remembering how she'd seen something on TV about how meditation could help clear the mind. Her eyes settled closed.

A frigid gust of wind followed by the jangle of the bell above the door made Steph's chin snap up.

"Good morning," Aaron greeted. "Everything okay?"

She yawned and rubbed her eyes. "I thought you said you had to take Georgette to the doctor's."

"I got a call last night. The doctor had to cancel."

"Still pretty early for you to come in."

His brow furrowed. "It's eight o'clock."

"What?" She looked up at the clock and gasped. She must have fallen asleep sitting up. She leaped to the counter.

"Are you all right?" Aaron asked.

She hurriedly started a fresh pot of coffee brewing, shaking the last of the cobwebs out of her fuzzy head as she tossed back the dregs of the pot she'd made earlier. "I've never missed opening time. Oh, God, I hope no one was knocking..."

"If they were *that* desperate for a muffin, I'm sure they would've kicked down the door." He set up the cash register with the daily float. "Have fun last night?"

She stared at him blankly.

"At Wyatt's," he prompted. The rough edge to his words scraped at her senses.

"Oh. Um, yeah." For a moment, all she could think about were the high school equivalency study guides and how *un*fun they were.

He didn't probe further, didn't chastise her for falling asleep on the job. He probably thought she'd gone out and partied too hard with Wyatt.

Well, what she did on her own time was none of his business. And anyhow, he'd practically pushed her out the door with the rancher. He hadn't taken the hint when she'd flagged him down with her eyes, hoping he'd give her an excuse to decline Wyatt's offer. Instead Aaron had shooed her out as eagerly as her mother would have. Men were so dense sometimes.

"I could use some help in the kitchen," she said. "Would you mind lending me a hand?"

He smiled. "Sure."

They prepared the day's goods in silence, interrupted occasionally by customers. She was surprised at how easy it was to work beside Aaron. He asked questions, but they didn't get in each other's way. They practically danced around each other, as if they'd been working together forever.

In the dining room the workmen pried and scraped as they pulled up the last of the scabby old vinyl, exposing the raw subfloor beneath. Steph had never realized how worn and dreary the orange, gray and brown tiles were. Seeing the place bared like this made her uncomfortable, but at the same time excited. Aaron showed her a picture of the gorgeous hardwood they'd be installing. She already could envision what the room would look like when it was done.

"Do you know what color you're going to paint the walls?" she asked.

He shrugged. "Thought I'd keep it simple. Eggshell white should do it."

"What? No way. White's boring."

"What are you talking about? White's classic."

"For an asylum, maybe. You want something warm and inviting. Something to match the bakery."

He frowned around at the burnt-orange walls, a color Steph suspected had been picked at the height of the seventies. "Not this color," she clarified. "But maybe something to complement it."

"I'm not going with avocado green," he warned.

"Ew, yuck. No. Listen, give me a day or two and I'll bring some paint chips." At his skeptical look, she added, "We're partners in this, remember? You said I could have a say. You don't have to agree with my suggestions, but I've redecorated my bedroom enough times to tell you I'm pretty good at picking colors."

"All right," he relented. "Show me what you're thinking in a couple of days."

She grinned. It was a small victory, but an important one. It made her feel as if what she thought mattered.

Outside, the wind picked up until a low moan whistled past the building and along the road. The temperature dropped after lunch, and then big, fat snowflakes started to fall, blanketing the roads and parking lot in a fluffy layer of slush.

"At this rate, it's going to be a really slow day," Steph said, watching the blizzard turn the world white.

"The weather reports are saying it's going to get worse. I already called Kira and told her not to come in. I should tell the contractors to go home, too. I don't want anyone driving in this."

"I wouldn't worry about it. Everyone around here knows how to handle a little snow."

Aaron frowned, and then Steph suddenly remembered about his parents. "I mean—not that accidents don't happen. I mean—"

"It's okay," he said quietly.

"I'm sorry." She tapped the heel of her hand against her forehead, mortified. "I wasn't thinking."

His jaw worked, and he pushed himself off the counter. "I'm going to work in the office for a while. If there aren't any orders to fill and you think we'll be okay stockwise for tomorrow, I think we should close early."

Steph watched him go, then pressed her palms against her hot cheeks. She'd known Aaron's parents had died in a car accident. It had been one of the worst crashes the town had ever seen, and it had forced the townspeople to take action to have that particular stretch of road properly widened, paved and marked.

Through the open office door, she could see Aaron resting his head against his fist, elbow on the table. He took off his glasses, holding his brow for a moment before sighing and sliding his glasses back on.

Steph quietly went back into the kitchen. She felt awful. She'd heard that back in elementary school, Aaron had cried a lot after his parents' death. She hadn't known him personally then. They'd been in different classes all those years. The one thing she had known was to keep away from kids who weren't cool, and Aaron had been like toxic waste. No one wanted a crybaby for a friend.

It was one thirty when she'd finished cleaning and packing up everything. Aaron sent the workmen home, then they closed the shop.

"Hopefully the snow won't stick around." He grimaced up at the sky. Large flakes settled in his dark hair. Steph stifled the urge to brush them away. "Drive safe."

She got into her SUV and turned on the heat and seat warmer. She took a minute to check her voice mail while the car warmed up and the windows defrosted. Maya had left a message telling Stephanie some of her consignment clothes had sold. And her mother had called to chat. When she looked up, Georgette's station wagon still hadn't moved from the parking lot. She could see Aaron fussing with the ignition. He popped the hood and exited the car.

She rolled down her window. "Is something wrong?"

"The car won't start," he said, glaring under the hood. Heavy, wet flakes pummeled him, and the wind picked up suddenly. "I think the battery's dead. Can you give me a boost?"

"I don't have cables," she said. "You?"

He rummaged through the trunk and groaned.

"Nothing here. Guess I'll have to call Frank." The town mechanic had a tow truck.

"He'll be busy as it is with this storm. He probably won't make it out here until after dark." She opened the passenger-side door. "Get in. I'll drop you off at home, and you can call Frank in the morning."

"I can't impose. Don't worry about me. I'll be okay."

"Don't be silly. I live around the corner from you. Now hurry up and get in. I want to get off the road before this storm gets any worse." When he didn't budge, she shouted, "Look, I'm not leaving until you're gone, too. So either we're bunking in the bakery tonight or you're going to get in here and toast your buns on my heated leather seat."

He scratched his hip, glowering at the station wagon as if that might get it to start. With a sigh, he shut the hood, grabbed his bag and slid into her vehicle. "Thanks. I appreciate this."

"No need to sound so grudging about it." She turned up the heat and patted the dashboard. "This baby's got four-wheel drive. It can handle anything."

She put the mini SUV into gear. It leaped forward into the dirt instead of reversing. Aaron clung to his seat and barely suppressed a yelp as she slammed on the brakes.

"Whoops." Steph chuckled weakly. She put the car in Reverse and pulled out of the lot.

CHAPTER TEN

STEPH TOOK THE road slowly. She wanted to reassure Aaron that despite her earlier blunder, she was actually a very good driver. Still, his fingers clenched around his knees. Out of the corner of her eye, she could see him glancing repeatedly at the side mirrors, and his right foot was unconsciously tapping a nonexistent brake pedal.

"Tell me about Boston," she prompted. She needed him to get his mind off her driving. His anxiety was making her nervous. "Where did you live?"

"I had a place in Cambridge near MIT," he said, his voice stiff. "The rent was pretty cheap for a one bedroom. Lots of grad students lived there. I liked the neighborhood."

"Was it hard to give it all up?" she asked. "I mean to come back here."

"I think I always knew I'd come home, but I didn't know when. It kind of snuck up on me when Gran had her stroke."

"But you were prepared. You must've had the idea for the bookshop for a while."

"It was something I'd been thinking about," he said mildly.

Clearly it had been more than a pipe dream. He'd been ready with a business plan and everything the moment he'd pulled into town. "What about your job? You spent a lot of time at your firm, didn't you?"

"About five years, so yeah, I guess it was a long time. Maybe too long. I was getting too comfortable. I would've been fine sticking around, but... well, when things get comfortable, I know I have to be ready for a massive change." He let out a breath. "I didn't *plan* for Gran's stroke, of course. She's always been in the best of health, what with all her exercising and tai chi or whatever she does now."

"Seniors' aquafit on Tuesdays," Steph supplied. "She hasn't gone since the stroke, though."

"Aquafit." Aaron chuckled. "She never told me that."

"She looks great in a bathing suit. For an eighty-two-year-old, I mean."

He groaned. "Please. She's my grandmother. I love her dearly, but I don't need to imagine that." He paused. "Oh, God, now I have. Cannot unsee."

Steph giggled. "I hope to be as fit when I reach Georgette's age. She's amazing."

"She is." She sensed his appraisal. "If I haven't said it, thank you for taking care of her and being here when I haven't been. I never realized how much she depended on you."

He hadn't even known she'd been working for her these past five years. She wasn't sure why Georgette wouldn't have mentioned her to Aaron, but then, employees were sometimes invisible to their employers, their presence only missed when something went wrong. Her mother took Lucena for granted all the time. So had Steph, until she'd moved out and learned that dust gathered a lot faster than she could ever have imagined.

"So, you live in town now?" he asked. "Don't your parents have a place by the lake?"

"I moved out a couple of months ago."

"Really? What made you do that?"

"It was time for a change, I guess." She sat up straighter. "I had an...eleph...epipen..."

"Epiphany?" he supplied.

"An *Aha!* moment," she returned with a decisive nod. "I wanted my independence. I've lived at home my whole life and I realized even though I've traveled all over the place on vacations and stuff, I've only ever stayed at five-star resorts and hotels. I don't really know..." She struggled for a way to explain her need to break away after her Christmas reunion. "I wanted to be more...normal."

He chuckled. "Normal's great and all, but being eyeball-deep in debt and living on ramen noodles isn't all it's cracked up to be."

"Yeah, I get it." She blew out a breath. "I know a lot of people think I'm a poor little rich girl."

"Whoa, now, I didn't say that."

"But you thought it, didn't you?" She turned to meet his eye.

He stared for a long moment and— "Steph!"

She jerked the wheel to the right, pulling the drifting vehicle out of the lane of oncoming traffic. The mini SUV fishtailed, but she regained control quickly. Aaron's nails carved a line of crescents on the leather seat, and his shoulders were hung up around his ears.

To ease his mind, she continued on casually, "Back in high school my parents bought me anything I wanted, and I let them." She tried to sound blasé about it, even though the admission burned a hole through her gut. "But later, when everyone else was moving on with their lives, I felt empty. Nothing I owned meant anything. It's pretty sad when you start to see that what you have doesn't amount to much if you didn't earn it somehow. That's why I started working for your grandmother." She smiled at the memory, proud of how far she'd come. "She wasn't going to hire me on at first."

"Really?"

"In hindsight, I couldn't blame her. I thought I could walk in, ask for a job and get it. But she didn't think I was committed enough. She wasn't about to waste her time training me only to have me leave once I got bored."

Aaron leaned closer. "So how'd you convince her to hire you?"

"Well, after she told me no, my parents called

Georgette to try to convince her I would be a good employee. She still said no, and then my mother said some pretty uncalled-for things. Georgette got so pissed off she refused to sell anything to us for a month."

His jaw dropped. "Are you serious?"

"Ask her sometime."

"But…your parents have friends—"

"Who would never challenge Georgette. They rely on her for all their good pastries, you know. If I didn't know any better, I'd think your grandmother was some kind of baking-mafia mobster who deals in illegal scones or something." She snickered. "Anyhow, it's not like the country club set would gang up on the little old lady who's been serving them cookies since they were kids."

"So what did you do?" he asked, clearly baffled by this revelation about his sweet old gran.

"At first, I did nothing. But my mom wouldn't stop harping about it. She thought I should file a complaint to someone for discrimination. She was even thinking about calling the sheriff, though I have no idea why she thought that was a good idea." She caught Aaron's stifled smile. "Eventually I realized that if I really wanted to work there, I had to make Georgette see that I was committed. At first, I offered to work for her for free, but she said money wasn't the issue. She knew I didn't need the cash.

"Suddenly, working for Georgette was the *only* thing I wanted, and my parents couldn't do anything to help me. I had to show her how serious I was, so I spent two days baking every single recipe I knew to show her I wasn't an amateur. I packaged everything up and took it to Georgette's and waited for her to arrive. It was four in the morning when she drove up, and I was sitting on her steps. I handed over the boxes and told her, this is what I can do. It's good, but I want it to be better.

"She thought I was crazy, but let me into the bakery. She told me to take down the chairs and make some coffee. That was my first day working for her." She slowed the vehicle to make the turn into town. "You know, looking back, I think she still thought of me as a kid or something. She asked if my parents knew I was out there, as if I were still a teen rather than a twenty-five-year-old woman."

Aaron gave a lopsided grin. "She does take her role as Everville's grandmother very seriously."

Main Street loomed ahead. The snow-covered roads were striped with muddy tire tracks. "The only things I was allowed to do at first were make coffee and serve customers. It was almost six months before she taught me her first recipe."

"So what happened to all the goodies you made?"

"She tried all of them and told me why they weren't any good."

"Ouch." He winced. "She probably didn't like the competition."

"She doesn't, but it was more than that. She was trying to toughen me up, make sure I wouldn't get all offended by her criticism and walk out of there. She wanted me to aim for perfection. She wanted to make sure I wasn't going to be okay with 'okay.' Nothing's more important to her than serving the best." She pulled up to the curb outside the Carutherses' bungalow. "Here we are, safe and sound."

He blinked, as if surprised they'd arrived alive. The snow was coming down in a thick flurry now, obliterating the view. Closing had been a good call.

"I've got to be at the bakery for four tomorrow. Since you don't have your car, I could pick you up, but that's early for you."

He surprised her by saying, "Four is fine. We'll have to clear out the snow, and I want to make sure Frank comes for the car. Besides, I'm supposed to be learning about the business." He smiled faintly. "No better time to learn."

WHEN AARON ENTERED the house, he found Gran dozing in her chair, a book resting in her lap. He draped a blanket across her and paused to watch her breathe. Every time her chest rose, he felt a little better. It was those too-long moments in between breaths that made him quake. She looked so tired.

Don't worry, Gran. I'll take care of everything. You focus on getting better.

In his bedroom, he sat at his desk to study the bakery's ledgers. He'd started going through them last night after Steph had left with Wyatt, but now he found a little knot of guilt lodged inside his chest. Hearing about how Steph came to work for his grandmother had opened his eyes. She'd worked hard to earn Gran's trust. It made what he was doing that much harder. He'd found discrepancies in the bookkeeping almost every week. The receipts simply didn't match what was in the till. And those errors, he discovered, had only begun a little after Steph had started working there.

He didn't want there to be a problem. Moreover, he wanted a reason—some way to explain it all away. Gran kept all the paperwork about the bakery in a four-drawer filing cabinet in the living room. He tiptoed out and opened it, riffling through the yellowing files until he found Steph's employee file. There wasn't much in there apart from her résumé.

He read through it. Did a double take. Read through it again.

"What are you doing home so early?" Georgette yawned and stretched.

He closed the drawer. "We shut down early for the storm."

She looked out the window. "Goodness, that's a lot of snow. Smart of you to come home when you could." She started to push herself out of her chair. Aaron hurried to help her up and then broke the news about her car. "I'll call Frank Konietzko, then make you a nice dinner," he said. "Why don't you lie down awhile, sleep in a proper bed so you don't hurt your neck?"

She didn't argue, which was both a relief and a worry. "What are you doing with that?" She indicated the file under his arm.

He didn't want to voice his suspicions now, and certainly not to Gran—not before he got a chance to talk with Steph first. "Just trying to familiarize myself with the business," he said.

When Gran simply shuffled off into her room, he swore he'd do right by her. The bakery was her life. He would do whatever he could to save it.

STEPH PICKED AARON up at 3:45 the next morning, and they drove through the slushy dark in silence. Maybe Steph wasn't the morning person he'd thought she was. He didn't try to start a conversation, enjoying her quiet company and the absolute stillness of the predawn hours instead.

"Sorry, I'm not much of a conservational...*conversationalist* in the mornings," she said, shaking her head. "Mind if I turn on the radio?"

"You're the driver."

She switched it on to a station that was playing an old power ballad from their youth. He found himself humming along, his thoughts drifting back to those days. At least the music had been good back then.

Stephanie snickered quietly.

"What?"

"Just remembering something about this song."

"Oh?"

"Dale used to love it," she said after a beat. "I always thought it was kind of cheesy."

Aaron stopped smiling and turned to stare into the darkness.

While Steph went into the bakery, Aaron quickly shoveled the thick slush out of the parking lot. The temperature was going up, so he figured he might as well save a few bucks and let nature do the work for him instead of calling a plowing service. Once he got into the bakery, Aaron got to see how things happened at four in the morning. He was surprised by how much work needed to be done. Aside from the baking, displays and counters had to be cleaned and disinfected, orders had to be filled and supplies needed restocking. Together they managed to get ahead of schedule by an hour, which pleased Steph.

Taking a break, Aaron sat at the table by the window to enjoy a cup of coffee. Dawn touched the sky, a silvery-blue veil that lit the snow-covered ground. With the sound of Steph working in the kitchen and the warm smells of coffee and baking, he felt closer to his grandparents than ever. He imagined Gran and Gramps waking up every morning to bake, cozy in the knowledge that their work brought smiles to the faces of everyone who came in.

It was a simple life, one Aaron wanted for himself. Baking might not be his forte, but he would never allow his grandparents' legacy to die. Soon, people would be flocking to Georgette's to satisfy their intellectual palates as well as their taste buds. Hopefully, the extra traffic would keep the bakery from hovering so close to the red.

Later that morning, the bell above the door jangled and in walked a flower arrangement with legs.

"Stephanie Stephens?" the vase overflowing with lilies and roses said.

Aaron called for her, and she came out of the kitchen, wiping her flour-dusted hands across her apron. The delivery man set the vase down gently, the curly mop of reddish-brown hair escaping from his baseball cap bouquet-worthy in itself. He took a slip from his pocket, and Steph signed it. "It was supposed to be delivered yesterday, but the roads were way too dangerous to come out here."

"I don't blame you. Thanks, Pete." She passed him a freshly baked banana muffin as a tip, but when he stuck his nose into the brown bag and inhaled, he groaned aloud.

"Better get me two more of these. I can't go back to work empty-handed and covered in crumbs. Janice would wring my neck. And three coffees with cream, please."

"Coming right up," Steph said brightly.

As he departed, Aaron realized this was how the freebies paid off—Gran always said good food was better when it was shared, after all. By handing out a fifty-cent muffin, Steph had made a ten-dollar sale. Even the construction workers with their daily free coffee and pastry habits were taking home boxes of treats for their families. A pretty good return on investment, now that he thought about it.

Steph pulled the card from the arrangement. She seemed to take a long time to read it, but Aaron had a feeling he knew who the flowers were from. "Wyatt?" he asked.

"He said thanks for coming out to the ranch." She primped the flowers. "Silly man didn't need to do this."

Aaron sipped his coffee to purge the bitter taste from his mouth. "He must be pretty serious."

"He is." She sighed. But she didn't sound wistful or lovesick. She sounded…resigned.

Treacherous hope flared bright inside him. "And…?" He bit his tongue, kicking himself for sounding so interested. "Sorry, it's none of my business. You don't have to answer that."

"No, no, it's okay. I don't mind. You're my… friend." She smiled tentatively. Something inside Aaron's chest unfurled, expanding until he was afraid he'd never be able to jam it back down into the tightly packed ball it had been. Like carefully packed baggage, he thought as he wrestled his emotions back under control.

"I'm not really looking to date right now," she went on. "I want to focus on me, figure out a few things. I'm still getting used to living alone, and it's been kind of tough."

He wondered how tough she thought she had it. With her parents' money, he doubted she was starving.

Then he chided himself for being so disparaging. After the story she'd told him about how she'd come to work for Gran—a story Georgette had verified word for word over dinner last night—he'd gained a lot more respect for Steph. It was unfair of him to keep judging her because she'd been born with wealth and privilege. The Stephenses were hard-working folks. They'd donated thousands to the town's various charities and works, and they volunteered at all the community events. They were good people, and they cared about Everville and its citizens. It wasn't their fault their daughter had dated a guy who represented the exact opposite of all that.

In fact, the only redeeming thing about Dale McCarthy, as far as Aaron had been concerned, had been Stephanie.

He stared at the flower arrangement and reminded himself Wyatt Brown wasn't Dale. Steph had said she had zero interest in dating *anyone*. And even if she did, Aaron didn't have any reason to want to throw the arrangement, vase and all, into the middle of the road.

Yet, the urge remained.

"He seems like a nice guy," he said instead of acting on his impulse. "You two seem to get along."

"He's looking for a wife." She said it bluntly,

almost disdainfully. "It would put my folks over the moon if I married him."

"You could date casually," Aaron pointed out, slurping his coffee loudly. Why was he encouraging her?

"I don't like to play games." Her sharp tone surprised him. She fidgeted. "I mean, he likes me, and he's told me he wants a wife and five kids, white picket fence, four pickup trucks and two dozen horses..." She tucked a few loose strands back under her hairnet. "It's ironic. At one point, I would've jumped on this. I would've jumped *him*. I mean, *look* at him."

Aaron supposed that if he leaned that way, he'd agree. But it didn't keep jealousy from kicking around the insides of his chest.

"It's not fair." She leaned against the counter. "All my life I thought I was ready to settle down and have a family. I thought I'd meet my soul mate and we'd ride off into the sunset. And then I had that stupid ep...ephi..."

"Epiphany," he reminded her carefully.

She scowled. "Suddenly I can't move on with my life." She scrubbed her hands over her face. "It used to be so much easier in my head. All I wanted was Mr. Merkl's house and a husband and kids and a dog and a cat. Why isn't it enough now?"

He recognized the heat in her eyes, even if she didn't know what her own feelings were; it was her ambition kindled to a blaze. He smiled inwardly.

"It's because you realized you could do more, that you *wanted* to do more, for yourself and for others."

"But…I barely know what it is I want to do, apart from work here. What if I've given up on what I'm *supposed* to want? What if I *never* get what I really want?"

He chuckled softly, sadly. "There are no guarantees in life." Boy, did he ever know that. "Gran says life happens at its own pace. If you'd gone off and gotten married right out of high school, who's to say you wouldn't have failed in marriage and family and burned down Mr. Merkl's house?" He spread his hands when horror bloomed on her face. "Hey, all I'm saying is, if you fail, you move on to plan B. You get up and try again. Or you figure something else out."

Her lips quirked in a sardonic smile. "That's not really reassuring."

He leaned his hip against the counter. "Do you remember Mr. Murray? The high school counselor?"

"I remember he used to tell horror stories about people who didn't finish high school." She crossed her arms over her chest.

"He used to say we can't all be the best at everything. That our wildest dreams were just that. Dreams."

"Again, not reassuring."

"The point he was making—" he plowed on "—was that it would take a long time and a lot of work for each of us to discover what we were good at, what would actually make us happy and what would pay enough to keep us in the lifestyle we wanted." He took out a sheet of paper and drew a Venn diagram—three circles that interlocked in the center and overlapped on each side.

"Oh, God. Don't tell me you actually memorized that stupid graph he made."

"What can I say? I like graphs." He drew a happy face in one circle, a dollar sign in another and a check mark with an exclamation point in the third. "This is where you are." He pointed in the space where proficiency and happiness overlapped. "You want to be here." He pointed at the minuscule center space where money was included.

Mr. Murray had claimed that the trifecta was nearly impossible to achieve. He'd said most people were never satisfied with what they earned, no one was ever truly happy and that people usually weren't good enough at the things they would've liked to do to meet the money or happiness quotas. It'd been a harshly cynical view; Mr. Murray's diagram probably said more about the guidance counselor than it did about life, but at least he hadn't left anyone with any illusions about what their futures would look like.

Of course, Aaron had already known life threw curveballs all the time. Being prepared was the key to survival.

Steph tapped the drawing with a grimace. "I

don't see where family and Mr. Merkl's house are on this thing. All Mr. Murray cared about were grades and college and careers…" She let out another long sigh and waved her hand. "It's way too early to talk about heavy stuff. Help me with the cookies, will you? I've got a couple of cakes to make."

She was walking away from the conversation. It wasn't the first time she'd shied away from talk about academics, either, and if what he'd read last night meant anything, this avoidance tactic made sense.

She paused on her way to the kitchen to fidget with the flower arrangement. She pulled an anemic red rose out of the bouquet, and its head suddenly dropped off. She stooped to pick it up. Aaron studied her look of dissatisfaction. "Are you going to go out with him again?" he asked. She stared at him confusedly. "Wyatt."

She looked back at the bouquet. "I said I'd go horseback riding with him when I get a day off."

She almost sounded ashamed. Then again, maybe he was hearing what he wanted to hear. "That's…good."

And it was. If she dated Wyatt, Aaron wouldn't need to worry about getting too close to her. He wouldn't have to risk pain and humiliation again. They might be better acquainted now than when they'd been in high school, but that did not put them in the running for that white picket fence or a happily ever after in Mr. Merkl's house. He was not going to risk losing everything they'd built and the future of Georgette's because he still had *feelings*.

Keeping it professional and friendly was the only way to deal with Steph. And it was all he was willing to risk.

CHAPTER ELEVEN

THE NEXT FEW weeks went by without incident. Gran never found out that Aaron was learning her recipes from Steph. If it felt as though he was keeping secrets, he rationalized they weren't harmful ones, and that the thrill he got out of it came from getting to know Steph better. She was a decent teacher and clearly knew her craft, even if she couldn't always explain the whys of what she did.

By mid-April, the drywall and plastering was complete. While the contractor began working on the patio, Aaron and the man Gran had insisted he hire, Jimmy Tremont, painted the walls. Steph had picked the color—a deep purple she called eggplant. He'd worried the dark shade might make the shop seem smaller, but as the color went up, it really connected with the rest of the bakery's warm, homey feeling. Aaron was glad he'd listened to her. White would have made the place feel sterile. Once the paint was dry, the new flooring went in, and they began installing the shelving units.

With warmer weather came more business for the bakery. Easter was especially busy, and Georgette, who'd recovered most of her mobility and sensation, had decided she would work on weekday afternoons and on the weekends. Aaron had tried to convince her not to push herself, but she'd complained she was bored at home.

"It's not that I don't trust you," she said matter-of-factly. "I just hate having folks think I'm wasting away. I feel fine, really."

"I know you are," he said it even though he wasn't fully convinced. "But you have to speak up if you don't feel well or you get tired."

She agreed, but he asked Stephanie and Kira to keep an eye on her just in case. Working on the bookstore meant he didn't always have a direct line of sight to the bakery, and he was afraid he wouldn't know if something happened to his grandmother. He still felt guilty about not being there when she'd had her stroke. It had been pure luck that she'd been having tea with a friend when she'd collapsed. What if she'd been at home alone and no one had found her until it had been too late?

That prospect haunted him. A part of him felt that he should have stayed with her 24/7 or hired someone to take care of her. He knew, though, that she never would have allowed him, much less a stranger, to hover over her like that. And Gran was far too independent to ever agree to live in a care facility.

In the bakery, Steph laughed at something Gran

said. After nearly two months back, he couldn't help but feel this was…right. He snuffed out the feeling and looked away. He shouldn't allow other things to distract him from what mattered.

Not that he'd been distracted by Steph. She'd gone on at least one more date with Wyatt Brown that he knew of. The cowboy had sent flowers again a week after the first bunch showed up, and he swung by the bakery weekly to buy whatever cookies and squares were left in the display cases at the end of the day. Aaron was glad for the business, of course, and when Georgette had met him, she'd been charmed. His grandmother was a good judge of character, so he trusted her assessment. Steph was in good hands.

More importantly, they weren't his hands.

There was another problem, though. He'd been silent about Steph's sluggishness lately because he hadn't wanted to stick his nose where it didn't belong. She'd probably been staying out too late with Wyatt, but it wasn't his business what—or whom—she was doing in her spare time. She was an adult. As long as it didn't affect her performance.

But it was. The till had been off nearly a hundred dollars on Easter weekend. He didn't want to bring it up, but he couldn't let her mistakes continue. Broaching the topic wasn't going to be easy. He didn't want her storming off again. He just wanted to be helpful.

At the end of the day, he clapped the fine plaster dust from his hands and clothes and slipped from behind the plastic that separated the bookstore from the bakery. Steph glanced up from behind the counter.

"Hard day?" she asked, eyebrow cocked.

He lifted a shoulder, feeling the ache there. "Some of those shelving units are crazy heavy is all. We had a hell of a time assembling them. Then I had to resand the plaster in one corner of the bathroom. Things are coming along nicely otherwise."

"That's good." She looked away demurely, cheeks tinting pink. Even with the shadows under her eyes, she was the epitome of fetching. Heat suffused him head to toe—whether it was out of embarrassment at the strength of his reaction or because he was gearing up to tell her she needed to address some deficiencies in her work, he couldn't exactly say.

He coughed discreetly to quell the feeling squirming through him. "Listen...there's something I need to talk to you about."

"Oh?"

He tugged at his collar. "I don't want you to take this the wrong way... I'm just *concerned.*"

She leaned one hip against the counter. "Really."

"You've been kind of...tired-looking lately." Her well-being was first and foremost. This wasn't about the money, he reminded himself. He was worried about *her.* "Is everything okay with you?"

She pushed a hand against the hairnet holding down her blond locks. "I've been busy. A lot of special orders coming in, plus the extra hours."

Extra hours? He didn't know she'd been putting in overtime. "You haven't had any days off lately. Maybe you should take some vacation time."

"I'm fine. Really."

"Maybe there's something I can do to help." Now would be a good time to revisit her mistakes at the register. But another part of him couldn't help but think she was in trouble and hiding it. What if she was sick? What if she was going through some personal troubles? Not that it was any of his business…except he *wanted* it to be his business. "Will you tell me what's going on?"

Her expression puckered. She turned away from him sharply.

"Steph? What's wrong?" Was she crying? Her shoulders were shaking and she was gripping the edge of the counter. He reviewed his words carefully, trying to figure out what he'd said to offend her.

A strangled noise stuttered out of her. Aaron hurried behind the counter and settled a hand on her shoulder, ready to apologize, to offer comfort…

She turned, took one look at his face and burst out laughing.

"I'm sorry…I tried, I really did. But…your face…"

His face? What did she…?

"Here." She pushed a shiny chrome napkin holder at him and he peered into it.

At first he thought it was the light, but then he saw it. His hair and face were powder white with plaster dust except where he'd been wearing goggles.

"You look like Snoopy!" she choked out.

"Good grief."

"It's in your hair, too." Steph giggled, reached up and ruffled his hair. Wood bits rained from his head. "I wasn't going to say anything. But then you got all serious and I was trying so hard not to laugh…"

"Ha-ha." She was making fun of him, but it wasn't mean-spirited the way it had felt in high school. He laughed it off as he brushed his face. "Better?"

"Not quite. Here." She grabbed a dish towel and cupped his chin, then methodically swiped at his cheeks, fingertips trailing across the rough stubble prickling his jawline. Aaron stayed perfectly still, unable to wrench his eyes from her face as she studied and cleaned him, treating him as though he were a precious museum artifact.

She threaded her fingers through his hair. Sawdust fell from his head like snow. One of her hands rested lightly on his shoulder. She was so close he could've leaned down and kissed her. His lips tingled.

"There." She held him at arm's length. "Good as new. Though I suppose a shower wouldn't hurt."

His mind immediately formed an image of the two of them in the shower together. His vision went fuzzy as if he were looking at her through a lens where all his fantasies were layered one on top of another. What was he supposed to talk to her about again?

"Steph." He wanted her closer. The warmth of her skin and the smell of vanilla and chocolate wafted from her. He forced his next words past a lump in his throat. "I really do care...about whatever is going on in your life." He clawed some of his senses back and more stiffly said, "You don't have to talk to me about it, but if you need to I'm here for you."

Her face softened. "Thank you. Really, I'm fine. It's nothing you need to worry about."

He wanted to worry, though. He was supposed to. Why was that again? Oh, right—the money. It didn't seem so much of an issue now.

Any price was worth seeing her smile at him like that.

THE DINING ROOM was a bookstore.

That was Steph's thought as the plastic sheet separating the bakery from the newly renovated space was torn down at the end of April. Over the past six weeks that semitransparent bubble had obscured the transformation happening on the other side. Now that it had been ripped away, all Steph could think was that things would never be the same.

The only thing that kept that shiny new room from bleeding into the rest of the bakery was the thin brass chain strung up in the double doorway that held a sign reading Opening Soon.

Admittedly, she didn't feel as threatened as she'd thought she would, and she acknowledged that part of it was due to her growing bond with Aaron. His excitement was infectious, and every hour the room evolved, his enthusiasm grew. Before, the dining room had been dated and dingy with its rough, scarred tables and vinyl-covered chairs. No wonder it had been rarely used. Now the room was cheerful and warm. Special energy-efficient track lighting had been installed, and the lights made the eggplant-purple paint glow.

With the display units in, the place looked smaller, but somehow deeper. The empty shelves made her feel sad for some reason, though. It was like when she walked into a doughnut shop and found only empty showcases. Maybe once the bookstore was stocked, she'd feel better.

Speaking of feeling better... She stretched and yawned, the kinks in her neck sending pain shooting through her back. She'd been spending three hours a night studying for the past two weeks, sitting on the couch with her laptop or the workbooks she'd ordered. Two hours hadn't been cutting it, especially when she allowed herself to be distracted. It went against everything Kitty had ever told her— studying while she was tired was about as effective as reading in a sports bar during the Super Bowl, but she had no choice. An extra hour of working on practice tests meant one hour less of sleep, and she was starting to feel it.

People had noticed, too, she was sure. Wyatt had called a couple of times last week, but she'd been in no mood to politely fend off his advances. She'd snapped at him rather than explain herself. It was so unlike her, she'd had to call to apologize the next day, and then promise to have dinner with him Sunday evening to make up for her behavior.

She wasn't looking forward to the date. Hanging out with him felt like hanging out with an older brother. Also, a night out with Wyatt would throw off her studying schedule even further. She should've explained her situation to him. She was sure he would understand and back off. But she didn't want to sound as if she were making promises, as if she'd be ready for him after the HSE exam.

Steph polished the counter during a quiet spell. Georgette had taken care of the special orders that morning, so Steph was free to relax. She was so used to being busy all the time she found the lull unnerving. In the bookshop, the first shipments of books had been delivered yesterday in heavy-duty stackable plastic crates. Aaron had opened them this morning, grinning like a child at Christmas. Now he was checking the inventory and shelving the books. Jazz music played from the little radio he'd brought to his side of the shop.

The double-wide doorway only gave her occasional glimpses of him as he worked. He carried a crate of books into view and set it down with a thump, then arched his back, stretching. When he squatted to grab an armful of books, the waistband of his gray underwear was visible above his belt.

She jerked her eyes away. She was *not* ogling Aaron Caruthers's butt. She certainly wasn't speculating what kind of underwear he wore, though on his frame, boxer briefs were really the only way to go. Preferably the tiny, skin-tight ones…

She shook the image out of her head. Idle hands apparently weren't the only thing the devil played with, because he was putting some wicked thoughts in her head. Needing some other preoccupation, she left the counter.

"Need any help?" she asked, standing behind the thin brass chain at the threshold of the bookshop.

He glanced around. "Uh…actually, yes. These books need to be shelved. I've sorted everything by section already. If you can work on this box for self-help, I'll get the next."

She hadn't expected him to say yes, considering how particular he'd been about his own books. But she'd offered and wasn't about to back out now. "How do you want them shelved?"

"Alphabetical by the author's surname."

Surname. Um…right. She lifted the books out and placed them on the shelves, then started sorting them.

Ten minutes into it, a customer entered the bakery. Kira wasn't in today, so she took care of it. Someone else came in two minutes later. Then a slow trickle of business kept her from the rest of the shelving job, and by the time there was another lull, Aaron was shelving the books he'd given her.

"Sorry. Things got busy," she said as she hurried back to the bookshop. "I would've finished it."

"Don't worry about it. Anyhow, it's probably a good thing you didn't get too far in. I did say to shelve them alphabetical by surname, right?"

She hesitated. "Yes…"

"You did it by first name."

Her face flamed. Fifty-fifty chance and she'd blown it. "Oh. Sorry."

He gave her a forgiving look that wasn't quite pitying and nodded to the display table. "If you have time, would you mind arranging those books on that table in some way that looks nice?"

"Yeah. No problem." She turned away, humiliated. *Surname.* She'd been sure that'd meant first name. Why couldn't he have said *last name*?

Yes, she could've asked. Or looked it up on her phone. But she didn't need him thinking she was any stupider than she already felt.

She yanked the mass-market paperback books from the boxes and stacked them on the table. The piles toppled and scattered, and she angrily gathered them back up and slammed them on the table.

"Everything okay?" Aaron asked.

"I... Yes, it's fine." She forced herself to calm down. It'd been a simple mistake. She was getting worked up over nothing.

She gave herself over to the task of arranging the books in a pyramid. She'd seen it done that way in other bookstores. It took a lot of playing with so the colors of the covers and the number of books all coordinated, but after twenty minutes, it was perfect.

"It looks great," Aaron said with the briefest of glances.

Great? That's all he had to say? All that effort and all he'd said was *great*? She puffed up her chest. "I wanted it to be perfect."

He must have heard the hurt pride in her voice because he looked her in the eye then. "Thank you. I appreciate your attention to detail."

"You know, I really would've finished that shelving eventually."

"I know. Listen..." He raked a hand through his hair, making it stick up. "There's something I've been meaning to talk to you about."

She took a deep breath as her walls went up. She willed her irrational fear down, stamping out her need to lash out before he'd even said anything, and stood straighter. "What is it?"

"I've been trying to bring this up, but I haven't been able to think of a way to frame it. I wanted to know…" His Adam's apple bobbed as if he was already trying to swallow back the words that streamed from his mouth. "Have you ever been tested for a learning disability?"

CHAPTER TWELVE

STEPHANIE STARED, JAW SLACKENING. Aaron cringed inwardly, mortified by his phrasing. Had years of living in Boston not refined his manners at all? Steph went from pink to pale white to crimson as his words sank in.

"It's not something to be ashamed of," he hurried to add, and felt even worse for saying it.

Oh, God. He wasn't trained for this. He wasn't remotely qualified to be confronting her about something he knew so little about. The websites he'd consulted when he'd first suspected Stephanie's problems hadn't exactly given him a step-by-step as to how to bring it up. And since when did he have the right to even ask?

Arrogant—that's how he sounded. Arrogant and condescending. As if he could simply label her problem to solve it. Somehow, the label made it worse.

"Why would you say something like that?" she asked in a harsh whisper. "There's nothing wrong with me."

"You're right, there absolutely isn't anything

wrong," he insisted quickly. "I'm not trying to hurt your feelings. But I've noticed a few little things—"

"Is this about shelving the books?" Her eyebrows slanted steeply down. "You said *surname*, and I thought you said—*meant*—first name."

"Actually, it wasn't just that. They weren't in alphabetical order," he said, and the feeling inside him got worse, as if he'd put both feet into quicksand. Dammit, he'd waded in this far...no stopping now. "But that's not all. Your handwriting and spelling...they're..." He wasn't going to say *atrocious*. But suddenly it was the only word he could think of.

She seemed to read his mind. "So what? Doctors have terrible penmanship, too."

He was making a hash of this, but he couldn't stop the flow of words. "I looked at your employee file and the résumé you gave Gran. You spelled the word business *b-i-z-n-i-s*."

"So what? Haven't you ever texted someone before?" She picked at her apron. "Why were you looking at my file? That résumé was from five years ago. Why does it even matter now?"

Aaron could have explained that there was a difference between instant messaging and writing a formal document to a potential employer. After all, she'd given that résumé to Gran when she was twenty-five, not fifteen. But it would've come off as patronizing and pedantic.

He was also wary of telling her what he'd gleaned

about learning disabilities in adults. She'd demonstrated quite a few of the signs of dyslexia, dyscalculia and dysgraphia, and when he'd thought about her years in high school, he'd started to wonder if what he'd mistook for flightiness was actually something else—ADHD, maybe. The more he'd read about it, the more confident he'd been that she had some broad-spectrum issues and the less qualified he was to be addressing this.

Regardless, this was about helping Steph. He might not be able to do anything himself, but he could set her on a path. That didn't make this any easier, though, and he'd clearly upset her. He had to make her understand his intention wasn't to belittle her, while showing her how her errors affected the people around her and her own life. "I noticed you still give change incorrectly sometimes...more often than not."

"This again? I told you, it was a mistake. I was probably having a bad day." Her tone rose an anxious octave. "Why are you hair...heresy..." She screwed up her face and hissed out a tight breath. "Why are you still *harassing* me about this? I always make up for it."

"Wait, what?" But she was already hastening back to the bakery side of Georgette's, retreating behind the counter as if it would protect her from his line of questioning. He followed. "What do you mean you make up for it?"

"I can't tell what I did wrong since you've started

counting the till." She started wiping the counter down furiously, leaving streaks all over the spotless surface. "I don't know what I still owe, but I can make up for it, I swear."

A cold feeling trickled through him. "Are you telling me you've been putting your own money into the register?"

She recoiled and started making a fresh pot of coffee, even though there was already a full pot there. "I know I make mistakes. I pay for them."

Aaron stood in shock. She'd been putting her own cash into the till. That explained why Gran had all those discrepancies in the books. Sometimes those numbers climbed into the hundreds. What was Steph living on?

She faced away from him, her trembling hands restlessly reorganizing the counter. What was he supposed to do now? Yes, she'd made mistakes, but it wasn't theft, and she was returning what she'd lost.

Still, he couldn't allow this to continue, for her sake as well as the bakery's.

"You're going to fire me, aren't you?" Her voice came out stiffly. "You think I'm an idiot."

"No. God, no." He wanted to hold her, to make her understand. "You know how much we need you. All I want is to help you." But seeing how he'd hurt her, he had no idea how he could've been helpful. No, if anything, he'd done this for himself, thinking he could be the hero, the leader, the mentor. He was still trying to play the white knight, and he sucked hard at it.

"Are you going to tell Georgette?" she asked, tears in her voice.

"There's no reason to, unless you want to tell her. I only asked you about this because...well, people with learning disabilities have it all their lives. It's never too late to get help and—"

"I'm not retarded," she lashed out, but clearly regretted the word as soon as it left her mouth. She looked down, red in the face. "I'm... There's nothing wrong with me. I make mistakes sometimes when I'm stressed out. I don't have *issues*."

They'd officially stepped into territory Aaron wasn't familiar with. He hadn't been ready to handle the emotional part of this, though—duh— maybe he should've expected to when he'd decided to confront her. Perhaps it'd be better to focus on solutions to her problems at work.

"Are you using the cash register?" he asked.

"Of course I am."

"But not all the time, I noticed."

"You've been watching me?" She took a step back, fists clenched in front of her as if she were ready for a fight. Aaron carefully moderated his tone.

"Of course I noticed. Not because I'm trying to find fault with the way you work. You're a great worker, a great baker and you relate to people around here in ways I never could. I couldn't manage without you." He let out a breath. "But I'm trying to manage my grandmother's business, too. You understand that, right?"

She didn't say anything, but then her chin bobbed in acknowledgment.

"You might think it's okay to keep giving away your money to make up for your mistakes, but the better solution is to cut down on those mistakes. That means we need to find other ways to do things."

She flicked him a skeptical look. "Like what?"

"Well, if you don't use the cash register every time, maybe you could keep a calculator on you."

Her jaw flexed. "I don't want to look stupid in front of people."

"No one's going to think that."

She sagged and turned away. "Of course they do. All my life they've called me a dumb blonde. You think it, too."

"You're not dumb, Steph." Clearly, her self-esteem had suffered, though he was only now beginning to see how much. She'd always seemed so cheerful and carefree, but beneath it all, she was scared of what people thought of her. He'd read that some people with undiagnosed learning disabilities did a lot to hide them. He knew how exhausting that could be, having hidden his own secrets back in high school. "You're not stupid, and you're not an idiot. You have to stop using those words to describe yourself."

She shot him a cynical glower. He didn't blame her for her uncertainty. After all, *he'd* labeled her with those words once, sometimes out of spite, sometimes out of a perverse sense of self-preservation.

Now, those labels were hurting her, pushing her away from him when they'd only just started bonding. He didn't want to keep her at arm's length anymore.

"Steph." He reached out and gently gripped her shoulder. She was firm and solid, with well-developed baker's muscles that shifted and bunched beneath his fingers. Warmth radiated from her, flowing to his hand, up his arm and to parts beyond. "I only brought this up because...I care about you."

She stared, her lips parted slightly. "You really do, don't you?"

His lungs squeezed, and he barely whispered, "Yes."

The space of a heartbeat put more distance between them than he could imagine. She shrugged off his hand coolly. "You've got a funny way of showing it."

If he'd thought he couldn't feel any lower, he'd been wrong. "All I meant to do was support you. I thought maybe if you talked to someone—"

"I'm going to get a head start on tomorrow's baking. Do you have a problem with that?" When he didn't reply, she trudged into the kitchen. The swinging door swayed on its double hinge and slapped the air behind her.

Aaron cursed himself. When it came to relating to other people, he was no genius. Even with the best intentions, telling Steph outright that he thought she had problems was hardly the way to help her, much less win her over.

If anyone had a problem, it was him.

THE BOOKSTORE'S OFFICIAL grand opening was scheduled for the second weekend in May, but Georgette's Bakery and Books was already a huge draw. An unseasonably warm and dry start to the month had drawn the tourists and weekenders, and the newly completed patio was soon filling up.

Aaron had planned an evening with hors d'oeuvres and wine. He'd wanted to do an author event or some kind of reading to kick off the celebration, but Steph had convinced him not to, explaining that as the newest addition to the community, Georgette's Bakery and Books would be the cool new place to hang out. He could organize special events during the slower months to inspire customers to visit. She might not have a business degree, but she did understand the folks in Everville.

Aaron agreed with her reasoning. He'd been asking for her advice or opinion often, and taking a lot of her suggestions. He'd even given her the go-ahead to start bagging and labeling cookies the way she'd recommended. She guessed he was trying to make up for telling her she had a learning disability.

She'd laid awake the night after that conversation, stewing over his accusation. She supposed Aaron had her best interests at heart. Still, Steph wasn't ready to believe something was actually wrong with her. She'd struggled for a long time knowing people thought she wasn't very bright. And maybe she'd perpetuated that by living up to everyone else's low standards.

It'd bothered her so much she'd called her mother.

"I don't know what gave you *that* idea," her mother had said unequivocally. "There's absolutely nothing wrong with you. We've talked about this."

"But…did the teachers say anything? Did they notice…?"

"What do teachers know? They're only concerned about the overall GPAs of their classes. Baby, believe me. If we'd thought anything was wrong, we would've fixed it."

They'd left it at that, but Steph couldn't shake that nagging feeling. It was confusing to think about. On the one hand, denying she might have a learning disability made her feel righteous but low. On the other hand, acknowledging the possibility that she might have LD gave her a weird sense of relief, as if finally there were an answer for why she'd never been able to keep up in class. Mixed in with all that were feelings of anger, frustration and resentment. It was all too much to think about. She wasn't prepared to deal with any of this.

Even if Aaron was damned wrong about her, she wouldn't hold it against him. She was a professional, after all, learning disability or not. He'd tested the limits of their new friendship, but she was willing to forgive him. They still had to work together, after all. If she could just make him see her value in the business rather than her failings, he wouldn't have to worry about her mistakes.

Admittedly, keeping a calculator on hand had proved pretty useful. And to her relief and surprise, no one ever commented on it when she pulled it out, which she'd done plenty of times that evening at the bookstore's grand opening. They were so busy, Steph couldn't spare a brain cell to do math while she and Kira rushed around making sure all the food was ready, the drinks filled, the space kept clean and clear of stray wineglasses. The caterer had taken over the kitchen. Since they didn't have the budget for waitstaff, Steph had to keep replenishing the platters of food in addition to running the counter.

"What a terrific turnout," Georgette said as she reached for the coffee. Steph hurried over and snatched up the pot before the older woman could, pouring her a cup. Georgette frowned. "Really, Stephanie, I'm not an invalid. You've got plenty enough to do that you don't need to be looking after me, as well. Are things all right over here?"

"Things are great," she said, giddy from exhaustion.

"Aaron's about to give a speech," Georgette said. "You'll mind the shop while he's out on the patio, won't you?"

A little twinge went through her. "O-of course."

"Thank you." Coffee in hand, Georgette walked sedately back out onto the patio.

It took Steph a moment to recover from the pinch to her pride. She would like to be there when Aaron delivered his speech, but Georgette was right. Someone had to stay in the bakery. Enjoying the party was not part of her job. Steph was the hired help.

Her mother would have had a fit.

During a brief pause in the steady flow of customers and catering, Kira answered a call on her cell phone. She seemed to shrink down into a ball of fury as she cupped the phone close and whispered harshly.

"I can't… No, I…" She bit down on her lip. "Okay. Just…hang on, all right?"

"What's wrong, Kira?" The teen's features were pinched.

"Something's come up. I have to go home." A sheen of anxiety glistened behind her glasses.

"Are you kidding me?" Steph gestured around at

the crowd, but immediately felt bad for snapping at the girl. Clearly, Kira knew this was a bad time. Something had to be really wrong at home. "Can't you stay another hour, at least?"

"No. It's…" Her face screwed up as she pressed her hands to the sides of her head. "Please. I wouldn't ask if it wasn't an emergency."

Several times now Kira had left early or missed work altogether, claiming she was sick. It was happening often enough that Steph was beginning to worry, and had even suggested a trip to the doctor's, but the teen had refused. She wondered if Aaron had noticed her absences.

Of course he'd noticed, she thought with a frown. He would probably bring it up with Kira at some point and try to *help*…even if it meant firing her.

Ultimately, as the bakery's assistant manager, Steph was Kira's supervisor. If Kira needed to leave, she needed to leave. And she'd defend her against Aaron if he had a problem with it.

"Okay. Go ahead." But her conscience pricked her, and she stopped Kira before she pushed her way outside. "You'd tell me if something were really the matter, right?"

Kira gave her a forlorn look. "There's nothing to tell."

Things got too busy for Steph to worry about Kira once she'd left. The sun that had been shining so earnestly earlier in the day disappeared, and an early summer storm blew in. Everyone who'd been on the patio rushed into the shop, their skin and clothes splattered with fat drops of rain.

"I guess those spring showers we were supposed to get decided to come late," Aaron mused. Droplets shone like silver in his dark hair and on the lenses of his glasses.

Steph smirked. "I told you it was better to keep the food indoors."

"I concede to your infinite wisdom." He staged a little bow that might have been meant to mock her, but she couldn't help but chuckle. "Guess I'll have to give the speech inside."

He disappeared into the crowd of well-wishers once more. Even when she meant to be cool toward him, it was hard to stay angry. She wasn't good at holding grudges, and she hated fighting with people, even Aaron, especially on a day meant to celebrate good things. He was all smiles and bright eyes, handsome in a clean shirt, a touch frazzled and vibrant with nervous energy. She'd called him a friend; she supposed that didn't end with one disagreement.

Many of the townsfolk had come to congratulate him and say hello to Georgette, including the mayor, Cheyenne Welks. The fortysomething woman with long, curly red-gold hair wore a loose, flowing green dress and mingled with the crowd with stately grace. Maya was here, too, wearing a red-and-black polka-dotted fifties-style dress with red pumps. She stood by the food table chatting with some of the other Main Street business owners. Stephanie's parents had wanted to come, but they were attending a friend's charity fund-raiser in New York.

"Mighty fine turnout." Wyatt appeared next to the counter, cowboy hat in hand. For someone so big and broad, he certainly moved quietly. Or maybe she just hadn't noticed him.

"Nice of you to come out all this way," she said in greeting.

"Any excuse to see you is a good one." He flashed his pearly whites. "Besides, I ordered some books from Aaron, and he got them in today. Thought it'd be neighborly to swing by for the party."

"Speaking of neighborly…" She caught Maya's attention with a wave and beckoned her over. "Wyatt Brown, I'd like you to meet one of my dearest friends, Maya Hanes. She owns the consignment shop on Main Street."

"Nice to meet you." The rancher shook Maya's outstretched hand, and she beamed at him.

"Steph's told me all about you and your ranch." Maya gave her a wink. Steph hoped her friend would understand why she'd called her over, and Maya didn't disappoint. "I've heard your family runs a ranch in Australia."

"In Queensland, yes."

"By any chance would it be near Townsville?"

His face lit up with surprise. "A couple of hours outside Townsville, in fact. You've been to the area?"

"I spent a year backpacking across Asia and made a few stops in Australia. Ended up working on a sheep farm in Queensland for a few weeks."

The two got to talking, allowing Stephanie to quietly edge away and see to the refreshments. Halfway to the punch bowl, she bumped into Aaron.

He looked around nervously. "Guess I'd better make this speech fast so I can ring in some sales." His fingers were trembling. She picked up a cup and filled it with punch.

"Dutch courage," she said, handing him the drink.

"You spiked the punch?"

"Huh? No. Why would you say that?"

"That's what Dutch courage means. Alcohol for settling the nerves."

"Oh." She'd only heard the expression because her mother used it frequently. She hadn't thought it actually meant anything. And why would drinking be a Dutch thing? That seemed discriminatory somehow. She stared into the cup. "Would it help if I said it was spiked?"

He gave the drink a critical look, shrugged and downed it as though it were a shot of tequila. "Good enough. Wish me luck."

The chatter died down as Aaron stepped onto

a milk crate and held up a hand. "Thank you all for coming." His voice boomed through the space. Steph had never really thought about the sound of his voice—not deep or gruff or anything she would've thought of as manly, but clear and precise, his words carefully chosen without all the *ums* and *ahs* and *likes* she was used to hearing or saying herself. She liked how he sounded. Confident. Direct.

"Almost fifty years ago my grandparents, Malcolm and Georgette Caruthers, spent their life savings on this building, two ovens and some supplies, and started a simple roadside bakeshop on the outskirts of Everville. At the time the town was a thriving little trading hub. Since those days, Everville's seen a lot of change, not all of it good, but it has lived up to its motto. It has endured, just as my grandmother's legacy has."

The crowd gave murmurs of assent and nods of approval.

"Georgette's has always filled stomachs with good food, and now, I hope it will also fill minds with great books. It's with great pride and joy that I welcome you to the newly renovated Georgette's Bakery and Books."

Everyone clapped. Steph wished she'd thought to string up a ribbon that Aaron could cut to mark the occasion. Seeing how excited people were and how proud Georgette was of her grandson made her happy for him.

"There are some people I want to thank…" He

went on to thank the mayor for her personal support, then thanked the contractors and caterer, the Everville business association, the customers and his grandmother, who gave him a big hug.

Steph zoned out and leaned against the counter, absently scratching at a bit of crusted-on jelly that had welded itself to the glass.

"There is one final person I want to recognize," Aaron announced. "Many of you know my grandmother has been ill. I think it's quite clear to everyone in this room that Georgette's would not still be up and running if it hadn't been for the tireless efforts of one individual. I've come to appreciate her more and more each day, and I've learned that without her, none of this would be possible."

Slowly, Stephanie looked up. Everyone was staring at her, but her eyes honed in on Aaron's. Her heart stopped. She couldn't look away.

"Stephanie Stephens—" Aaron's voice seemed to come from far away "—come up here. I have a surprise for you."

Her numb feet carried her forward, buoyed by a wave of applause and whistles, and she was urged toward Aaron by a sea of hands clapping her on the shoulder. Smiling faces she'd known all her life congratulated her and told her what a wonderful job she'd done.

Something inside her blossomed. Her eyes began to sting.

The space in front of her opened up, and all of a

sudden it was just Aaron standing there with a sparkling pink gift bag. "I wanted you to have something that was both useful and showed how much you're appreciated."

She had no idea what could possibly do that. Right now she felt so full of love and awe, there was nothing that could make her float any higher.

She reached into the bag and felt something made of stiff fabric. She drew it out and unfolded it. It was a plain brown apron—practical and so very Aaron. Embroidered on the front in pink letters were the words Sweet As Sugar. He pulled out a matching cap with Georgette's logo on the front. "Custom made for you," he said.

She showed the crowd, who voiced a collective "aw." Aaron slipped the apron over Steph's head as if it were a medal. "Thank you so much," she said.

"I'm the one who's thanking you."

Gripped by joy, she threw her arms around his shoulders. His arms twined around her waist. He was so easy to hug. No extra meat or muscle to get in the way. No hulking shoulders or thick thighs. And when he hugged her back, he didn't squeeze her too hard or let his hands roam. It felt natural.

She absorbed the moment and then eased back slightly so she could tell him thank you.

And then he kissed her.

The applause fell away as a rushing sound filled her head. Time trickled like flowing molasses, and she lingered, absorbing the sensations shivering through her. She could smell the soap and shampoo he used—nothing overpowering, just clean. He tasted like an intriguing combination of coffee, chocolate, mint and something uniquely Aaron. His lips were soft and firm all at once, and his warm hands rested lightly around her waist.

The moment he broke away, she knew she wanted more. She wanted to dive back in, memorize his taste and make a dessert out of the flavor. She felt as though she'd tasted chocolate for the first time ever—mind opened to a world she'd never imagined. In that moment she saw Aaron Caruthers as more than the guy who'd taken over Georgette's Bakery, more than the geeky kid who'd once had a crush on her in high school.

He was a guy she wanted to sleep with. Bad.

CHAPTER THIRTEEN

IN HINDSIGHT, THE KISS had probably been a bad idea.

Not that his body believed that. Aaron had replayed the scene over and over until his mind had distorted the memory, magnifying it till he'd convinced himself it'd been one of those big romantic Hollywood moments.

He still had no idea why he'd done what he'd done. He'd never been into public displays of affection. Kissing Stephanie Stephens, a woman he had no claim over, in full view of practically everyone in town had not been on his agenda. It'd just happened. He'd wanted to acknowledge her, show her she was appreciated. He'd wanted to make her understand how vital she was to Georgette's. Maybe he'd even wanted to smooth things over after their confrontation. A handshake would have been the proper etiquette.

But then she'd hugged him, and he'd felt all that warm, soft, cinnamon-perfumed flesh pressing against him. It'd felt so right that his instincts had simply taken over.

He wiped away the smile creeping onto his lips

at the thought of her flushed cheeks. Her lashes had fluttered like ruffled birds' feathers. She hadn't seemed offended—surprised, maybe. Or had that been the reaction of an assaulted employee in shock?

And then awareness of the outside world had seeped back in. Had there been hoots and whistles? Murmurs of speculation? Of disapproval? He wasn't sure.

He did remember the look on Wyatt Brown's face. Surprise, disbelief…maybe envy, or was it anger? A tiny knot of dread tangled with smug satisfaction deep down inside him. He knew it was petty to revel in the fact that he was finally the guy on the other side of Steph's lips. But he did.

Not that he'd been staking his claim or anything. That was a bad idea all around. They were coworkers. And they had baggage.

He started up the station wagon as Georgette climbed into the passenger seat. She was looking a lot better these days, but still had to see the doctor for regular checkups. He was sure all that time off had renewed her strength. Going years without taking a vacation couldn't have been good for her. She attributed her improving health to the fact that she was working again and not feeling like a lump at home. Regardless, he'd make sure she took it easy.

He was taking Gran to the physical therapist before he went to the bookshop that morning. He'd expected to spend a lot more time in the initial days running the place, but Kira had proven quite adept at managing things in his absence. Maybe she was trying to make up for bailing out on the grand opening two nights ago, but Steph had explained later that Kira had had some kind of family emergency. That must've been the fifth or sixth time this month. He was starting to wonder if she was as reliable as Gran and Steph seemed to think.

"Is there anything you'd like to tell me?" Georgette asked after a beat.

He diligently checked left and right along the empty stretch of highway before turning onto it. He'd avoided this conversation with his grandmother as long as he could. "About what?"

"About what happened Saturday night."

She was referring to Stephanie, he knew, but he pretended to misunderstand. "Actually, I wanted to ask you about Kira." He paused. He didn't want to pry into the girl's private business, but he had to plan for the worst if Kira had to leave again... or for good. "She's been away from work a lot. Sometimes she leaves in the middle of her shifts."

"Family emergencies," Gran said with a nod.

Aaron knew that, but his concern was more for Kira than the bakery. "I'm worried that work might be distracting her from school. She's still...what? Sixteen? Seventeen?"

"People do what they have to do, Aaron. We don't get to judge them for their choices."

"I'm not judging. I'm just concerned that she's spreading herself too thin." He didn't mention he was also concerned that Kira wasn't as dedicated as Gran thought she was. "She's a great worker, but she needs to have fun and be a normal teenage girl. Isn't her family worried about her?"

They were coming up on the turn where his parents had been killed. It was the most direct route to Gran's therapist. They were both silent as he negotiated the bend, mindful of all the signs marking the road. Georgette didn't reply until they'd cleared the spot. "Kira's parents aren't in the picture."

His grip on the steering wheel tightened. "What? Where are they?"

"Some things don't get talked about in town, and the Wests are one of those things. You never met them, I suppose?"

"No."

"Her father lost his job at the plant a few years back, and her mother hasn't been employed for some time. She and Kira live in a camper in the trailer park outside town. I don't know what happened to the father, but from what I gather, he's no longer in the picture. Their mother—"

"Their?" he interrupted.

"Kira has a younger brother, Tyler. He's eleven," she explained. "Their mother fell in with some bad people and… Well, let's just say I pray for her every day. She's practically abandoned the children…" Gran's lips pursed. She didn't like speaking ill of anyone. "Kira's the one holding everything together. She's the breadwinner at home. Pays the rent and cares for her brother. She knows that child welfare will get involved and take Tyler away if they get wind of their home situation." She cut him a look. "I trust you won't spread this any further."

"No." But then he rethought that. Maybe child services *should* get involved. That couldn't be a good environment for either of those kids. Still, if the children weren't being abused and Kira was handling everything, he didn't want to break up the family and send them to foster homes. "Does Stephanie know anything about this?" he asked.

"Unless Kira told her, I don't think so, and I think Kira would rather keep it that way for her brother's sake." She paused. "It's not that I don't trust Steph with secrets. Helen Stephens, however…"

"I'll keep quiet." Still, he wondered if they were doing the right thing by letting Kira shoulder the burden alone. Pride was one thing, but if Kira and her brother, Tyler, were in danger, Aaron would be complicit in his silence. It didn't sit well with him.

They were quiet for a time. The flourishing spring greens and browns of the land whipped by. The sun shone through silky-thin cloud cover, making the sky glow silver.

"So about Stephanie…"

He'd wondered when she would circle back to that. He concentrated on the road. "There's nothing to tell, Gran." When she didn't respond, he added, "We're just friends."

"In my day, friends only kissed like that in front of big crowds at their wedding."

"I was trying to show my appreciation for her hard work. I got caught up in the moment. Anyhow, you like Stephanie. I don't see the big deal."

"But it *is* a big deal." Her mouth was set in a tight line. "I remember how you said she treated you in high school. Why do you think I never told you about her working for me? She made you... unhappy."

That was only half true, and Gran knew it. They were both skating around the real reason he'd been unhappy back then. "We're not teenagers anymore. Besides, I wouldn't date her now."

Georgette's gaze whipped around. "And why not? She's a perfectly nice girl, you know."

Jeez, now she sounded as though she were pushing them together. He wondered whether the stroke had affected her judgment. "We're too different. She's not my type."

"Why? Because *you* happened to go to college and she didn't?"

The comment corkscrewed through him. "What? No. Why would you say that?"

"You put a lot of stock in formal education, Aaron. I remember how much you clung to your studies and your work."

"I didn't cling, Gran. I did what I had to do so I could make sure you were taken care of."

"And I appreciate it," she said kindly. "But you're well past those days. Not everything is as perfect in reality as it is in theory. It's time to look up from your neat little graphs and binders. You can't plan your whole life out. Live a little."

"I appreciate the advice—" he didn't "—but Steph really isn't my type."

"It wouldn't hurt to try something different now and again."

She'd often said the same thing when he was growing up and she'd put some new dish or pastry in front of him. "Try it and maybe you'll like it," she'd say, and Aaron would dutifully, if grudgingly, sample the alien confection. It usually turned out fine, but he knew what he liked and knew what was good for him.

Bran muffins might be boring, but too many cookies would rot your teeth. He didn't see a need to deviate from what he was content with...no matter how mouthwatering the alternatives were.

"You have to set a date."

"No, Maya."

"Yes, Maya." The consignment store owner picked up Steph's laptop and went to the high school equivalency testing website. "It says here all we have to do is email them and they can set up a date for the examination."

Steph broke into a sweat. "I'm not ready."

"Yes, you are. Holding off will only make you more and more reluctant to do it." Maya had been working with her all night to complete the language and reading section of the HSE workbook Steph had ordered. She was good that way, forcing Steph to concentrate. If only she'd hung out with her more in high school instead of spending every spare period with Dale, maybe her marks wouldn't have been so dismal.

Steph dug her fingernails into her palms. "I don't feel ready. I'm still..." She ground her jaw. Even the word *exam* made her sick.

On top of all that, she was still thinking about Aaron's suggestion about her having a learning disability. What if he was right? What was she supposed to do about it? It wasn't as if she could flick a switch to suddenly make her smarter.

She hadn't even told Maya about what Aaron had said because she was afraid her friend might confirm his suspicions.

"Hey." Maya patted her clammy hand. "Listen. It'll be okay. I'm not making you do the exam tomorrow. I just think we should set a date so you don't put it off. This is what you wanted, right?"

More than anything, except maybe owning Georgette's. She'd prove to Aaron once and for all there was nothing wrong with her. She'd see it through, dammit. No flaking out.

She relaxed her grip and stared at the half moons

of her fingernail marks crisscrossing the love lines on her palms. "Okay. Do it."

"Atta girl."

They decided she'd do the exam in the third week of June. That gave Steph about a month to prepare.

"You know, I bet Aaron would be great at helping you prep for the test," Maya said, clearly fishing.

Steph didn't give her the satisfaction. "He doesn't know I'm doing this. Besides, he's too busy with the bookshop and taking care of Georgette. I don't want to bother him."

"I don't think he'd mind." Maya waggled her eyebrows. "Especially after kissing you in front of all those people. Ballsy of him."

"I was just as surprised," Steph replied, unable to stop the warmth and giddiness rising through her. "Call me crazy, but…it was kind of hot."

Maya chuckled and got up to open the bottle of cabernet sauvignon she'd brought as an incentive to study. "From where I was standing you two were practically smoking." She poured the wine. "Good kisser, then?"

"Omigod, like you wouldn't believe." Her skin buzzed just thinking about it…and she'd thought about it a lot. "You know I've kissed a lot of frogs—"

"Humble brag—" Maya sang.

"—but I didn't realize how warty they were next to Aaron. How did this never occur to me before?"

"Clarification—toads are the ones with warts,

not frogs." Maya gave a small shrug. "And you didn't have the exposure to him that other people had. He was kind of geeky, but there were plenty of girls who had crushes on him, you know."

That caught her off guard. "Really?"

"You sound surprised."

"No. I mean, yes. I thought he was..." She was about to say "a loser" but then she rethought it. How was calling Aaron a loser any different from anyone else calling her a bimbo? She pledged to erase the word from her vocabulary. "I thought he wasn't that kind of guy."

"Well, he was kind of hung up on one girl, and everyone knew it." Maya gave her an arched look.

A deep sense of shame filled her. She realized now how badly she'd treated him, stringing him along, pretending to be kind when she'd been laughing at him behind his back. She'd been cruel and shallow...and for what purpose?

Maya toasted her. "Drink your wine. Then tell me if I need to smack some sense into you about Aaron."

"What are you talking about? I've got plenty of sense."

"But none of the you-should-hit-that sense, apparently."

Steph rubbed her knees compulsively. "I dunno. I mean, yeah, I'd do him in a heartbeat now that I know how he kisses."

"But?"

"But…" She nibbled her thumbnail, a habit she thought she'd broken a long time ago. "I'm not sure we're…compare…compatible." Or that he would go for a one-night stand. He struck her as being the serious, long-term-relationship type.

"Do you think you're more compatible with Wyatt?" Maya asked.

"No." She said it so quickly she surprised herself. "No," she repeated more slowly, turning the word and everything it meant over in her mind. "Me and Wyatt…I'm not feeling it." And she doubted she ever would. He looked good in theory—nice body, great smile, personality, money, goals, influence and the desire to have a family. He might as well have been a freaking candidate for *The Bachelor*. But they simply didn't have the chemistry she apparently had with Aaron.

"Oh, goody. Cuz I wanna ride that cowboy all the way home." Maya sipped her wine and licked her lips. "But seriously, Aaron is, from what I know of him, a decent guy. I'm not saying you should start picking china patterns or anything like that—"

"Leave that to my mother," Steph said with a snort.

"But what harm could a little dating do?"

"And by dating you mean sex."

She toasted her. "Of course I do."

"You know we work together, right?"

"All the more reason to hook up. Otherwise, you've got all that unresolved sexual tension building up. It'll be like the worst parts of high school with all those raging adult hormones floating through Georgette's." She snickered. "C'mon, you don't see a lot of single guys coming into town. If you don't snatch Aaron up, someone else will."

Maybe Maya was right about that. She'd seen the way women had checked him out.

"Just so you know," Maya added, "Wyatt was not pleased by that little show Aaron put on. The game is afoot."

Steph blanched. She hadn't even considered Wyatt's feelings in all this. "Was he mad?"

"Not mad. But he did say 'Challenge accepted' to himself."

Steph scoffed. "No, he didn't."

"Okay, he didn't," Maya relented. "But that was the look on his face."

Steph hoped Wyatt wasn't too upset. She hadn't meant to lead him on. She'd made her disinterest pretty clear, or she thought she had.

Maybe dating Aaron wasn't a bad idea, especially if it encouraged the rancher to chase someone else.

She was still trying to figure out who she was, after all. Part of that meant rediscovering what she liked. And the more she thought about it, the more she realized she liked Aaron.

CHAPTER FOURTEEN

STEPH'S LIKING FOR Aaron didn't lessen as the days went on, even though he was clearly avoiding her. The strength of her growing attraction was baffling. She found herself studying him while he worked on the bookstore's computer. He was so...average. If she passed him on the street, she wouldn't give him a second look. And now she was giving him a third, tenth, twentieth...

When the bakery was slow, she asked if he needed help in the bookshop, but he always said no. Maybe he didn't trust her since the shelving debacle. Instead, Kira worked in the bookshop when shipments came in, running both registers on slower days. Aaron had even raised her pay since she was technically doing two jobs.

The only time he asked for Steph's help was when he wanted her opinion on the way a display looked. He didn't say much to her apart from the usual greeting. If he'd thought the kiss was a mistake, she figured he would've apologized by now. But he hadn't. Instead, it was as if he was pretending it had never happened; he'd drawn a line between them and was staying firmly on his side.

After more than a week of near silence, she was fed up. She brought him his post-lunch coffee and bran muffin, then lingered, studying the books on his recommended titles shelf. The tension between them thickened.

She blurted, "Are these all nonfiction?" then cringed inwardly. She could've figured that out for herself if she'd stopped and taken a moment to think.

"All but two," he said. "They're the most recent books I've read, so I feel like I can sell them."

She stared at the rows of books with little framed cards next to each describing the content. She read a couple and blinked hard. Books about oil production and the firebombing of Dresden weren't exactly her idea of fun summer beach reading, but to each his own. "You should talk to Chris Jamieson. I don't know if you know him—he was a couple of years ahead of us in school. He likes reading this stuff."

"Chris Jamieson? The quarterback?"

"I'm surprised you haven't bumped into him since you got back. He came back to Everville after his first year of college to take over his dad's farm. He's the one who got the city council to agree to build the wind farm outside town."

"No kidding." He scratched the back of his

head. "Wow. I never thought he was into that kind of thing."

"Guess we all sorta grew up and branched out." She stuffed her hands in her pockets and shuffled her feet. "Y'know, I bet Kira would have some great recommendations for young adult books. And I bet you could get lots of folks to write reviews for you. That way you don't have to do all the work of picking books yourself."

"And they wouldn't all be boring-as-hell reads." He glanced at her and laughed. "Oh, c'mon, I can see it in your face."

She raised her hands. "Your words, not mine."

"What do you like to read?" he asked.

She shrugged. "Mostly thrillers, sometimes a romance or two. I try to keep it light. I do a lot of books on tape. I don't have much energy at the end of the day to read."

"I can imagine with your early hours. If you have any favorites, let me know. I'd love to see reviews from you."

The *L*-word, even out of context, gave her a little thrill, and she lifted a shoulder shyly. "I'm not much for clitoral analysis," she said.

There was a beat of silence before she registered her gaff. "*Critical* analysis!" she blurted. Dear God, that was a Freudian slip if ever she'd heard one.

Aaron smothered a huge grin behind his hand and coughed. To his credit, he didn't laugh at her. "I don't need a doctoral thesis, just a couple of sentences that say thumbs-up." She couldn't detect any irony or sarcasm in his words, but her self-doubt lingered. "In fact, borrow any books you'd like. Think of this as your own personal lending library."

"That's really nice of you. But I can pay for my own books."

"Ah, but this way, you'll be pressured to read and return them."

"Sneaky. I'm beginning to think you've got an agenda."

"What can I say? It's all about the bookstore." Pride shone in his face.

Steph smiled. Aaron had achieved his dream. She'd seen the place go from drafty underused dining room to this warm, friendly space that people were excited about. She'd been wrong to be afraid of change. She was proud of what he'd accomplished.

"Go out to dinner with me," she said before she could think of a more elegant way to ask.

He blinked owlishly. "What?"

"Dinner. Like a date." Her heart hammered. She'd never asked a guy out before. She'd flirted, sure, and sometimes she'd tricked a guy into asking her out, but in the end, they always did the asking.

As his stunned silence lengthened, she grew clammy all over. What if he said no? What if he laughed at her? They hadn't exactly had the smoothest of working relationships. And she hadn't forgotten the whole LD thing. Maybe he thought she was crazy to think he'd ever go out with her after the way she'd treated him. She was starting to regret asking when he answered. Sort of.

"*You*...want to go on a date...with *me*?" He enunciated it slowly, as if he didn't understand her meaning.

She kept her expression bright, despite her doubts. "Yes, you. This Thursday after we close. I'll take you to Greenfields."

"You want to go to the country club?" Apparently, all he could do was ask questions.

"They have the best prime rib dinner. It'll be my treat."

"Why?" Aaron pulled back slightly, as though he was preparing for her to kick him in the nuts.

"Because...because I like you." Her whole body flushed hot. When his lips parted in surprise, the urge to bite down and suck on them blew through her like a blast of heat from an open oven.

Aaron's face glowed red. He glanced around as if searching for hidden cameras.

Steph toed the ground. "You're making this really hard for me. I swear I'm not pulling a prank or anything. I want to take you out to dinner."

"Sorry." He made a giddy sound between a giggle and a cough. "Sorry. Um..." He shifted his weight, trying to lean against the counter and look casual. "Yes? Yes."

"Great!" And they were left facing each other, grinning awkwardly. "Right. Thursday night, then."

"Okay." His head bobbed as if his neck were a spring.

"Okay." Another beat and she turned away and hustled back to the kitchen where she stopped and let out a long, quaking breath. Her heart was racing and her skin felt tingly, as if someone had tickled her all over. She hadn't felt this light-headed since she'd been asked to her first dance.

She was going on a date with Aaron Caruthers. Back in high school the idea would've sent her into a howling fit. Now all she could do was grin.

ON THURSDAY AARON found himself watching the clock and not getting much done. His face hurt from smiling all day, but he didn't care. He counted down the minutes as Kira and Steph washed up and put things away. The moment the clock reached five, he hurriedly flipped the shop sign to Closed.

A date with Stephanie Stephens. Not only that, but *she'd* asked *him*. She'd said she *liked* him. It was hard not to wonder if he'd stumbled into the Twilight Zone.

That moment of fear gripped him again. He should call this whole date off. So many things could go wrong, the least of which were tripping and throwing up all over himself. Getting involved with Steph put everything at risk—his grandmother's business, their friendship and his personal feelings. But no matter how much he tried to convince himself, and against all his better judgment, he wanted this. His eagerness made him certain he should call it off.

"Go on home, Kira," he called as he shut off the lights in the bookshop. "I'll handle the rest of the cleanup."

The teen cocked her head to one side. "Are you sure?"

"Absolutely." Ever since Gran had told him about the girl's home situation, he'd been more mindful of her hours, making sure she didn't overwork herself. He'd tried to buy her lunch a few times, but her frown had made it clear she didn't like accepting charity, so he did his best to help her in other ways. A small but affordable raise and flexible hours were important. He also had her work in the bookshop when he thought she could use a mental break. He even encouraged her to do her homework while watching the register when it was slow.

Tonight, though, he was sending Kira home early because he didn't want her wondering why he and Steph were leaving together. Not that he was embarrassed, but he wanted to keep gossip to a minimum. He hadn't even told Gran. Their talk in the car the other day had made him hyperaware of how he behaved around Steph, and he was bent on being casual about this.

In the kitchen Stephanie was loading the dishwasher. She looked over her shoulder and smiled when he entered. "Hey."

"Hey." Even with her dark blond hair confined beneath a hairnet and her T-shirt and apron stained with chocolate, she was still one of the most beautiful women he knew.

"I'll be done soon," she said. "But I need to swing by my place and get changed. Is that okay?"

"No problem." He indicated his own outfit, which he'd painstakingly assembled that morning in an effort to look casual, clean, but not nerdy. Charcoal-gray dress pants and a light blue shirt with a tie were as close to nice as he had without sliding into the wedding-guest look. "Am I okay?"

The way she checked him out had his blood surging south. "Hang on." She wiped her hands on a tea towel and walked up to him until they stood toe-to-toe. Her hooded storm-blue eyes fixed on his lips. His mouth went dry.

She reached up and undid his tie, then drew it off with a yank, the slick fabric making a *ziiiip* sound as she did so. "There." She thrust her fingers through his hair, mussed it up. "And there. Greenfields isn't as uptight as all that. You can go there in jeans if you want, actually. Maybe not with flour and caramel stains, though."

He smoothed his hair back automatically, and she reached up and ruffled it again. "Stop that," he said, even though he wouldn't have minded her fingers in his hair all night. She snagged his wrist as he reached up to straighten his cowlick once more.

"Nuh-uh. Messy is best. You look much sexier all tousled and hot and bothered."

His mouth gaped open, but whatever witty retort he'd intended came out as a prepubescent squeak. Him? Sexy? Not in a million years would he have imagined Steph calling him that. She giggled and whipped off her hairnet, pulling out the elastics of her pigtails and shaking out her hair. "I'll go get my purse, handsome." She winked.

Jesus. She was going to kill him flirting like this.

In minutes they were on the road. Steph insisted on driving him to the club and then dropping him off at the bakery after dinner to pick up the station wagon. Normally, he preferred to have his own vehicle, but saving gas was good, too. They went to her apartment first, a cluttered but well-lit space above the pharmacy on Main Street. She settled him in front of the TV with a glass of wine while she took a quick shower and changed.

As he sipped the sweet chardonnay, he marveled at the surrealism of the evening. Knowing Stephanie Stephens was naked in the shower only a few feet away was like something out of one of his teenage fantasies. He'd had to turn up the TV to drown out the sound of running water and the squeak of her bare feet in the tub. When the TV proved to be no distraction, he studied his surroundings in a desperate attempt to keep his wicked imagination from embarrassing him before the date had even begun.

The apartment was small and looked smaller because every surface was covered in haphazardly piled papers and magazines, pamphlets and junk mail. Swarovski crystal figurines and ceramic piggy banks took up valuable space on the bookshelves. Aaron had never liked to keep *things*. Of course, he owned a few mementos and keepsakes that had belonged to his parents, but apart from his books, he didn't hang on to knickknacks that could break, be lost, gather dust or otherwise be forgotten. Gran used to say it wasn't what he received that mattered—just the thought and the people behind the gift. Maybe that was why she only gave baked treats as gifts.

He glimpsed the spine of a book on the bottom shelf of the coffee table and pulled it out. It was a high school equivalency workbook. He flipped through it briefly, recognizing Steph's gawky handwriting.

He'd had no idea she was trying to earn her diploma. He was delighted for her. His blood rushed thick and fast with a weird sense of excitement and hope for Steph…and for him. It made him feel…

Like she's worth it.

He set the wineglass down, appalled at himself. That was a genuinely dickish way to think. Maybe Gran was right about him. Maybe he was a snob. All of the women he'd dated had at least a bachelor's degree, and that had been a conscious decision on his part. It simply made sense to him that he'd date someone who had a comparable level of education.

So what was he doing here? Academically slumming it? He shook his head, disgusted with himself. Gran was right. He did put too much stock in formal education. It was no guarantee of happy ever after, obviously, since all those past relationships had fizzled out. He shouldn't be so hung up on a piece of paper with some letters on it.

The bathroom door opened. He hastily stuffed the workbook back under the table. He didn't want to look as though he'd been snooping.

When he looked up his heart stopped. Steph had her hair wrapped in a towel. She wore a short white terrycloth robe that gaped in the front to reveal a V of smooth flesh between her breasts. The scent of rosewater tickled his nose as a cloud of steam wafted out behind her. "I'll be dressed in a few minutes. Our reservation isn't till seven."

He breathed deep as the blood rushed back into his brain and took a big swig of his wine.

Before long she emerged from her bedroom dressed in a pale blue top and khaki-colored skirt with ballet flats. It had been years since Aaron had seen Steph dressed in anything other than jeans and her Georgette's Bakery T-shirt and apron. She'd left her hair down. She looked good. Better than good. Yet, somehow, nothing like the girl from high school.

"Before we go," she said, "I have something for you."

She whipped out a bundle from behind her back tied neatly together with gold ribbon. He thought it was a small bouquet of some kind at first, but then he looked closer and gasped. "My pens!"

"Not *your* pens." She grinned. "Those dried up years ago. I had to special order these online. Had a hell of a time finding them, too."

He took one out of the bouquet and uncapped it with openmouthed glee, testing it on his palm because he was too excited to find a piece of paper. He drew a smiley face.

"Here." She took the pen from him and wrote something across his palm, her soft hand lightly cradling his.

He stared at the series of digits on his suddenly too-moist skin. "What's this?"

"My phone number." She winked. "I've been told you always wanted it in high school."

A feeling like the purr of an engine started at the base of his spine and rumbled upward. Back in school he used to get nervous and irritable whenever she talked to him. This reaction was completely different and decidedly adult.

And why shouldn't it be? He was a grown man. Confident. Experienced. Worldly. Fully capable of taking care of himself. He wasn't that awkward teen anymore. He'd left that dork far, far behind.

Now Stephanie Stephens was someone he actually might have a chance with.

"There're a lot of things I've always wanted." He caught the tips of her fingers and sent her what he hoped was a roguish smile. "This is a good start."

Her pretty blush had him mentally punching the air.

He could handle himself. He could handle her.

CHAPTER FIFTEEN

GREENFIELDS COUNTRY CLUB was located on the opposite side of Silver Lake. It was a sprawling resort in one of the most scenic spots in the county. The club was reserved for the wealthiest and most privileged members of the community. Even Terrence Stephens had had a hard time being vetted for membership. Helen had made that very clear to Steph when she was young. She'd been told she always had to be on her best behavior or risk having the family banned for life.

Greenfields featured a world-class eighteen-hole golf course, squash and tennis courts, swimming pool, bar, five-star restaurant and on-site spa. Steph and her parents had spent many weekends at the club when she was young, but despite all the facilities, she'd been bored and lonely. There hadn't been any kids her age there, and she hadn't been allowed to bring her friends.

Aaron sat forward as they drove up the cobblestone path to the enormous manor house.

"Jesus." He ogled the three-story building that looked a bit like the White House. "It must cost a fortune to heat this place in the winter."

She chuckled as she pulled up to the front doors. Only Aaron would think about a detail like that. A pair of uniformed valets rushed out and opened their doors for them. The younger of the two took her keys and surprised her by saying, "Good evening, Miss Stephens."

"Come here a lot?" Aaron asked as they walked up the front steps.

"Not for a long time. I don't recognize any of the staff, either. I don't know how they know me."

"The guard at the gate might've radioed up ahead and let them know you were coming," Aaron reasoned. "If this place is everything I've heard it is, they'll be greeting you at the door with your favorite drink in hand."

She'd never thought about that. She took a lot of this stuff for granted, she supposed. It made her feel strangely self-conscious.

When they walked in a concierge was, in fact, waiting for them, though she didn't have a glass of good red wine waiting. Too bad—Steph could use it. She was growing steadily more nervous. Aaron had said he'd never been to Greenfields, and she wondered if he would be comfortable. She was seeing it all through Aaron's critical eye now, and even though she'd been here countless times, the place felt alien to her. The main reception hall reminded her of a hunting lodge from a cartoon with overstuffed leather club chairs and lots of masculine oak furniture covered in deep greens and rich browns. The deer heads mounted over the mantel glared down at them from their posts. A chill came over her as she stared into the fireplace. It was as if the hearth threatened to swallow anyone who entered the club.

She was glad when they went straight to the dining room.

Once the waiter draped their napkins over their laps and left them to read the menu, Aaron gazed around, tugging at his shirtfront as if it couldn't be straight enough. "I feel underdressed," he whispered.

"You're not. Trust me. You look great."

He slipped on his glasses as he settled down to read the menu. She had to say, she actually really liked the glasses on him. The trendy black plastic frames suited his sharp features. He pursed his lips. "Um…there are no prices on this menu."

"Don't worry about that. I said this was my treat." As soon as she said it, she felt as though she were waving her family's money under his nose. Her doubts crowded in on top of one another. She should've picked a different place to eat. A restaurant in town or something more casual. She'd wanted to impress Aaron, but she should have known the posh club would only make him uncomfortable.

"I thought I'd get to fight with you over the check, at least."

"You'd never win. I'd tell the waitstaff to hold

you down." She chuckled when his jaw slackened. "I'm kidding."

He refocused on his menu, the fine lines around his mouth deepening. She could almost hear the gears turning as he tried to figure out which of the meals was the least expensive. She'd noticed he didn't treat himself a lot. His clothes were simple, durable and classic. He rarely ate any of the bakery's goods apart from his daily bran muffin, and he almost always packed a lunch. She liked that he was practical. But tonight, she wanted Aaron to have a good time and relax.

She ordered a bottle of her favorite French merlot and a calamari appetizer and Caesar salad to share. Aaron looked as though he might have objected, but she insisted. After a few sips of wine, he relaxed a little, and she convinced him to order the prime rib dinner.

"Thank you very much for dinner tonight," Aaron said.

"You haven't even tasted the food yet. Who knows? Maybe you'll hate it and curse my name forever."

"I doubt that. You can tell a lot about a place by their bread basket." He selected a Parmesan-crusted bread stick from the fine arrangement of rolls and crackers and took a bite. "Mmm. That's mighty fine eating."

"Glad you like it. Don't fill up on bread, though. You'll love the au jus that goes with the beef. If being a spoiled princess has taught me anything, it's that I have a well-developed palate."

"Hey." He set the bread stick down. "Don't talk about yourself that way."

"What?"

"Don't call yourself a spoiled princess. You're not like that at all."

She shrugged. "But it's true. Look around you." She gestured. "I'm not just blessed, I'm *privileged*. Anything I've ever asked for, my parents have bought me. And I throw tantrums when I don't get exactly what I want."

Aaron sat back, regarding her, head tilted to one side. "I might've believed that of you at one point, but I haven't seen a hint of selfishness in you since I came home."

He was lying, of course. She'd been very selfish. She'd quit Georgette's in a huff because she hadn't been able to handle the threat Aaron's arrival had posed to her future.

"Let me tell you a story. On my fourteenth birthday, my dad got me a horse. I'd wanted one since I was six—a strawberry roan with a white mane. I was going to name her Jewel and she'd be my best friend forever. But Dad got me one with a *black* mane...and I flipped out on him in front of all my friends."

Aaron frowned. "So what happened to the horse?" he asked.

Steph picked up a dinner roll and twisted it into

smaller pieces. "I refused to accept it. I cried and screamed at him like a total diva. My birthday party was packed with friends from school. All I remember thinking at the time was how embarrassing my parents were, when *I* was the embarrassing one." She knew she was running her mouth off, but she needed to share these details. To let him really look at her, know her, know who she was and who she was trying not to be.

"Dad sent the horse back. The next week, he got me a strawberry roan with a white mane. Exactly what I wanted. And I remember saying something awful to him like, 'You should've got me this one in the first place, idiot.'" She pinched the bridge of her nose. "I called my own father an idiot."

"I think every kid does at some point." He stared morosely into his wineglass.

She bit her lip. "Turns out *I* was the idiot. I only got to ride Jewel once. She got severe colic and had to be put down."

Aaron moaned and wiped a hand down his face. "That's awful."

"I felt so guilty—like maybe I hadn't taken care of her right. The thing was, the breeder didn't want my dad to buy Jewel because she'd shown signs of sickness. He'd tried to tell me that, but I wouldn't listen to him. I guess I thought nothing bad could possibly happen once I had her. So the man got his money and I got one ride and a lifetime of guilt." She looked down at her plate, covered in

me, ...ys be. Spoiled prin-
...ned me. And they were right. Peo-
...e still talk about it even now..." She trailed off,
suddenly aware of how much she was wallowing.
"I'm sorry. I don't mean to throw a pity party. I'm
just trying to get you to understand...I don't want
to be that girl ever again. I've spent a long time
trying to escape her."

"We're all weighed down by our pasts." He drew
a finger down the side of his water glass. "I mean,
just look at me. Micromanaging every aspect of my
life because I'm..." He trailed off and smiled apolo-
getically. "Well, I'm sure you don't need to hear it."

"Hey, I showed you mine." She quirked her lips.
"But I won't be offended if you wanna zip it."

His gaze lifted and he gave a short laugh. "When
I was a kid...when my parents died...I realized life
could throw anything at you. That nothing was safe
or sacred. I started seeing it everywhere...in the
newspapers, all these stories about families being
broken up by tragedy, freak accidents, random

cess, they all called

that's who I am and will always remembers ma

"To everyone at that party who remembers

girl anymore." And you're not that

was just a thing that happened. You didn't 'deserve that. H

"You were fourteen. You didn't deserve."

tees or protect me from heartache. And that bei

a brat got you what you deserved."

first time I realized that money didn't buy guar

the mangled pieces of bread.

"I w   ng."

He shrugged. _____ gro-
ceries stashed under _____ an was
mad when she found out w_____ sta had
been going."

Steph couldn't help a smile, but knew this story
was actually more sad than funny.

Aaron scratched his head. "I still do it now. Plan
for every crisis. Even though I know there's no way
to protect myself from…everything." He let out a
long breath. "Boy. Things totally got heavy here,
didn't they?"

"I started it." She gave a watery laugh. "Thanks for letting me run my mouth off. I talk too much."

"You don't." She was filled with reassurance when he reached out and squeezed her hand on top of the tablecloth. Their fingers laced, and neither of them moved to disentangle themselves. A little throb began in the center of Steph's chest and slid lower. "You're a sweet, gifted, intelligent, beautiful woman. You made some mistakes in the past. We all did. All you can do about it is forgive yourself and let it go."

He thought she was intelligent. No one had ever said that about her. And it wasn't a line, either. She'd heard a lot of them, knew when a guy was just trying to flatter her. He was sincere. "Thank you."

"You know, back in high school I would've given my right hand to have you sitting across from me and talking like this," he said.

Her mouth quirked. "Your *right* hand? Aren't you left-handed?"

He snapped. "Curses. Foiled again."

She laughed, and it felt so easy. She didn't have to pretend to like him or force herself to be enthusiastic. It was almost *too* easy.

"Stephanie?"

The familiar voice popped their little bubble, and she looked up. "Wyatt." She let go of Aaron's hand dazedly, reluctantly. "What a nice surprise." The corners of her mouth hitched up and froze there.

The rancher rotated the brim of his cowboy hat in his hands. "I'm sorry. I'm interrupting something here, aren't I?"

"We're having dinner." She glanced at Aaron, whose smile reminded her of the Cheshire cat's. Wyatt's face was more like Grumpy Cat's. "How about you?"

"Just...stopped in for a drink." The two men locked gazes. "Aaron."

"Wyatt."

They seemed to carry on a silent conversation in that loaded look, gray clashing against green. The air grew heavy around them, as if a storm were about to erupt. Steph edged her seat closer to Aaron's.

Two heartbeats passed, but neither of them invited Wyatt to join them. Truth be told, she didn't want him to, even though it would have been the polite thing to do, the thing her mom would've done. Wyatt looked kind of lonely standing there with only his hat to keep him company. But Steph wanted to be with Aaron. Alone.

"Well, I better leave you two to your dinner." She thought the rancher's words were a little curt, even though he was still smiling. He saluted Aaron with two fingers. "Nice to see you."

"Likewise."

Wyatt strode toward the bar on the opposite end of the manor house. A held breath hissed out between Steph's teeth.

Aaron took off his glasses and polished them nonchalantly. "Are you two still…?"

"No," she said emphatically. "I mean, Wyatt's nice. But that's all he is to me. Nice." Poor guy. She really ought to hook him up with Maya.

Their food arrived, and they were quiet as they dug into their prime rib dinners. Steph's self-consciousness grew as the meal went on. She didn't want to ruin the evening by talking about herself any more than she had. But Aaron seemed content over his slab of beef, chewing slowly and deliberately as if he were meditating over each bite.

"You know, they say a good relationship is one where you can endure ten minutes of comfortable silence together," she said.

He blinked at her. "Really?"

"I read it in a magazine." And then she discovered she had nothing else to say about it. She felt stupid for even mentioning it. She shoved a forkful of mashed potatoes into her mouth. Maybe she should just shut up and eat.

"So I read an interesting article in the *Economist*," Aaron piped up.

She chewed her food. "Oh?"

She stopped listening about ten words into his lecture about technology and its effects on employment…at least, that's what she thought he was talking about. She'd tried to pay attention, but her thoughts strayed, and by the time she tuned back in she had no idea what he was saying.

"Aaand I'm boring you, aren't I?" He rubbed his temples, grimacing. "Sorry. I do this a lot on dates, apparently."

"No, no, not at all." And here she'd thought she'd used her smile-and-nod technique to great effect.

"I'll go on for twenty minutes given the opportunity. Please, next time I do, stop me."

They fell back into awkward silence, picking at their food. For someone who'd been on as many first dates as she had, she thought she should be better at small talk.

"Did you read *The Great Gatsby* yet?" Aaron asked hopefully.

"No. Not yet."

"Oh." He swirled the gravy around on his plate. "So…what do you do when you volunteer at the retirement home?"

"Mostly I play board games with the residents. They have a Wii, too. It's fun to watch them play Wii Sports. It helps with their coordination."

"It's nice of you to spend time with them," he said and cast his gaze down. He was probably thinking about Georgette. It was hard to picture someone as vivacious as the baker sitting in the retirement home's lounge staring listlessly at the TV. "With a full-time job and the hours you keep, I think it's admirable that you volunteer there."

"I know they appreciate me visiting." She didn't have much more to say about it, or anything else. Apart from studying for her HSE, she didn't have a lot going on. Baking was her life, and Aaron already knew all about that. She supposed she could talk about getting her high school diploma, but if she told him he might make fun of her. Or worse, start hoping and expecting things of her—and she wasn't willing to disappoint him or anyone else.

"So…see any good flicks lately?" Aaron asked.

She thought hard. "I haven't seen a movie since last summer. The Crown Theater in town closed, and I haven't made the trip out to the big theater in Welksville."

"I haven't been there, either. Maybe we can go sometime."

Was he saying what she thought he was saying? That he wanted a second date? They hadn't even finished this one yet, and so far it hadn't been the most stellar night. She felt all at once excited and full of dread. "What kind of movies do you like?" he asked.

"Oh, you know…I love to laugh, so I watch mostly comedies and rom-coms. I'm a sucker for old musicals. That's Mom's fault. And I admit, I'm still kind of a Disney girl, so I'll watch anything animated with singing. How about you?"

"I'm more of a documentary kind of guy. I saw this one recently…" He started to go on about venture capitalism or something—she wasn't sure. She tried to listen, really. But her brain shut down the moment—

He stopped abruptly. "I did it again, didn't I?" Aaron covered his face with both hands.

"I'm sorry," she blurted on a mirthless half-laugh. "It's me. I'm not... You're just so... When you start talking, my brain goes *pbbbt*." She blew a raspberry. As hard as she tried to listen, she'd get hung up on a word or idea she didn't understand and then lose track of everything else he was saying.

Aaron rubbed the back of his neck. "Sorry," he murmured and tucked his chin against his chest. He used to turtle like that back in high school, too, whenever he'd said something embarrassing.

She felt bad that her own definite...define...deficiencies were causing him pain. But then she wondered: Was this part of that learning disability she supposedly had? Or was it that she couldn't understand what he was saying because she simply didn't know? Like when he'd said *surname*.

Don't think about that now. It doesn't matter.

She steered the conversation to more neutral areas. There had to be something they had in common they could talk about. "Okay. Name your top five favorite movies of all time. No thinking about it. Go."

He blew out a breath and counted them off. "In no particular order, *Star Wars*, *Dr. Strangelove*, *Citizen Kane*, *Seven Samurai* and *Jurassic Park*."

"*Jurassic Park* is one of my favorites, too!"

Thank God. "Every time it's on TV I have to stop everything I'm doing and watch."

"Clevah girl," Aaron quipped. She laughed as they traded quotable lines from the film. "How about you?" he asked.

"Well, apart from *Jurassic Park—Dirty Dancing, Princess Bride, Ever After, Titanic* and *Maid in Manhattan.*"

"The Jennifer Lopez movie?"

"Hey, don't judge me. My list changes every time I get asked that question. That's the thing about not thinking about it. It tells you about your mood and shows you how you change as you get older. My list used to be all Disney movies. I said *Maid in Manhattan* because I saw it on TV the other night."

"Now that really is interesting. Can I change my mind?"

"You can always change your mind."

They fell into discussing other films from when they were in high school. It led to discussions about music from the era and favorite bands. They were as different as two people could be when it came to tastes—she'd loved the boy bands and pop divas of the era; he'd been into classic rock, grunge and, to her shock, heavy metal hair bands. And yet, the era linked them, grounding them in shared history.

When she started talking about high school dances he told her he'd gone only once, and it was to play "an epic game of D&D" with a few of his friends in what had been known by all as the "nerd room," where all the kids who didn't want to dance hung out to play board games.

"So, wait, you didn't even go to prom?"

He shrugged. "I didn't really want to. It just seemed like a huge waste of money on a single night, and I didn't want to go through the hassle of dressing up and stuff."

Typical Aaron answer. "Well, you didn't miss anything."

"Really? How's that?"

"I mean, it was fine. The DJ was awesome. But it wasn't, like, magical."

"I thought it was about getting drunk beforehand and making an ass of yourself." Aaron chuckled wryly, but his comment hit home.

"I was on antibiotics at the time—I got an infection from a scrape during cheerleading practice—so I couldn't drink. But Dale and his friends each had a mickey of whiskey and rum that night. Things got pretty sloppy and I ended up going home, even though we'd rented a cabin out by the lake. It was supposed to be a romantic getaway for the two of us."

"That's too bad."

"I guess I built up a lot of expectations for that night. It was, like, a rite of passage, you know? And it was ruined thanks to Johnnie Walker and Captain Morgan." She traced a pattern in the condensation on her glass of ice water. "I guess I've watched too many movies. Still, I miss the good ol' days in high school."

"They certainly were *days*," he acknowledged drily.

"Oh, c'mon. It couldn't have been that bad."

The bleakness in his expression struck her like a punch to the gut. She winced. "I mean, you did have some high points, right?"

The shadows in his face deepened as he looked down at his plate. Whatever rapport they'd developed dribbled away. The past was tricky that way; bad times oozed to the surface no matter how deep you tried to bury them.

Well, Steph sure was going to try. "For what it's worth now, Aaron…I'm sorry about the way I treated you in high school. Now that I've gotten to know you better… Any girl would've been lucky to be with you."

"Thanks. But you don't have to say that," he said quietly.

"It's true. You've turned out to be so…so different from what I expected." In reality, he was so much more. He'd grown up, sure, but it was more than that. The way she viewed him had changed. She'd somehow gone from thinking he was a geeky loser to being…well, someone she could be with. Which sounded so snobby in her mind; she wondered when or why she'd ever thought of herself as being above him. Maybe she'd thought that way because of how scared she was of her own shortcomings. "I misjudged you," she said. "I wasn't very nice."

He gave a harsh, humorless laugh. "Anyone who's ever liked someone who didn't like him back would've felt the way I did. I don't blame you for it, and you don't owe me anything." He wiped his mouth. "It wasn't about you."

His voice was laced with something like resentment. "I don't understand."

Aaron's fingers clenched, and he hid his fists under the table. "Let's drop it. It wasn't your fault."

"Fault? For what? Aaron, who hurt you?" But even as she asked, she knew exactly who, though she should've known long before now. "Dale?"

His face remained impassive. Coolly, he picked up his wineglass and swirled the contents within. "I tell myself in hindsight it was because I was a threat to him. That he had a bad childhood or something that made him feel the need to beat up on a guy who tried hard to stay off his radar." He regarded her stonily. "In reality, I'm pretty sure he was an asshole who got off on picking on guys who were weaker than him."

The words sat between them like a rotting piece of food that had suddenly been revealed to be the thing stinking up the room, only they'd both gotten so used to the stench they hardly even noticed anymore. Steph felt nauseated. She wanted to believe he was exaggerating, but she knew deep down every word he spoke was true.

Aaron sipped his wine. "One time, he beat me so bad he cracked one of my ribs. He never touched my face, though." His cold smile chilled her. "He never gave me anything worse than a split lip above the neck. His thing was body shots. And he was a kicker."

Hot fury funneled into her roiling stomach. She couldn't believe the boy she'd thought she'd loved, the man she'd once dreamed of marrying and having a family with, could have been so cruel and hateful. How could she not have seen this in him? Or had she known all along and ignored it? As a running back at over six feet and two hundred and fifty pounds, he'd earned a reputation for sending guys out on stretchers. And Dale had had a mouth on him. He shit-talked just about everyone... including her.

Her thoughts jumbled as she recalled all the things Dale had called her. Blondie. Bimbo. Ditz. Stupid bitch. All she'd done had been to laugh it off because, well, what else was she supposed to do? Laughing had been easier than fighting with him.

"Why didn't you ever tell anyone?" Her words came out like an accusation, one she knew was aimed partly at herself. He scoffed.

"A man solves his own problems. My father told me that when I was really young. Besides, there were never any witnesses. Dale always cornered me alone after school or whenever he spotted me in town. You'd think a guy like him would want his buddies around to watch, but he didn't." He fidgeted with his wineglass. "I solved my own problems. Or at least, I tried to."

"How?"

His head lolled to one side almost languidly. "One day, I packed a lead pipe in my backpack. But Gran found it and made me tell her what was going on. She practically begged me not to go to school that day. She wanted me to clear my head. I did it for her, and I'm glad I did. Otherwise…"

Otherwise, he'd probably have ended up in jail for assault with a deadly weapon.

She reached for her water glass with a trembling hand. She wished she'd allowed herself more than one glass of wine, but she was driving tonight. "I'm so sorry. I had no idea about any of this."

"You didn't, did you?" She looked into his face and saw the pity there. "I always wondered how you could be with a guy like that unless…"

Unless she was like Dale, too. Maybe she had been. It made a kind of perverted sense; hooking up with Dale had distracted her from her personal frustrations with her grades. Maybe she'd even encouraged Dale to beat up Aaron without meaning to. Hadn't she once complained how annoying he was, pestering her about those pens of his?

She pushed her dinner away.

"I'm sorry. I didn't mean to bring this all up. I didn't say it to upset you." He tossed his napkin onto the table. "I think I've officially set the record for the worst first date ever."

"No. You...you had every right to tell me this. I..." Apologies seemed worthless at this point. Even though he'd absolved her of any wrongdoing, guilt sat as heavily in her stomach as the cold slab of meat congealing on her plate. "After your grandmother found out...what happened?" she asked.

He lifted one shoulder. "He stopped beating me up after the Christmas break in our final year. I thought maybe he finally got bored or didn't want to jeopardize his football scholarship or something. But then..." His lips pursed. "Well, it was just a rumor."

"What?"

"Someone told me they saw Gran talking to Dale after school near the football field. I heard some other stuff, that she'd followed him around and pushed him under the bleachers, but I think that was all hearsay. She denies it, of course. I think she was trying to preserve my dignity. No guy wants his grandmother fighting his battles for him."

She'd never heard that rumor, but knowing Georgette as long as she had, she could imagine the old woman doing and saying whatever it took to protect her family. The sweet, grandmotherly exterior hid a core of iron, and Steph had no doubt Georgette would've done much worse than withhold a few croissants from Dale's family for what he'd put her grandson through.

Now that she thought about it, she'd never seen the McCarthys in Georgette's.

The waiter came around, brow furrowed as he spotted their half-eaten dinners. He brought them a round of free dessert and coffee, afraid something hadn't agreed with them. But even the smooth and delicate crème caramel didn't do anything to sweeten the bitter turn the evening had taken.

Steph grimaced. This certainly wasn't how she'd hoped the evening would go.

CHAPTER SIXTEEN

STEPH DROVE AARON back to the bakery in silence. Her lips were pressed into a tight line. He couldn't blame her for being upset. Why had he told her about the way Dale had humiliated him? Maybe he'd been subconsciously sabotaging his chances with her. He hadn't meant to make her feel bad, but how else was she supposed to respond to the fact that her ex-boyfriend had been a violent psycho?

She parked and turned off the engine, and they sat in the dark, cricket song and a light breeze their only companions. The motion sensor-activated floodlamp on the patio had flicked on as they'd approached. It cast sharp shadows into the vehicle's interior.

"Thank you for dinner," he said. "I'm sorry I wasn't better company. I guess I'm out of practice."

"Don't apologize," she said tightly. She blew out a breath and unbuckled her seat belt, turning toward him. "This is on Dale. If I'd known back then what he was doing to you—" She shook her head. "But that's the thing. I don't know what I would've done. I keep thinking...maybe I *did* know what he was like. That I might've ignored what he was doing to you…"

He held up a hand. "I already told you it's not your fault. And it was years ago."

"So what? It doesn't matter how many years ago it was…it doesn't make it right. You're still hurting from it."

True. But he hadn't told her for selfish reasons. "I'm not looking for apologies or payback, Steph."

"Then what is it you want?"

"Nothing," he said. Truthfully, he didn't know. This from a guy who always knew exactly what he had to do to get what he wanted, who usually had everything planned out to within an inch of his life, with plans B and C already prepped if something failed. He scrubbed his hands over his face. "I'd better go."

Before he could do anything stupid, he popped his seat belt and reached for the door handle. But Steph snagged his arm. He turned to ask what was wrong when she grabbed him by the collar and hauled him across the console, smashing her lips against his.

Her kiss was rough, demanding and generous all at once. Her eyes were squeezed shut as if she were pouring everything she had into it, as if she could give and give and always have something left over.

Aaron moved a hand up to push her gently away—not because he didn't want this, but because maybe this wasn't what *she* wanted. But when he cupped her cheek, a stray curl of silky hair brushed against him, and he was lost. His fingers raked upward gently. Touching her hair was everything he'd dreamed it would be. He wanted to twine it around his fingers, spread it out on a pillow, have it brush down his chest and lower until...

He pulled away sharply. He'd had too much wine. But Steph's grip slid around his neck, and she held him so close their lips continued to brush.

"Kiss me," she rasped. Their ragged breaths mingled. "Aaron, kiss me."

"Steph—" He wanted to. He really did. But what if she were only kissing him because she felt sorry for him? What if she was simply trying to make up for the torment he'd suffered at her ex-boyfriend's hands?

That hadn't been why he'd told her about Dale. He was *not* playing the pity card.

Then why did you tell her? a tiny voice demanded.

Because he was trying to put some emotional distance between them, afraid of being hurt? No, the way he looked at her, the way he *wanted* her, was not rooted in fear, anger or resentment. The truth was he'd needed to share this piece of him with her, to have her see that broken part of him, just as she'd shown him the spoiled princess she'd been. He'd needed her to know this about him, to expose the festering wound that had infected so much of his life, as if in doing so it would heal. And as selfish as it was to think it, it had helped.

Her lips brushed his again, as soft and sweet as their dessert. He gave in with a moan. She climbed into his lap, attaching her lips to his while her tongue invaded his mouth.

The passenger seat, while roomy for one, was cramped for two. Steph pressed tightly against him, her legs dangling over the center console. Aaron feared she might accidentally kick the parking brake off and roll them into a ditch. But the gentle tugging on his tongue and the sweet, firm warmth pressing into him reminded him he should be paying attention to other things.

Except he couldn't. As eager as his body was, his mind was pulling him in a dozen different directions. It didn't feel right.

"Steph…" He gently held her back by the shoulders when she came up for air. "Let's…let's take this slow, okay?"

Her brow furrowed and she frowned. She clambered off him and slid back into the driver's seat. They stared out the windshield in silence.

Aaron struggled to explain. "It's not that I don't want you. We had a…weird kind of night. Good, but…" He didn't want to talk or think about Dale anymore. But his secret was out there now, and he wanted to make sure this wasn't some kind of pity move on Steph's part. "I want this, really. But… not like this."

She glared at him. What was she mad about?

Wait. That wasn't anger. She was embarrassed. He rushed to reassure her. "If we move forward, I want things to be right. Special."

"You've never parked before, have you?" She gave a brittle laugh.

He blushed. "Call me old-fashioned, but I have a three-date policy."

She sighed and rolled her head back to stare at the roof of her car despondently. "You're one of the good ones, Aaron. It's a shame."

Yeah, real shame. He ran a hand through his hair. There was nothing left to do now but leave. "I'll see you tomorrow."

"Sure you can drive a stick?" she asked.

"What are you talking about? I drive an automatic."

Her arch look dropped to his lap. When he realized what she meant, his face flamed.

"*Good night*, Steph." He opened the door and hurried to his own vehicle before his humiliation could be any more evident.

His mind didn't rest as he drove home, Steph's bright headlights watching him in his rearview mirror. He shouldn't have said anything about what had happened with Dale. But the moment they'd gotten to talking about high school, it'd all come out. It'd been cathartic in some ways, sharing his personal shame openly like that. Maybe it was a bit manipulative, though, too. He'd always wanted her to see Dale for who he really was.

Maybe he was no better than Dale.

Good God. Forget about a second date—he should worry about her quitting tomorrow and hating him for the rest of her life.

STEPH LAY AWAKE alternately smiling and frowning.

Kissing Aaron had been the best and worst idea. Best because, wow, was he ever a good kisser. Tonight had confirmed his gift in that department. Her whole body was still tingling. She knew with bone-deep conviction they'd be phenomenal together in bed.

But it'd been the worst idea ever because he thought she felt sorry for him. He was exactly the kind of guy to overthink things that way. Yes, a part of her had wanted to make up for the crap he'd been through. The other part of her simply *wanted* him. Fiercely.

Guilt over the past churned through her like too-wet cookie dough. She'd always prided herself on being a good judge of character, but obviously she had missed a few important details when it came to Dale. She supposed love made a person willfully blind…if she ever had loved Dale. Had she been so set on marriage, kids and Mr. Merkl's house that she'd overlooked all Dale's faults? Because he'd certainly had them.

She thought back over the years they had been

together, ever since her second year of high school. He'd hit on her when he'd tried out for the football team and she'd been on the cheer squad. She'd been trying to study during a break in practice, determined not to fail yet another test.

"Forget about studying," he'd said, taking the book out of her hands. "Sit next to me and I'll pass you the answers."

She'd declined at first, but then he'd sat next to her during the test anyhow and had made it impossible to refuse his help. And she'd passed.

He'd helped her cheat her way through a lot of her classes after that. He brought her prewritten essays to turn in, helped her fudge assignments and showed her how to get by doing as little homework as possible. He'd convinced her to skip more and more classes so they could make out in his car or go to the mall. He'd used his status as a star football player to get out of detention or schoolwork, and his charm or his massive size to get everything else. Real smarts, he'd used to say, didn't come from a book, but from knowing how to work the system.

He'd made everything so simple for her. It'd been much easier to pretend not to care, to stop living up to everyone else's expectations and let him do the thinking for both of them, rather than constantly failing no matter how hard she'd tried. Even her parents had liked him. He came over a lot, pretending to help her with her schoolwork, and they'd loved his supposed studiousness.

Then came the day they'd broken up, literally the night before he'd left home for college. "It's not that I don't want to be with you, babe," he'd explained. "But I've got my whole life ahead of me, and it wouldn't be fair to you to string you along. You want me to be happy, don't you?"

She had. She'd actually convinced herself his happiness was more important than hers. And then he'd left her. It had only been after he'd gone that she'd understood how much she'd depended on him. Maybe that was why she'd spent so much time grieving over their breakup. Because she hadn't known how to function without someone to give her all the answers.

And then when her parents had learned about the breakup they'd been devastated for her and had immediately taken up the slack to see to her every need.

Agitated, she threw off the covers, got out of bed and went to the couch where her HSE workbooks were piled together. All those years of depending on others was over. She'd never let it happen again. She'd broken her studying streak tonight, too upset by Aaron's revelation and too overstimulated by his kiss to concentrate. She wasn't sleeping. She might as well study. The exam was next week, after all.

Unfortunately, her mind kept sliding back to thoughts of Aaron. Unable to shake her guilt, she opened her laptop. She'd already replenished his pen supply. How else could she make amends?

Her Google search turned up surprisingly little about Aaron Caruthers. He hadn't left much of an internet footprint, but he was on Facebook. He didn't update his account very often, though. Most of the posts were articles about the things he seemed to enjoy reading about. The latest one had been about declining household incomes across the country. The status before that one read, "Headed for home: Everville, NY. New beginnings."

She kept scrolling, skipping all the articles, seeking some clue about him in his updates that would give her what she needed. She knew he'd said he didn't want anything from her to make up for what he'd been through, but she couldn't let it be.

Further back into Aaron's profile she spotted a picture of one of his grandmother's bran muffins with the caption: Gran's Bran Muffins. Mmm. Fiber-y Goodness.

She smiled. He was so wholesome and practical he'd *fill* cavities.

Well, maybe not too wholesome if tonight's romp in the car told her anything. She'd felt that tremor within him, as if his leashed libido was straining to escape. She'd practically *begged* him for more. She'd never had to beg.

She kept scrolling. Finally, she found it: the solution that would set things right—some of them, anyway. It was a close-up photo of a perfect chocolate soufflé dusted with icing sugar. The caption read: THIS IS THE CURE TO ALL EVIL IN THE WORLD.

Steph laughed out loud. She couldn't imagine Aaron ever feeling so strongly about anything, much less a dessert. But here he'd posted a picture of something she'd never seen him eat, never heard him mention. For a guy who claimed he didn't like sweets that had to be one hell of a soufflé.

She had to make it for him.

Like Aaron and his gift of books, this was the one thing that meant something to her that she could share. It wouldn't make up for the torment he'd suffered. But it was a start.

AARON WALKED INTO the bakery at eight the next morning feeling a little sluggish after a fitful night's sleep. He was surprised to find Kira at the front. Usually, she had class on Friday mornings.

"I hope you don't mind," she said. "I wanted to make up for the hours I've missed."

"No classes today?"

She bit her lip. "Yeah. Something like that."

He frowned. He'd rather she not skip school to work, but maybe she needed the money. Asking seemed too personal and intrusive, though.

"Is Steph in the back?"

"Yeah. She said she wanted to work on a new recipe or something and didn't want to be disturbed."

He hadn't realized Georgette allowed any other recipes outside of her own. Perhaps Steph was just making an excuse not to talk to Aaron after last night. Ugh, had he ever screwed that up. Still, they'd have to talk eventually. He'd known it would be one of the drawbacks of dating someone he worked with. Yet, when he thought of that kiss, he couldn't muster any regret.

Unsure of what he was going to say to Steph, he decided to leave her alone for now and opened the bookshop. It was probably for the best. Things would get extra weird if Kira suspected anything going on between them. She was already giving him fishy looks, though thankfully she didn't ask questions.

Aaron didn't see Steph all day, not even during the lunchtime rush. It must've been one hell of a recipe she was working on, because though he smelled the mouthwatering scent of baking chocolate, he didn't see a single sample or taste test pass through those doors.

By closing time, she still hadn't emerged. He wasn't even sure she'd stopped for lunch.

He was worried. It seemed kind of extreme to avoid him like this. They'd have to see each other eventually.

He glanced at Kira, who was wiping the counter listlessly. Dark bags hung under her eyes and her cheeks seemed more hollow than usual—bruised, almost. As she pulled off her hairnet, a clump of knotted hair went with it, and she gasped.

"Kira? Are you all right?" He tried hard not to stare at the hairball in her hand.

"I...I'm fine. I...pulled too hard." She hastily tossed the clump of hair into the garbage.

He studied her a little more closely. Her hair hadn't been ripped out. It was falling out.

"Listen, Kira," he said carefully. "It's none of my business, but...I'm really worried about you. Georgette is, too. We know you have...*challenges* at home. If you need help with anything—"

"I'm fine. Everything's fine." Her teeth flashed white against too-red gums. She pushed up her glasses and he noticed the little chip in the corner of the lens.

"You know I want to help, right? I know about your mom—" her face turned gray "—and I know you're struggling to get by. If there's some way I can help—"

"There's nothing you can do." She said it quickly, the hurt and anger lashing him as she spun away and grabbed her backpack. "I can take care of things. I'm done here. Can I go now?"

He pursed his lips. "Sure."

She hurried out, jumping into the old clunker of a car he now realized wasn't a hand-me-down gifted from a parent to a child, but the family vehicle. It coughed as it started, but the engine caught and it chugged out of the lot and down the road.

Maybe he shouldn't have confronted her like that—it seemed he was just plain bad at talking to people about anything really serious—but something clearly needed to be done. He had to think of a way to help Kira without hurting her pride or getting her in trouble with the authorities.

He locked the doors and turned the sign to Closed, then steeled himself to walk into the kitchen. Talking to Steph about Kira would be a good way to break the ice between them.

He stumbled over a bag of flour which had, once again, been left in front of the swinging door. With a muttered oath, he grabbed it and shoved it out of the way. When he looked up, he nearly yelped. The worktable was littered with eggshells, wrappers and sheaves of computer printouts. Chocolate was splattered and smeared everywhere, as if someone had filled a blender with hot fudge and switched it on without securing the lid. Cocoa powder, flour and sugar dusted the counters. He'd never seen the place this chaotic.

"Oh. My. God." He stared around. "What happened in here?"

Stephanie looked up from the far end of the kitchen. She hadn't heard him come in at first because she was wearing her earbuds. She quickly draped a large cloth over whatever she was doing and stepped in front of it, yanking out the earbuds.

"Sorry. I've been..." She gestured around as if that was explanation enough. Chocolate was spattered across her apron, and a smear adorned her cheek. She studied the room as if she'd only just noticed the mess. "Don't worry. I'll clean up before I go."

"Let me help."

She looked flustered. "Oh, no. I can manage."

"I insist. I need to talk to you about Kira." He rolled up his sleeves and grabbed a clean apron off the hook, then slipped on a pair of rubber gloves. As he scrubbed chocolate off the counters, he told her about the teen's hair falling out, and about how tired and upset she'd been. "Do you know what's going on with her? Has she said anything to you?"

"Honestly, no. All I know is that she's had to leave a few times for emergencies."

"She has a lot of emergencies." He grimaced. He didn't think Kira was the type to shirk her responsibilities so she could go out and have fun. "I'm worried about her. If she tells you anything, even if it's something small, will you let me know?"

Steph sucked in her lower lip. "Maybe it's better if she handles things on her own."

"Why would you say that?"

"She's mature and responsible. Georgette wouldn't have hired her otherwise. Kira only wants to make up for the hours she missed. I was the one who told her that was fine. I need the help." She sounded defensive, as if Aaron was attacking *her*.

"This isn't about her performance or attendance. She's great at her job. I'm worried about *her*. Whatever's happening, I want to make sure she's taking care of herself and that we're doing everything we can to help."

Steph gave him a steady look, then nodded. "Okay. I'll let you know if she tells me anything."

"Thank you." Was she trying to protect Kira? Did she know something and wasn't telling? Or was it because of last night she was reluctant to help him with this?

He put those thoughts aside and focused on cleaning off the chocolate crawling up the walls. "What on earth were you making in here?" he asked, exasperated as he followed the blast radius higher and higher. "A bomb?"

"Just...an experiment."

"An experiment in what?" As he moved some ingredients off the worktable, he picked up a familiar metal box and his heart sank. "This is Gran's special chocolate. She only uses this for shavings for her special German chocolate mousse cake." It was one of the most expensive ingredients in the bakery, and it looked as though Steph had used half the tin.

She had the gall to look sheepish. "Oh...yeah. Um..."

His blood pressure spiked. "You can't use this for...for *experiments*." The one time he'd eaten a piece out of that tin when he was eleven, Gran had had a fit. He'd never seen her so angry before.

Then he started noticing the other ingredients scattered across the worktop: real vanilla beans,

Grand Marnier, caster sugar, about two dozen eggs and what looked like five pounds of unsalted butter. "How much of the supplies did you use? What were you making?"

"It's private." She gathered the printouts off the counter. "I was testing a bunch of recipes."

"Private? For who?" His thoughts zoomed to Wyatt, and his chest felt as though it might be on fire. Dammit, he had no claim to her. She could do as she liked, just not on his grandmother's dime. "Where are these tests?" He squinted at the garbage can, adding up the dollars that might have been binned. "Don't tell me you *ate* all that butter."

"No." Her gaze shifted to the table covered with the cloth.

He frowned. He hated that he had to use his business voice with her after everything they'd been through, but despite the high season, the bakery still hovered on the edge of black. "We can't afford to waste ingredients, Steph."

"I'll pay for what I used."

That wasn't the point. "We're in this business together, remember? I thought you trusted me enough to share the decision making. That includes any new recipes or stock you want to try selling." He went to the cloth-covered table.

"No, wait—" Steph rushed forward as he drew the cloth off.

Thirty small ramekins filled with some kind of chocolate pastry at various heights and textures sat dejectedly on the table. Each seemed to have its own personality, some of them grotesque—runny, flat, burnt, pockmarked...

"It's chocolate soufflé." Steph sighed.

He stared at them. "Who's going to buy these? They're way too delicate and pricey for our clientele."

"I didn't make them to sell," she said impatiently. "I made them for you."

He startled. "For me? But...why?"

Her chin lowered, and she traced a pattern in the icing sugar on the table. "Because after last night... I wanted to do something for you... But you didn't want..." She trailed off, wringing her hands. "It's your favorite thing," she blurted.

Now he was really confused. "What are you talking about? My favorite thing is Gran's bran muffins. I don't like chocolate soufflé."

"Yes, you do!" she insisted, reminding him of a small child stamping her foot. "You say you like bran muffins, but you just eat them because they're safe. You like sweets. Stop denying it. I looked at your Facebook profile. You love chocolate soufflé. I asked Georgette and she said you had it at a restaurant in Boston, but they shut down."

Of course Gran would remember that birthday treat—she had an incredible memory for those kinds of details. He squeezed the flesh between his eyes. "So all these..."

"I couldn't find the chef from that restaurant

listed anywhere, so I went online and…" She held out the pile of printouts. "I had to see which one was best."

Oh. Oh, wow. All at once, Aaron felt like a heel, while a weird feeling puffed up his chest. Maybe it was an allergic reaction to flattery combined with being a jerk.

Steph twisted her apron in her hands. "I wanted you to have something to make you happy. I wanted you to have something…good. From me."

He laughed then. He really had no other response. "You didn't have to do this."

"Yes, I did." Her tone was defensive. "Baking is what I do. It's the only thing I know how to do that makes people happy."

His chest ached. It wasn't true. She had to know that. "Steph—"

"When you told me about what Dale did, I couldn't stop thinking how I might have made things worse. How I didn't know any of this was happening to you. I can't change the past, and I know you said you don't expect anything from me, but…I want to make up for everything bad you've *ever* been through, even if it means baking you a chocolate soufflé every day for the rest of my life." She grimaced at the ramekins. "As soon as I can actually make one, that is."

The walls around Aaron's heart gave beneath the barrage of feeling behind her words. Her speech rang with self-recrimination and remorse, and all he wanted to do was wipe it away. There was only one way to do that.

"What are you doing?" she asked as he grabbed a spoon.

"Well, we don't waste butter, right?" He picked up a ramekin.

She flapped her hands in horror. "You can't eat those. They're disgusting."

"Watch me." He put a spoonful of fudgey goo in his mouth. Chocolate flooded his senses and made his teeth twinge as he slowly chewed. "Mmm…interesting…" He worked on swallowing the taffy-like abomination. "Maybe a little underdone." He put that one down, wishing he hadn't started with throat glue, and picked up another. The spoon clinked against the rock-hard crust, and it took a few tries to get a mouthful in. "Hmm…burny."

"Give me that." She swiped the ramekin from his hands. "You're going to hurt yourself. Or go into a sugar coma."

"I've always dreamed of death by chocolate," he said, determinedly picking up another soufflé. Steph tried to take it away from him, but he held it above his head as he spooned out some. "Oh, looks like this one might be the magical one. It causes girls to touch me."

"Give me that!" She strained up, pressing the length of her body against his. The ramekin tipped, and a drizzle of dark chocolatey syrup splashed down on them both. Steph squealed, and Aaron quickly lowered it.

"Well, that was unexpected." He wiped goo from his cheek.

"It's a cake with a chocolate liqueur filling. It's called a…" She trailed off as her face turned deep red.

"What?"

"It's called a chocolate orgasm."

Aaron went very still. Steph pressed against him, and he could see the chocolate in her hair and on her chin and shoulders. She smelled like cocoa and buttercream icing. They licked their lips at the same time.

"Have you tried some?" he asked thickly.

"I can tell on sight it's wrong."

"You don't know till you've tried it." He raised the spoon to her mouth. "Taste."

It should've been weird holding that little spoon to her mouth while he was still wearing yellow rubber gloves and an apron, but when she slipped her lips around the spoon and sucked, he felt it right down to his…toes.

She glided her palm up his chest. "Actually, that's not bad."

"I think it's my new favorite dessert."

She leaned into him. "You haven't tried the other twenty-seven yet."

"Sometimes a guy just knows." He leaned in and brushed his mouth against hers. Both of their lips were sticky sweet with chocolate. In the next moment, they were devouring each other, licking and sucking and purring as they kept finding more chocolate. Aaron tore off his rubber gloves and plowed his fingers through her hair, but they snagged on her hairnet.

She giggled as he tried to take it off. "Maybe we should clean up first."

"Leave it till tomorrow," he growled, surprising himself and, clearly, her.

CHAPTER SEVENTEEN

THE DRIVE BACK into town was excruciating. They'd barely gotten out of the bakery with their pants on. Every time they came within orbit of each other, he'd reach out, grab her and kiss her senseless.

Steph was practically drunk on the taste of him. Or maybe it was all that chocolate giving her a sugar and caffeine high.

She parked and hurried up to her apartment above the pharmacy. She paused, wondering if she had condoms that weren't expired, but knew better than to buy supplies downstairs where Mr. Keegan would know exactly what she would be up to tonight. She trusted the pharmacist's discretion, of course, but Mrs. Keegan was friends with her mother. She wouldn't put it past her mom to call in the middle of the night to interrogate her about ongoing activities.

Aaron had been to her apartment before, of course, but giving the place a quick cleaning wouldn't hurt. She kicked her stray shoes out of the entryway and hung up the jackets she'd left lying on the back of the couch. In the bathroom, she swept the assortment of makeup from the countertop into a basket, then gave everything a wipedown.

Once that was done, she felt she had to give herself a scrub, too. There was still chocolate sauce in her hair, and her skin was covered in cocoa, butter and sugar.

She stripped and jumped into the shower, and was only just getting out when she heard a knock on her door. Crap. Aaron was early.

She threw on her bathrobe and finger-combed her wet hair. Ugh, that didn't help. Well, if he was interested in the same thing she was, her hair wouldn't be much of an issue. Maybe she should open the door naked.

She grinned to herself. No, better to leave something to the imagination. Adjusting the front of the robe so it gaped open seductively, she went to answer the door.

It was Maya. She glanced down at Steph's partially exposed chest and snickered. "Something tells me you forgot about our study session."

Steph slammed the heel of her palm against her forehead as she clenched the robe closed around her neck. "Can we postpone?"

"You know the test is next week, right?"

She sucked in her lip. So much had happened in the past twenty-four hours that she'd practically forgotten about the HSE exam. "I was thinking... maybe I can move the test date back. It's been really crazy at work and I—"

"No way." Maya propped her fists against her hips, frowning. "The whole reason I agreed to help you out was to make sure you didn't do this exact thing. If you back down now, you might never take your test. You've come so far already. Why stop now?"

"Look, I know I have, but I'm not ready." She felt a weight lift from her chest. She hadn't realized how hard it'd been to admit that to Maya. She'd kept her fears to herself, afraid to disappoint her after all the time she'd spent helping her study.

Unfortunately, it looked as though Maya was disappointed anyhow. Steph sighed. "Please, Maya. Some stuff's come up and…I want to be sure I'm ready. I want to reschedule the exam."

Maya scowled and heaved a frustrated sigh. "Are you gonna tell me what's so important that you're putting this off?"

At that moment, the door on the lower landing opened, and someone came marching up the steps. "Steph?" Aaron rounded the corner of the stairs. He stopped abruptly at the sight of Maya. "Oh. Hi, Maya." He was carrying a bouquet of flowers and a bottle of wine, and he tucked them behind his back. As if he could hide his intentions now.

"Aaron." Her gaze skated toward Steph. "Ah. I was just leaving." Maya's final sharp-eyed look said she'd let Steph off the hook this time, but that she'd better make up for it with juicy details and a full explanation. And maybe a batch of chocolate-dipped macaroons. With a short wave, Maya headed down the stairs.

"We were totally made," he said sheepishly as he closed the apartment door behind him. "She's not likely to tell anyone, is she?"

"I doubt it." She pointed to the bottle of wine and the bouquet of flowers. "Are those for me?"

"I thought it was the least I could do." He held them out, straight armed.

"Thank you. This is sweet."

Aaron looked away modestly. "If I'd known you'd be showering, I would've taken time to freshen up myself."

She remembered then why he'd come…how they'd been so hot for each other barely an hour ago. It should've been an easy matter of slinking up to him and taking off her robe, but she was nervous all of a sudden.

"Are you hungry?" she asked instead. "I've got frozen pizza in the freezer. I mean, of course it's in the freezer. I didn't say I'd defrosted it." She cringed.

"Actually, I am kind of hungry." He rubbed the back of his neck, gaze darting all around. "I was thinking I could get some takeout from the Good Fortune Diner."

"That sounds great." She said it almost a little too enthusiastically. She wanted this to be special and she needed time to prepare.

She listed off her favorite menu items and Aaron

scurried out. Once he'd left, she quickly dried her hair, applied a touch of makeup, then stared into her closet. She was well-stocked in the lingerie department, but none of her clothes seemed appropriate for seducing Aaron. She had silky things and lacy things, naughty things and nice things. She even had a few sexy Halloween costumes to get her kink on. But when she thought about Aaron and what he would like…she had no clue.

There was really only one answer to her wardrobe dilemma.

HE WAS REALLY going to do this, wasn't he?

Yes, he told himself firmly as he waited in line at the Good Fortune Diner. *You are going to walk back there and tell Steph you're not ready.*

The fact was he didn't know the first thing about how to please Stephanie Stephens. He understood basic female anatomy, of course, but he still saw Steph as kind of alien—a woman of an entirely different species. Whatever his expectations of her were, he knew she'd defy them all.

If he screwed this up now, he'd lie awake overanalyzing it every night for the rest of his life.

"Hey, I remember you." Daniel Cheung, the son of the diner's owners, pointed at him with a pair of tongs. He was a few years older than Aaron, but he remembered him from school. The guy had tutored him when he'd been struggling with calculus. "Aaron, right? Good to see you. It's been a long time."

They caught up briefly and then he ordered. Daniel filled Styrofoam containers with food from the steam table. "Taking this home to your grandmother?" Daniel asked. "I didn't think Georgette liked sweet and sour chicken balls."

"No, I'm having dinner with someone," Aaron said before he could think to lie.

Daniel looked thoughtfully at the dishes. "Well, considering I only know one woman who regularly orders black bean eggplant with extra chilies, I'm going to guess you mean Stephanie."

Aaron was too caught-out to respond, and Daniel chuckled. "Don't worry. I don't involve myself with local gossip. But here." He grabbed a handful of fortune cookies and put them in the bags. "She can't get enough of these. And she's one of our best customers."

"Thanks." He felt as if he should've known that. Being intimate with someone he didn't know some basic facts about didn't seem right. One-night stands had never been his thing.

So you expect this to go beyond one night, a voice in his head chimed in. He stifled it. He was going to deliver this food and bow out like a gentleman. That was all.

Once he'd paid, he hurried up the street, hoping no one spotted him and stopped to chat. The last thing he needed was more interrogations. He wasn't sure why he should feel the need to be so secretive. Maybe because in all his previous relationships he'd known exactly what he was looking for with the women he'd dated. With Steph he didn't have a checklist or an itinerary or a recipe for what their relationship should be like. He was just feeling his way through it. And it was terrifying.

He hated to think anyone would suspect that he didn't know what the hell he was doing.

He arrived at the apartment unseen. The door at the top of the stairs had been left unlocked for him.

He took a deep breath. They'd eat, and then he'd tell her they should take things more slowly, get to know each other better. Good things were worth waiting for, after all.

He opened the door.

His heart nearly exploded.

"Hey." Steph sat on her couch, facing the door, feet tucked up under her, arms spread across the back of the couch, wearing a smile...and nothing else.

His grip tightened on the bag of food. "Hi." His voice cracked.

"Hungry?" She shifted her legs. He'd been wrong—she was wearing a slip of pink lace.

He couldn't do more than breathe. Actually, he wasn't sure he was breathing. The edges of his vision were getting hazy.

There was a slightly nervous jangle to her laugh. She got to her feet and walked toward him, bare feet soft against the hardwood. The nail polish on her toes matched the dusky pink of her nipples.

And then he realized he was staring at Stephanie Stephens's bare breasts.

Oh, dear God. This felt like something out of a fever dream. He was afraid if he even blinked he'd wake up.

She finally reached him, standing barely an inch away, the tips of her breasts brushing his front. He could smell her light perfume, feel the heat coming off her skin, hear the tremulous intake of her breath. His heart thundered.

She took the bag of food from his stiff fingers and placed it on the table by the entrance. "Eat first?" she asked, coyly looking up into his face. "Or later?"

STEPH WASN'T PREPARED for the ferocity with which Aaron grabbed her. His mouth descended on hers, hungry, invading. He practically slammed her against the wall as his hands found her breasts, her belly, her hips, her thighs. He couldn't seem to decide what he wanted to touch first. His control had well and truly snapped, and Steph loved it.

She grabbed his shirt collar, the material chafing against her skin as he sought to get closer. His breathing grew harsh as his open mouth brushed the length of her jaw to her neck, nibbling until he found *that* spot, making her gasp and moan and fall open to him.

She'd never thought of Aaron as a particularly strong guy. He didn't have the build of most of the guys she'd dated. But he lifted her easily, hands cupped beneath her thighs. She wrapped her legs around his waist, loving the way he cradled her bottom, still kissing her as he carried her toward her bedroom.

He set her gently on the bed. She reached for the hem of his shirt eagerly, laughing as their hands tangled and he struggled to pull it over his head. Her fingers worked quickly to undo his belt and slide the zipper of his pants down.

She wasn't sure what she'd been expecting, but she wasn't disappointed. Actually, she was downright impressed.

Aaron looked frazzled, his chest heaving. "Should...should we put on music or something?"

Music? She snickered, not sure why he wanted music. "We'll make it together."

It was probably the cheesiest thing she'd ever said to a guy during foreplay, but for some reason he was making her feel sappy. Seeing his hair sticking up in all directions from wrestling with his shirt, his lean but well-defined chest with its sprinkling of hair rising and falling rapidly, reminded her of her first time, giddy and nervous and full of anticipation.

She fumbled with his pants as she tried to pull them past his knees. She couldn't help but notice the ripple of pale stretch marks around his waist and hips—the body's map of changes. He grabbed her shoulder and tried to step out of his trousers, stumbling, getting his toe caught. They both laughed as he pivoted around, one leg of his pants wrapped around his ankle. Finally, he freed himself and stood fully naked in front of her, taking off his glasses as he made his way onto the bed.

She gasped as the hot length of him pressed against her thigh. She skimmed her hands along his shoulders and down his chest, the sinews bunching beneath her touch. She went lower still until she grasped him and gave an experimental tug.

He hissed, then buried his face against her neck. "You like that?" She did it again, stroking him, loving the way he responded and the power she had over his body. She knew she was good at sex—good at figuring out what men liked. It came instinctively to her, a skill that was the polar opposite of baking, which required precision and careful measurements.

But with Aaron, she felt as if she had to employ all her skills to draw out his pleasure one teaspoon at a time. She wanted to make him groan and pant and beg and ache as tenderly as she did. But her needs were growing, too. She'd wanted this from the moment they'd kissed. She wanted to bring him against the razor's edge the way she'd felt for days after he'd kissed her. She wanted to punish him for making her feel so needy.

But that wasn't going to happen. Aaron grabbed

her wrist and turned her onto her back. "No more," he said through gritted teeth. "I want you. Now."

Thankfully, the condoms in her bedside table hadn't expired. She watched him roll one on, wanting to help—anything to touch him again. Grasping her, he settled himself, and then he was there, pushing into her, driving out every other thought except for the sheer feel of him.

Aaron held still, breathing. Lightning flickered in the storm-gray depths of his eyes. If there were such a thing as electricity between two people, she was feeling it crackling through her veins, gathering in hot knots in her nipples, across her lips and deep down where they were joined.

She didn't know what he did next, but could only describe it later in her mind as flexing. It seemed to touch her everywhere all at once from the inside, and her head lolled back as a wave of pleasure rolled through her. He did it again, coupling it with a slow thrust that had her arching and clutching him tight. And then he did it again.

Precision. Control. It permeated every sinew of his body, which was how he turned her body to liquid, flexing and thrusting and driving her hard against the edge of reason. He became bolder, stroking her faster, more fiercely, until she was as taut as a bowstring. And still he went on, relentless and untiring.

She'd known he was focused and dedicated. That he worked hard to get what he wanted.

He got exactly that when she came, hard, sweaty and clinging and calling his name over and over.

And still, he went on and on and on.

"YOU'RE A MONSTER," Steph said breathlessly hours later, lolling in the bed, her damp blond hair and a wide smile plastered on her face. Aaron lay on his side, one arm draped across her waist. He could barely move. Being with Stephanie had been better than any little blue pill. He couldn't get enough of her. And the way she'd screamed his name had only stoked his fervor.

He felt the residual tug of arousal but ignored it. If he went one more round now he'd probably have a heart attack. Or his dick would fall off.

She stared at him, shell shock clear in her features. "Where did you...? How did you...?"

"Tantric yoga lessons," he said with a straight face. But he didn't have the energy to keep up the act and laughed out loud as he squirmed closer. "Did I hurt you?" he asked, kissing her bare shoulder.

She shook her head dazedly and giggled. "I think I have orgasm poisoning, though."

"Oops. Sorry. I won't do it again."

A look of mock horror lit her face. "No. Do it again. I demand it."

He sighed dramatically and rolled on top of her. She squealed. "Not now! God, you're going to tear me in half."

He climbed off and flopped back down onto the mattress. He hoped his deodorant had lasted. A shower was probably in order. Then again, he wasn't sure his legs were working.

They lay side by side in silence, the sound of their breathing tapering off. He was exhausted, yes, but he'd never been comfortable falling asleep in someone else's home. He wasn't exactly sure what the protocol here was, either, which kept him awake. Were they going to have The Talk now? What was this between them exactly? Steph didn't seem averse to them going at it again, which he supposed was a good thing. But to what end?

Maybe *he* had orgasm poisoning. He always knew what he was getting into when it came to relationships, and never took things anywhere before he had a clear idea of what the other person wanted. But he didn't have a clue what was going on here. He didn't have a plan B or an exit strategy.

And the silence was lengthening.

"Y-you know," she stuttered. "They say a couple who can share ten minutes of comfortable silence are meant to be together."

"So you've said before." Only after the words had left his mouth had he realized how he might have made her feel, but by then it was too late to take them back. He clenched his jaw and stared at the ceiling.

"I read an interesting article the other day," he

said ten seconds later, unable to stand the stillness. He rambled on for a bit about the magazine feature about the mass extinction of the honeybee population, all the while wishing he could stop talking and instead tell her what he really felt. The problem was he wasn't sure what he felt...or maybe he was feeling too many things to put into words.

He trailed off, mortified. He got the sense she was trying very hard to stay silent. Her eyes darted around as if tracking a hummingbird flitting from thought to thought. Her brow was slowly wrinkling up. Maybe she was starting to regret this whole evening.

What if this was all he got? His chest tightened. He breathed deep and turned onto his side facing away from her. So what if this was it? He'd had a great time, and so had she, as far as he could tell. If this was all they ever had...

Damn. He hadn't thought she could still affect him this deeply. They hadn't even talked yet, and he was already bracing for heartache.

He hadn't wanted the intimacy that came with sex. That was what he'd told himself.

He closed his eyes. Who was he kidding? He wanted the whole package.

AARON'S BREATHING EVENED OUT, and when Steph shifted, he didn't stir. He'd finally, thankfully, fallen asleep.

She wasn't sure she could have stayed still any longer. She hadn't wanted to ruin anything by opening her mouth and saying anything more to shatter the bliss. She'd totally forgotten she'd said that thing about ten minutes of silence on their date. He must think she had nothing else to say. She didn't. Nothing as interesting as those honeybees, anyhow.

She carefully got out of bed and tiptoed into the bathroom. She supposed it would've been more polite to offer the shower to him first—or maybe they could have showered together. He probably wasn't ready for that, though. She could feel him pulling away from her already. Maybe that was a good thing.

It wasn't that she was having regrets. She was more than willing—no, eager—to see where things could go with him. She'd never felt that physically compatible with anyone before. But when it came to actual conversation she had nothing to say to him. And besides, what had happened to finding herself and learning to be independent? Clinging to Aaron—to any man—for support of any kind was so not the way to do that.

She showered, her muscles and emotions raw and aching. Her stomach growled as she dried herself off. It was way past her dinnertime. Then she remembered the Chinese takeout on the hallway table. She'd let Aaron nap while she warmed up the food and have it ready for him when he woke up.

She'd be the perfect little domestic goddess, having food ready for when her hungry man…

No, that was her mother's way of thinking. The first thing she should do when he woke up was ask how much the food was and pay for her half. Independent girls paid their own way.

As she waited for the microwave to heat up the food, her gaze landed on the HSE workbooks stuffed under the coffee table. Maya's look of disappointment as she'd told her she was postponing the test popped into her head. That frown superimposed itself on Aaron's face, and she faltered.

Aaron Caruthers had been the reason she'd wanted her diploma in the first place, as if that piece of paper would prove she was smart enough to run Georgette's by herself. But now…now she couldn't imagine running the place without him. Now, getting her diploma was about proving to herself that she was good enough for *him*.

"I think five minutes might be a little too long for that to be in the microwave." Aaron's voice startled her. Hurriedly, she hit the stop button and took out the scalding plate, putting in the next and setting it to a much more reasonable two minutes.

He'd put on his rumpled pants and glasses, but his T-shirt and socks were still missing. Not rushing out, then. Good. She was relieved he wasn't eager to leave now that he'd gotten what he wanted.

He wrapped his arms around her waist and rested his chin on her shoulder, kissing her neck.

She purred, but under all that, she was confused. How could she still want him with all these doubts circling?

"Do you want a shower before you eat?" she asked. Keeping their conversation to mundane topics would keep her from saying anything stupid.

"Nah, I'm starving. I'll eat first." He took the plate from her and gave her a peck on the cheek. Warmth filtered through her. It seemed he wasn't ready to have a conversation about how things would go from here, and she was fine with that. In fact, she was willing to put off that talk until she had her diploma in hand and they stood on more even footing.

Besides, she was hungry.

CHAPTER EIGHTEEN

AT THE END of May, the day-trippers were out in full force. Aaron kept a professional distance from Steph at Georgette's that weekend, but it was so busy, she couldn't tell if that was simply because he was preoccupied with the bookshop. No matter what she tried, he wouldn't cross the threshold to the bakery, especially when Georgette was around.

But sometimes Steph would catch him watching her with hooded eyes, and she'd feel a ghost of that flex. Her knees would go weak as a ripple went through her, and she'd curse him silently as he sent her a secret cheeky grin. Maybe it was a good idea that he stayed on his side—she might ravage him on the counter otherwise.

It was a full three days before he finally bridged the gap. They'd had a busy weekend, and he hadn't even called after work. They were all so tired, but by Tuesday, business was quiet again. Steph and Aaron had both insisted Kira take time off. The teen hadn't been happy about it, but her gray pallor and sluggishness worried them deeply.

It was about three o'clock when Aaron strode

through to the bakery. Steph assumed he was coming to help himself to a cup of coffee. She'd turned away for a moment to straighten the pastries in the display case. When she shifted back she bumped up against something warm and hard.

She straightened so quickly the blood rushed from her head. Or maybe that dizzying sensation was something else.

"Hi." That was all Aaron said before he glanced around surreptitiously, then leaned in and kissed her deeply, hands sliding around her waist. She melted instantly, running her fingertips up his arms and pressing against him, his arousal nudging against her thigh.

When they both came up for air, he leaned his forehead against hers. "Sorry," he murmured. She giggled and kissed the cleft in his chin. He captured her lips once more, as if he couldn't stand the teasing. "You've been driving me crazy being so close. All I've wanted for days was to touch you."

She pulled back a little to look into his face. "I thought you were avoiding me."

He shook his head. "I'm just trying to draw some lines here. This is your workplace, too. I shouldn't be…harassing you like this."

"Are you kidding me?" She turned in his arms to press her bottom against him, rubbing seductively as she curved her arms up around his neck. "Harass away."

He groaned, fingers digging into her hips as he

stilled her. "Not now. Not here." He buried his nose behind her ear, nipping at that spot that made her gasp and arch into him. His hot breath bathed her neck as he whispered, "Later. Tonight."

Her legs buckled as she craned her neck around to look him in the eye. "My place?"

He answered with one more kiss, his hands sliding down her front, giving her a taste of the evening to come.

They didn't even speak that night when he arrived. He simply pushed her up against the wall in the entryway, devouring her as if he'd been starving, stripping them both of their clothes right there. She couldn't stop touching him, exploring the smooth skin stretched over taut, lean muscles.

The first time had been all about technique. Tonight he showed her his wild side. He was an animal, driving her hard against the boundaries of pleasure, keeping her riding the fine line between ecstasy and agony. And Aaron had some serious stamina. Steph had never felt so alive, so decadently fierce. She was certain the pharmacy customers could hear their pounding and groaning, but she didn't care. When they finally came together, Steph's heart overflowed with emotions she wanted to name, each one frightening and perilous and wonderful, like lightning in a bottle.

It was close to midnight when Aaron got up and started dressing in the dark. They hadn't had dinner. Hadn't spoken a word beyond those said between lovers in heat.

"Stay with me," she said softly. She didn't want him to go. She liked having him here. She sat up and flicked on the bedside lamp.

Aaron looked away, dazzled by the light, maybe. "I want to. I really do. But…Gran's at home alone." He smoothed a hand over his hair. "She knows I'm here. I told her I was having dinner with you, but if I stay over… I don't want to give her the wrong idea about us."

And what, exactly, was the *wrong* idea? She didn't know, and it was eating at her insides. She'd jumped in with one simple goal in mind—to scratch an itch—but now she wasn't sure where this was all supposed to be leading. Or if she should want it to lead anywhere at all. "I understand," she said instead, which was laughable.

Aaron didn't catch the irony. "I'm not ready to let the world know about us."

It was probably better this way for now. It seemed neither of them knew exactly what was going on. "Okay."

She was determined not to let it bother her. She didn't want to be his dirty little secret, as if he was ashamed of her, but at the same time, she was also kind of thrilled. It was her first relationship with a guy her parents didn't know about. They'd introduced her to a lot of the men she'd dated—all of them nice enough, but the fact that they'd been her parents' choices and not hers hadn't endeared them to her. Having Aaron all to herself like this meant her parents weren't constantly pressuring her to like him.

Who knew that being with Aaron Caruthers, the high school bookworm, would be her way of rebelling?

It was only after he'd kissed her good-night and closed the door that her doubts overran her. She turned over on the bed, the sheets still smelling of Aaron's soap, deodorant and sweat. She gathered them close, breathed deep, wrapped herself in his scent. When she realized what she was doing, she turned onto her back once more. *Strong, independent women don't need men to define their worth*, she chanted to herself. She had to fight that impulse to *need* him.

To her surprise, Maya didn't totally agree with her when they met the following day.

"I don't see what the problem is," she said. Maya had invited Steph to come for dinner after her visit to the retirement home, eager to get the scoop on Aaron. "He's a great guy. If you like him, and he likes you, then why the hell *wouldn't* you date?"

"Because this isn't what I'm supposed to want. I'm supposed to focus on *me* and getting my diploma."

Maya sucked in her cheeks and leaned forward. "Listen, I might have reacted a bit harshly when you first told me you wanted to postpone. I was afraid you were giving yourself an excuse to give up. If you're not ready for your test, you're not ready. I don't want you to give up on a good thing just because of something I said."

"I didn't postpone because of Aaron. I wasn't ready. But I already called and rescheduled the exam for the end of June," Steph said firmly. "I'm going to do it, but I want more time."

Maya blinked in surprise. "Oh. Good. I'm glad you've got a plan in place." She grinned. "The old you would've put that off until I placed the phone in your hand and dialed."

That was probably true. But Steph had no wish to postpone the test any longer than she had to. As difficult and exhausting as studying and doing all those practice tests had been, she was set on her path, and she refused to stray from it.

As the days went on, it was tricky, though. Aaron came to her place after work almost every other night, and she found she couldn't say no to him. Even after a full day of work, all it took was a touch, a kiss, and she was ready for him. Naturally, all thoughts of studying flew out the window the moment Aaron carried her to her bedroom.

They had plenty of quiet moments, too. Sometimes he would come over with takeout, and they'd simply eat and watch TV. At one point, he picked up the copy of *The Great Gatsby* he'd given her and started to read it out loud while she cooked dinner. Steph didn't have the heart to tell him she'd listened to the audiobook version twice. She loved his voice, low and flowing over the words like melted chocolate. He was really good at performing, something she hadn't expected from someone so straitlaced. For several evenings she simply lay on the couch with her head in his lap while he read to her and stroked her hair.

One evening, they rented the DVD. After the viewing they compared notes and found they both liked and disliked the same things about the film, and they got into a long conversation about other movie adaptations they'd seen. It was one of the first times they'd been able to carry on a conversation that didn't end in awkward silence.

"It's kinda funny," she said at one point as she snuggled against him. "I had a babysitter who used to do this exact same thing with me."

"What do you mean?" Aaron cocked an eyebrow.

"She used to read to me all the time, and sometimes she'd rent a movie version and we'd talk about it."

"Sounds like the best babysitter ever."

She chuckled. He would think that. "Her name was Kitty," she said. "I think she was a college student or something. Almost every week my parents would go to some meeting. I don't remember what. And Kitty would come with a book. I enjoyed it sometimes, but there were days when I just wished she'd leave me alone to play video games or something. Man, that must've gone on for...years."

"What happened to her?"

Steph bit her lip. "I think I might have gotten her fired," she said bleakly. "I was sick of seeing her and being left at home every week, so my parents... They stopped going to their thing and I didn't see Kitty at all after that." She hadn't thought about that in a long time. She'd been twelve or thirteen, and growing more belligerent by the day. She'd thought she was getting too old to have a babysitter. Lucena had always been around to watch her, after all, and would have happily let her have the run of the house instead of making her do wholesome educational activities. Her parents had never seemed to trust their daughter to keep herself entertained.

Now that she thought about it, Kitty didn't live in Everville now. Where had she gone? Guilt and dread pricked her conscience. She hoped she hadn't inadvertently run her out of town.

As Steph drove to her parents' house later that week she debated telling them about the HSE exam. It didn't seem right to keep something so important hidden from them.

She could already predict their reactions— cautious optimism from her father, outright skepticism and disapproval from her mother. It was how they'd reacted any time she mentioned a desire to try something new. And it was no wonder, she mused now. She remembered her father shelling out big bucks so she could learn how to play the harp, but she'd given up two months into it when her fingers had started blistering and bleeding. When she was sixteen, she'd gotten it into her head that she wanted to become a champion skier, so her parents had sent her to Vermont for a winter. She'd spent most of that time in the lodge's hot tub, she'd been so sore and bruised after only three lessons.

Mom and Dad had never complained. Not really. Her mother told her it was good enough that she'd tried. Her father had simply sighed and shrugged it off as another lost investment. Even Maya knew her habit of quitting when the going got tough.

She never wanted to be that flaky girl again. Now she made commitments and stuck with them.

She parked in the garage and went into the house. The smell of roast beef beckoned her to the kitchen, where she found Lucena mashing potatoes. She greeted her as Steph grabbed a drink from the fridge. "Your parents are on the deck," she said.

"Thanks, Lucena. How've you been?"

The older woman gave a shrug. She'd been working for the family since Steph was four, and Helen had run her ragged, insisting she look after all of Steph's needs. At seventeen, Steph had had to beg the woman to teach her how to do her own laundry in secret. Helen had thought it unconscionable that she would have to do anything on her own when they were paying someone to do it for them.

"Make sure you see me before you leave," Lucena said. "I made you some soups and foods to keep in your freezer."

"Aw, thanks. You didn't have to do that."

"I do it anyhow. You need to eat better," she said pointedly, stirring the gravy. "You're too skinny."

Steph rolled her eyes. Like her parents, Lucena had never stopped seeing her as a child to be fed and coddled and cleaned up after.

On the back deck, Terrence and Helen sat in the lounge chairs, reading. Steph kissed them both before settling on a cushioned chair at the table. She took a deep breath, ready to declare that she was studying to get her diploma, but her mother set her magazine aside with an enthusiastic grin.

"Baby," she began in an excited voice. "Why didn't you tell us what you were up to?"

She stared. How had her mother found out about the exam? "I…I wanted to see how things would go."

"You shouldn't be shy about it," Helen said giddily. "I mean, at first I was a little sad that things didn't work out between you and Wyatt, but Aaron Caruthers is a fine young man. Practicing law is a perfectly respectable job, especially if that bookstore of his doesn't work out. Why, I bet he could handle running a firm out of that same space. Don't you think so, dear?"

Terrence barely looked up from his paper. "The boy's got a good head on his shoulders and good business sense. Practical. Decent. I've got no objections."

Steph's breath caught. "How did you—"

"Wyatt told us he spotted you two having dinner at the club." Helen tsked. "He was pretty crestfallen about it. I wasn't happy to see him so depressed. I'd hoped you two would hit it off, but this thing with Aaron is much better. Yes. I'm very happy you've made a choice."

Made a choice? Her mother sounded as though she'd picked a dress for prom...or worse, a wedding.

"I hear he's been bringing you takeout every other night." Her mother cut her a sly look, tapping a finger against the side of her nose.

"Don't tease the girl, Helen," her father said reproachfully.

"I'm not teasing. I'm just happy for her." She turned to Steph. "You'll invite him for dinner next week, won't you?"

"I-it's not like that," Steph sputtered. "We're just friends."

"With benefits, I'm sure." Helen gave her a condescending moue. "Now, I'm all for women's lib, and there are some impulses you can't deny." Terrence muttered a protest and buried himself deeper behind his paper as his wife went on. "But you know the old saying. A man's not going to buy the cow if he gets the milk for free."

"For God's sake, Mom, I am not a *cow*!" Steph

slammed her palm against the table, her chest heaving. "And I wasn't put on this earth so you could have grandchildren, so stop trying to sell me like I'm livestock!"

Helen sat back at her outburst. "Where's this attitude coming from? I only want what's best for you, baby."

Her blood seemed to be bypassing her heart entirely, pushing up into her head as her chest went cold. "*I'm* the only person who gets to decide that. What Aaron and I do together is our business, so please stay out of it."

Helen's brow lowered as she geared up for a retort, but Steph wouldn't give her the opportunity. She rose and marched off, heading back through the kitchen.

"I'm sorry, Lucena. I'm not feeling up to dinner tonight."

The housekeeper frowned. She'd obviously heard their argument. Lucena started toward the fridge. "Let me pack up some things for you to take home."

"No." Why was everyone always thrusting things at her? Men, money, food. Didn't they think she could manage on her own? Angry tears welled in her eyes. "I'm fine. I…I have to go."

She hurried through the house and got back into her mini SUV, but didn't start it up just yet. She gripped the wheel and breathed through her anger, alternately pissed off at her mother's attitude and at herself for flying off the handle. Was this any better than the tantrums she'd thrown as a child? Slowly, the red haze around her vision cleared, but her chest continued to quake.

A knock on her passenger-side window startled her. Her father opened the door and got in next to her. He sat for a beat and then asked, "If you're planning on leaving, can I come with you?"

She rested her forehead against the wheel, but didn't respond.

"I talked to your mother. Told her to stop egging you on. She didn't appreciate that. I'll probably be sleeping in the guest room tonight."

She wanted to say "I'm sorry," because she felt genuinely guilty for making her father pick sides. It felt good to know he was on hers, but at the same time she was still mad.

Steph released a long breath. Her father's hand came to rest on her shoulder and he squeezed. "Your mother's the way she is because she loves you and wants to make sure you're taken care of."

She shifted in her seat. "I can take care of myself."

"I know you can. I'm always trying to convince her you're a grown-up. Still…" He rubbed the back of his neck, and a spurt of indignity rose back to the surface. Maybe her father wasn't as confident in her as she thought he was. "No one really wants to be alone forever," he said finally. "Now I don't know Aaron half as well as I'd like, but he strikes me as being a good man. I'd like to get to know him bet-

ter, but you're right. What you do with him is your
business. I don't need details," he added hastily.
"But you should know that whatever you decide,
it's your choice to make. If your mom and I come
off a little heavy-handed at times, it's not because
we're trying to control you. You get that, right?"

She slumped her shoulders. "Yes."

"We only want you to be happy."

"I know." But being given everything, having all
her problems taken care of for her by other people
was not how she wanted to live her life. She wanted
to feel like she deserved happiness because she'd
earned it.

"Are you going to come back in for dinner?" her
father asked.

She stared at her hands, fingers still curled into
claws. She was too high-strung. "No."

He stared at her a moment longer. "All right." He
opened the door and got out.

"Please tell Mom I'm sorry."

"You can call and tell her yourself." He gave her
a sympathetic smile. "I love you, baby."

"Love you, too."

As she drove off she regretted her outburst. She'd
call and apologize tomorrow. Giving Helen the silent treatment would only make things worse.

Back at her apartment her regret deepened with
her hunger. She should've taken Lucena up on her
offer of food, but instead, she settled on a package of instant ramen noodles. As she ate, her gaze

landed on her phone. Her first thought was to call Aaron, tell him what had happened, find some comfort in his voice and maybe in his arms. He'd come over if she asked him to. But the moment she realized what she was pining for she snuffed out the urge.

She couldn't lean on him—or anyone—for anything anymore. She had to be her own woman and prove she could take care of herself. No more parental interference. No more relying on good intentions or sympathy. Aaron had to stay out of the picture until she knew she was standing solidly on her own two feet.

Her exam was a week away. Once she got her diploma, she'd show the world she could do what she wanted on her own. That was all that mattered.

She needed to study.

CHAPTER NINETEEN

AARON HAD NO idea how his grandmother could bake when it was as hot as an oven outside. He kept peering over from the bookshop, afraid he'd find Georgette passed out on the floor. Kira was running the front counter, but he wasn't certain she would hear above the rattle of the monstrous old air-conditioning unit if something happened to Gran. Better air-conditioning was something he'd have to look into. The heat couldn't be good for his grandmother's health or for business.

That Wednesday was particularly quiet, giving Aaron a chance to do some inventory. Gran was in the kitchen baking. Steph had taken the day off to visit a friend in Hudson Falls. He told himself that was good. She needed time off. At the same time, she hadn't said who she was visiting. He didn't want to get possessive about her, but every night over the past week, she'd told him she was too tired to have him over.

Maybe she was mad at him for not staying. But what was he supposed to do? He couldn't sleep over. That would raise far too many questions, and besides, he had to think of his grandmother.

Maybe Steph was simply getting tired of him and this was her way of breaking things off gently so they could go back to the way things were. The way they'd been before he'd seen her naked...

He sucked in a deep breath, trying to stay calm, cool and in control. He'd always known it would end sooner or later. Frankly, it was a miracle it'd lasted as long as it had, despite how comfortable they were getting with each other. If she didn't want to see him anymore there was nothing he could do about it.

Nothing.

Yet his chest tightened with panic as his mind spun out a dozen different ideas for how to hold on to her. Another part of his mind was formulating a plan B, preparing him for the bitter end of their relationship...such as it was.

He hated that he was so wrapped up in her. God, what was it about her that made his insides soft and his outsides hard?

He heard the bakery door open, but didn't pay attention until someone peered into the bookstore. "Hello?"

Aaron looked up to see a vaguely familiar-looking blond man. "Hi. Can I help you?"

"It's Aaron, right? Chris Jamieson. We went to school together."

The name and face struck a chord as he remembered the high school quarterback Steph had mentioned. He shook the man's outstretched hand. "How's it going, Chris?" He found he didn't have the negative visceral reaction to this former football player that he usually had with guys from his set. Huh.

"Not bad. Great bookshop. I've been meaning to get down here." He gazed around smiling. "Listen, I don't mean to bug you, but I was hoping to get some doughnuts."

"Oh. Kira's not there?" He abandoned his task and accompanied Chris into the bakery. The teen was missing. She must have gone to the bathroom. "Well, no problem, I can get you what you need. Sorry about the wait." He filled Chris's order and they chatted. The former QB told him about his father's farm, and Aaron was surprised to find out Chris had a teenage son. He asked about the wind turbines along the highway, and Chris got to talking about the project he'd helped launch, which led to Aaron recommending several books about alternative energy. They talked for almost an hour before Chris realized he'd dawdled for too long. They ended up making plans to continue their talk over coffee.

Even after Chris had left, Aaron was still grinning. He'd made a new friend in town. He'd never have thought that he and the former golden boy would have anything in common. But then, he'd never thought he'd get a chance to date Steph, either.

Kira still hadn't appeared after Chris, and then two more customers, came and went. Concerned, he knocked on the bathroom door, but she wasn't in there. A bad feeling churned through him as he peered out at the parking lot. Her car was missing.

He hastened into the kitchen. "Gran, did Kira tell you she had to leave?"

"Leave? No. She's not here?"

"Her car's gone." A new fear gripped him. "Hold on." He went to the register and ran a summary of the day's sales, then counted the cash against the float.

The till was missing a hundred dollars.

A sour taste filled his mouth. His first instinct was to be angry, but dread hung over him like a thundercloud. Something wasn't right. Kira couldn't be a thief. She wouldn't have taken off without telling someone. And if she'd wanted money, why hadn't she taken it all?

He called her cell phone and got her voice mail. "Kira, I don't know where you are or what's going on, but I need you to call me." He tried to sound concerned rather than angry, but wasn't certain he'd succeeded.

By midafternoon she still hadn't called back. He considered calling the police, but then remembered what Gran had said about her home situation. He didn't want to be responsible for breaking up her family because of a misunderstanding.

The door opened. His heart shot into his throat in the hope it was Kira.

It was Steph. She looked pale, her mouth pinched in the corners. "I thought you were going to be in Hudson Falls all day," he said.

"I wanted to get back before nightfall." Her smile was small, tentative, her voice rusty.

His worry shifted temporarily. He wanted to go to her, to ask her what was wrong, to hold her. But there was something in her look that told him to keep away, that she was somehow…fragile. "How was your visit with your friend?"

She blinked at him, then shook her head. "Fine. It was fine." She noticed Georgette standing behind the counter, frowning. "What's going on?"

"Kira's missing. She's taken a hundred dollars from the till, and I can't reach her on her cell." He paced. "I think I should go and see her at her home, maybe talk to her mother if she's there. I'm worried about her."

"What if she didn't steal the money?" Steph said, wrapping her arms around her waist. "What if… what if someone held her up and kidnapped her?"

"I doubt that." He hadn't meant to sound so curt, but his worry was getting the better of him. "She took a specific amount of money, grabbed her things out of her locker and left without a word.

She wasn't kidnapped out of the store. I've been here all day. I would've seen or heard something."

Gran's brow pleated. "It's only a hundred dollars, Aaron. I'm sure there's a reasonable explanation and that she'll tell us what's going on as soon as she can." She cast him a meaningful look. "It's not worth stirring the pot over."

"But what if she's in trouble? What if something's happened?" He chewed his lip, unable to stop himself from imagining the worst.

He squeezed his eyes shut, trying not to think about a wrecked car in the middle of the highway. "I need to make sure she's okay. The only thing I can think of doing right now is going to her home to see if anyone might know where she is."

Georgette folded her hands in front of her as if locking her decision between her palms. "All right. But I'm going with you. If her mother, Darlene, is there, she'll be more likely to talk to me than to some stranger."

"I'm going, too," Steph said, her expression grave.

Aaron hesitated, exchanging a look with Gran. They'd been reticent about sharing what they knew about Kira's home life with Steph. Perhaps it was best to keep the circle of people who knew as small as possible.

"What?" She caught their looks. "What aren't you guys telling me?"

Georgette let out a long breath. "Kira and her

brother are alone for the most part. Their mother comes and goes, but she's essentially abandoned them. It's been that way for a while now."

Steph glowered. "You knew this and didn't tell me?"

"It wasn't for us to tell," Aaron said and felt his justification fizzle away at her hard glare. "We don't want child services to get called in."

Her look hardened further. "We need to find her."

"You don't have to come…" He was about to say it would be better if someone stayed at the bakery to take care of things. But the conviction setting her jaw told him she would not be deterred.

"I'm Kira's supervisor. I sensed something was wrong, but I never asked her about it, even though it was affecting her work." She raised her chin. "I didn't do my job. She's my responsibility, too."

He didn't argue with her. They'd both been too distracted to focus on the teen's problems. Or maybe they'd been too squeamish to confront her, convincing themselves it was none of their business and that Kira was capable of handling her own affairs.

Clearly, she was not. Whatever had happened, Aaron felt responsible. Everyone needed help now and again, and despite knowing what she'd been facing, he hadn't done nearly enough.

He just hoped they could help her before it was too late.

THEY CLOSED THE BAKERY, and Aaron and Georgette got into the station wagon. Steph followed in her mini SUV. It was a forty-minute drive to the trailer park where Kira lived. Along the way Steph conjured up the most dramatic daytime talk-show scenarios in anticipation of what they might encounter, what kind of troubles they were about to face. As they drove into the wooded lot sparsely inhabited by some truly frightening-looking trailer homes, she was glad none of them had come here alone.

They found the Wests' dingy trailer sitting on cinder blocks, paint peeling from its sides. The crumbling wooden steps listed to one side. Aaron started toward the door, but Georgette stopped him. "Wait, Aaron. If Darlene answers, it's best she sees me first."

"Gran, those stairs are going to fall apart any second. I'm not letting you climb them."

"Let me talk to her," Steph insisted. His eyebrows knitted together, and she explained, "I've met Darlene a couple of times before. And Kira's known me for longer. Besides, you look too angry."

"I'm not," he snapped. Steph gave him a flat look. He rubbed the back of his neck and said more softly, "I'm not angry. I'm worried."

"I know." She rested her palm on his shoulder. "But you can be intimidating. Just let me talk to her."

She carefully climbed the rickety steps and knocked on the screen door while Aaron and

Georgette waited below. She could hear a TV inside, and a light was on, but no one answered.

"Hey, you." They turned to see a portly older woman with wild, wiry graying hair standing in the thoroughfare. "What're you doing here?" She glared at Aaron and Georgette in turn, then turned her look on Steph's mini SUV.

"We're looking for Darlene West," Aaron said. "It's concerning her daughter."

The woman gave him a suspicious look. "What do you want?" she demanded.

Steph intervened. "Please, we're just trying to make sure Kira is all right. We work with her at Georgette's Bakery. She left work suddenly without telling anyone, and we're concerned."

The woman gave her an assessing once-over. Whatever she saw seemed to satisfy her, because she gave a short huff. "Hang on." She went up to the trailer beneath the small port window and banged a fist against the siding. "Kiki! It's Velma. There're some people here who wanna see you. Don't be rude and leave them out here."

A second later the door unlocked, and Kira's pale face peered through the broken screen on the storm door. "What do you want?"

Steph's heart eased, seeing her alive and, for the most part, healthy. "Kira, we were so worried. You left work without telling anyone."

She looked away. "I'm sorry. There…there was an emergency."

"What kind of emergency?"

Kira's eyes darted toward Aaron and Georgette. She shrank. "I'm so sorry. I know I let you down—"

"What emergency?" Georgette repeated in a no-nonsense tone. Steph knew it wasn't impatience, but concern that made her sound so sharp.

"I'll pay you back, I swear. But I didn't know what else to do and…"

There was a hacking noise from within, dry and violent, followed by a small, raspy moan. Kira glanced in nervously.

"Who is that? Your brother?"

"He's really sick," Kira said. "Please, don't come in. He has a fever and he's coughing a lot."

That didn't sound good at all. "Where's your mother?"

"I…" Her eyes darted to Velma, who was standing by. She shook her head. "Not here right now."

Steph wondered if maybe the woman was the landlord and knew about Kira's family life. Did she care? Would she report the West children if she knew they were on their own?

She couldn't chance it. "Kira, if your brother is that sick, he needs to see a doctor."

"I can't afford it," she said quietly. "He'll be okay. He just needs…"

"If he's got a fever and is coughing a lot, it could be any number of problems." She knew from working with the seniors in the retirement home to watch out for particular symptoms and when it was important to call a nurse. She lowered her voice. "If he has tuberculosis, you could have it, too. It's very contagious, and if you've been exposed, so have we." She had to make it clear to her that it wasn't only her brother who was in danger.

Another plaintive moan had Kira darting back in. "Wait here," Steph said to Aaron and Georgette. If the boy was contagious, Steph could afford to get sick. Aaron, however, couldn't risk catching something and spreading it to his grandmother.

The inside of the trailer was tidier than the exterior let on, but the air was stuffy. A bag from the pharmacy rested on the small table, and an empty children's cough syrup box sat on the counter. In the back of the trailer, a small boy swathed in blankets was curled in the double bed built into the wall. The TV played a fuzzy feed of some cartoon. His eyes were glazed, his cheeks ruddy.

Steph suppressed the urge to cover her face as the boy hacked helplessly into the blanket. Kira helped him sip water from a glass, and he gave another plaintive moan. She forced herself forward. "Hey there." She smiled down at the boy, who watched her warily. "I'm Steph. I work with your sister. What's your name?"

"This is Tyler," Kira said for him when the boy looked to her.

"Feeling kinda sick, huh, Tyler?" She reached out and brushed his hair away from his forehead. He was dry and burning hot. She kept her smile fixed and said quietly to Kira, "How long has he been like this?"

"He's had the fever for almost three days now. And he keeps throwing up."

She chewed her lip. "Okay. I'm not a doctor, but I know that's bad. We need to get him to the ER right away."

"We can't. They'll ask questions." She gnawed on her lower lip. "They'll ask about our mother." As ragged as she looked, her eyes gleamed with fear, conviction, dread and anger. She was trying so hard to hold it together it made Steph's chest ache.

"Listen, Kira." She drew the girl away from the bed and touched her shoulder. "I know your mother's not really in the picture. I know you've been doing the best you can. But we can't leave Tyler like this."

She shook her head as she started to weep. "I can take care of him. We can take care of ourselves." Fat tears fell from her eyes.

"But what happens if *you* get sick?" Tuberculosis wasn't out of the question. Steph knew that was always a big concern at the retirement home. She'd had her shots for it, but Kira probably hadn't. And there could be dozens of other reasons for Tyler's illness, none of them good. "You can't work when you're sick. What if you've passed something on to a customer?"

Kira wiped her nose across the back of her hand. "I didn't mean to! I—"

"You haven't done anything wrong," Steph

rushed to assure her. "You were doing the best you could. But you can't do this on your own forever. I want to help you and Tyler. Will you let me help you?"

FIVE HOURS LATER, Steph sat in the ER waiting room, rubbing a groove into the top of her thigh with the heel of her hand. She'd told Aaron to take Georgette home in case the children were contagious. He'd come to the hospital afterward and was getting coffee while Kira sat with her brother.

The doctor's questions about the siblings' mother were predictably tricky. At first, Kira said she was working, but when the doctor had asked for a contact number, Steph had blurted that she was a friend of the family and was taking care of the kids while their mother was out of town on a business trip. The doctor had left it at that.

Tyler was put on an IV drip and oxygen. He was severely dehydrated and was having trouble breathing, most likely because of inflamed lungs. They were waiting for test results. The doctor wanted to make sure it wasn't something like TB. If it was, Kira and Steph, and probably Aaron and Georgette, would all need to get tested.

Steph silently berated herself. She should've confronted Kira after Aaron had mentioned the girl's hair falling out. She'd thought it was the stress of school. Steph had gone through it herself, after all. If she'd known what was really going on, she could have done…well, something. Despite Kira's fear of child services, Steph wasn't sure how much longer the West kids could survive on their own. Tyler was thin as a twig. Steph had carried him out of the trailer and put him in her car, and he'd barely weighed anything.

She tried to distract herself by watching the news flickering across the TV screen, but she was exhausted from the HSE exam and the long drive to and from Hudson Falls. It felt like a million years ago. Her nerves ratcheted tighter thinking about the test. She'd been so nervous. Her stomach had nearly gone into convulsions, the way it used to during tests back in high school. She'd powered through the queasiness, though. She wasn't exactly sure how she'd done. She'd answered all the questions, but some of the writing and reading comprehension stuff had stumped her, and she'd had to give her best guess. She'd second-guessed herself a lot, too. Plus, doing all the writing by hand had made her fingers cramp. She hoped penmanship didn't count toward her score.

Aaron came back with a coffee and a sandwich from the cafeteria. She hadn't eaten since lunch, but she had little appetite.

"You don't have to stay here, you know," she said to him as he sat next to her.

"Of course I do. Those kids don't have anyone else." He lowered his voice. "If the doctor thinks it's okay when they send Tyler home with Kira, Gran and I are going to ask them to stay at our place for a while. Just until we can figure out where their mother is."

Keep a teen and a young boy in that tiny bungalow? "But...where will they sleep?"

"They can have my room. They need someone to look after them."

Steph's heart melted. Aaron barely knew the Wests, but he was willing to give up his bed for them.

The doctor emerged from the ER unit an hour later. She and Aaron stood.

"Luckily, it doesn't seem to be anything more serious than bronchitis," he said. "But I'd like to keep Tyler overnight just in case."

"Thank God." Steph sagged.

"If you like, you can go in to see him before we move him to his room."

They did. Tyler was already looking and sounding better. He lay dozing in his bed, while Kira sat next to him, watching his chest rise and fall. Steph sat next to her. "You okay?"

"How am I going to pay for this?" she asked hollowly. "My mom never signed us up for health insurance."

"Don't worry about that." Steph had money in her trust fund. It'd been one of those things she'd refused to touch once she'd moved out, but this wasn't for a pair of jeans or a bottle of wine. This was for something that mattered. "It's been taken care of."

"That's right," Aaron said. "And don't worry about work or anything. Focus on Tyler for now, okay?"

Kira nodded mutely. Tears streamed down her pale cheeks and dripped off her chin. She hid her face in her hands as exhaustion took over. Steph gathered her close and let her cry. The poor girl needed someone as much as Tyler did. She'd been shouldering this burden on her own for far too long, and her strength had finally given out.

When her tears subsided, she told them she would stay in the hospital overnight so Tyler wouldn't wake up alone. She'd smartly packed a bag for both herself and her brother, so they were set. Aaron told her about his plan to have them stay with him and Gran. Kira looked a little wary and said she'd think about it. She hadn't outright rejected him, though, so that was something.

Steph and Aaron left once the orderly wheeled the boy off to his room. They walked out to the parking lot together to their respective vehicles.

"Gran's already agreed to pay Kira while she takes this time off," he said. "We're going to make her officially full-time, if she wants it." He rubbed his chin. "Maybe I can look into getting her and Tyler enrolled for health insurance. Not sure how it'll work if her mom's not around. I should see about group coverage for Georgette's, too. It might cost a lot, but for cases like this, it'd be worth it."

He was speaking mostly to himself, but Steph

could almost hear the gears turning in his brain as he planned for future emergencies, thinking up ways to keep all the different balls in the air. He was already doing more than she ever could for the siblings. He was so generous and confident. He took charge and didn't hesitate to do the right thing. She'd thought her attraction to him was part of some experimental phase, seeing what it'd be like dating a smart, adorable geek. But Aaron Caruthers was so much more.

She threw her arms around his shoulders, cutting off his words. He stiffened, then folded her in a hug. It had been more than a week since they'd touched, but this embrace somehow felt more intimate than anything they'd done before.

"What's this for?" he asked.

"For being you," she said into his chest. "For caring so much and for helping them."

"Hey, you're the one who managed to talk to Kira, and you walked into that nest of germs without a mask."

She looked into his face and said drily, "It wasn't *that* bad."

"It's not just that you went into a virtual quarantine zone." He cupped her cheek. "You were great with those two. You were calm and you didn't freak them out. I would've terrified them with all the things going through my head. I've read way too many articles about infectious diseases, you know." He clasped her more tightly. "Thank you."

Her heart warmed as if a ray of sunlight had broken through the day's gloom. "I have something to tell you," she said. He gave her a quizzical look. "I wasn't in Hudson Falls visiting a friend. I was there to do my high school equivalency exam."

The grin that lit up his face dispelled the last of the day's gloominess. "That's...that's great. How did you do?"

"I'm not sure. I won't get the results for a few weeks." The weight in her chest eased. She hadn't realized how keeping this secret from him had affected her.

He stroked her hair out of her face, tucking it behind her ear. "I'm sure you did fine. But I have something to confess. That first time I went to your place, before we went to Greenfields, I saw the workbooks on your coffee table. I wasn't sure what you were up to, and I didn't bring it up because... well, I didn't think it was my business. But I'm so happy that you went and did it."

"Maya's been helping me study," she said. "I would've asked you, but I didn't want you to know."

His brow furrowed. "Why not?"

"Because..." She didn't want him to know his opinion of her mattered so much. "Maya's my best friend. And you were already busy with your bookshop and Georgette. I didn't want to add to your burden."

"It wouldn't have been a burden." His brow furrowed. "Is this why you've been so distant this past week?"

"I've been studying. I'm sorry." She sent him a wobbly smile. "Anyhow, if I'd let you help me study, we'd never have gotten anything done."

The shift in his stance and gentle prod against her hip told her he'd already forgiven her. "Am I that irresistible?"

She peered up at him shyly from beneath her lashes. "Come over tonight and we can test that theory."

He gave her a hot, brief kiss. "Keep the porch light on."

CHAPTER TWENTY

AFTER TYLER WAS discharged from the hospital, he and Kira moved in with Georgette and Aaron. While they were quiet, ultrapolite and did everything they could to stay out of the way and not make a fuss, Georgette did everything she could to get them to come out of their shells. When Aaron mentioned his concern that his grandmother was overtaxing herself, Steph started coming over after work to play board games, watch DVDs or do homework with Tyler and Kira.

She didn't mind spending time with the West kids. It took her mind off the fact she and Aaron hadn't had The Talk yet, even though the whole town seemed to know something was going on between them. She'd gotten more than a few sly remarks at the bakery.

Hanging out with Kira and Tyler also distracted her from the anxious anticipation of waiting for her exam results. She'd been told the average wait time was six to eight weeks. Every time she approached the mailbox, her lungs filled with leaden dread, only to be replaced by a confusing sense of simultaneous disappointment and relief. The rest of the time, she felt as though she were stuck at the top of the roller coaster, waiting for the screaming plunge.

"Hey." Aaron nudged her. "Your turn."

She stared at the Scrabble board, the letters blurring together. Her tiles sat before her untouched. "Oh. Sorry. I'm thinking."

It was another minute before she put down *cat*.

Aaron added his tiles and turned her word into *category*.

"Show-off." Kira noted his point score as Tyler focused on the board. His sister peered at his tiles over his shoulder and helped him put the word *guise* together.

"What's a guise?" Tyler asked.

"It's a facade." When the eleven-year-old simply stared at him, Aaron elaborated. "As in *disguise*. Like a mask. The face you put on to hide yourself."

At that moment, Steph felt as if she were wearing the mask of an adult. She'd always thought that word was pronounced *gweese*.

She didn't say anything, though. The game went on for another thirty minutes before Kira shooed her brother off to bed.

"Have you heard from your mother at all?" Steph asked when the teen came back.

Kira pushed up her glasses. "I don't expect to. She doesn't usually come back unless she needs something." She said it matter-of-factly, without a trace of bitterness, and Steph marveled at how mature she sounded. This was a girl used to taking care of herself, to having no one else to rely on. She felt a pang of sympathy for Kira in addition to admiration, but layered under that was a deep sense of shame. Steph's parents had given her everything; no matter how screwed up her life got, she knew they'd be there to prop her back up. Kira had no such support system. Yet Steph had criticized her parents for everything they'd done for her.

"When we do find her, I'll have a chat with her," Aaron said. "Maybe you and Tyler can stay here with me and Gran on a more permanent basis."

Kira sucked in a cracked lip and stared at her hands. "It's not that we don't appreciate it," she began in a low voice. "But we *have* a home. I've been taking care of things all right."

"That doesn't change the situation. You're only seventeen now. Doing this for even another year more… It's not tenable, Kira. You need to be in school."

"Of course, we love having you at the bakery full-time," Steph hurried to assure her. "I couldn't run the place without you." She looked to Aaron for confirmation. But his mouth had become a tight line, and he gave her the slightest shake of his head, shutting her down. She suppressed the urge to ask what was wrong. He'd already committed to taking her on full-time. Why was he backing out now?

He went on, "You've only got a year left before you graduate, right? I mean, you could complete your credits in summer school and get your diploma by the end of the year if you have to. In that time, you and Tyler can stay here. We can take care of you."

"I can't accept," Kira said. "Georgette is sick. And you've been on the couch all this time."

"My grandmother's fine. She's happy to have you here. And don't worry about me. I've spent plenty of nights on that couch."

Steph knew for a fact that the couch had been putting kinks in Aaron's back. And while Georgette had made a full recovery from her stroke, she was eighty-two, and her home was tiny. Sharing one bathroom among four people, including a teenage girl, was unthinkable to Steph. Besides, what would happen once Kira turned eighteen? They couldn't let the West kids move back to that dingy little trailer. Even if Kira became his legal guardian, Tyler was still a boy. He needed someone to be there for him.

"Food costs money," Kira said in that same hard, practical tone. "And the way Tyler eats…"

"You won't eat us out of house and home. Gran's thrilled to be cooking for more than two again. I am, too. She's been making things she hasn't made since…" He trailed off and smiled sadly. "Well, since my parents died and it's just been me and her."

The teen glowered at her hands, trying to come up with a valid reason to refuse. Money seemed to be her main focus. She insisted on paying to keep the spot at the trailer park. Steph understood her need: however beat-up and tiny, that trailer was the only thing that remained of their family that was solid and relatively more dependable than her parents had been.

"Think it over," Aaron urged gently. "You're welcome to stay here as long as you need."

Kira went to bed soon after that. Nothing had been settled, though, and clearly Aaron didn't want to push her. None of his solutions were ideal, and both of them were too stubbornly polite to put the other out.

"Why'd you shake your head at me when I mentioned working full-time?" Steph asked in a whisper. "Can't we pay her?"

"It'd be a bit of a stretch, but that's not the issue. I want her to finish high school."

"There's nothing wrong with taking time off," she argued.

"If she stops, it'll only get harder to start again. She's smart, and she's so close to finishing. If we let her give up her studies, she might lose her incentive to complete her education. When you have to focus on living hand to mouth, you can't climb any kind of career ladder because you don't have the educational requirements to get better-paying jobs. That's how poverty is perpetuated—people get stuck in ruts because they literally can't afford to better themselves." He shook his head. "I won't let her end up like that."

Every word stung. Maybe he hadn't meant to criticize Steph directly, but she could read between the lines. What he really meant was that he didn't want Kira to end up like *her*. That piece of paper still meant more to him than job satisfaction or happiness. He would always aim for the center of Mr. Murray's stupid Venn diagram, and he'd always judge other people for not trying to do the same.

She breathed deeply, pushed down her righteous indignation. Of course that piece of paper meant something to her, too. Why else would she have done the HSE exam? And it meant something to Kira, obviously. She'd been working so hard to keep up her marks and had only started skipping school when things had gotten desperate. Steph couldn't impose her values on the teen any more than anyone else could on her. Ultimately, she wanted what Kira wanted for herself—to be able to fulfill her dreams. For Kira, that meant she had to finish high school.

The realization made something inside Steph shift. Aaron had steepled his fingers and was resting them against his lips as if he were breathing deep thoughts into the cradle of his palms. And she understood now why he wanted Kira to go back to school.

"You think she's too proud to ask for help," she said.

Aaron's jaw clenched. "For some people it's one of the hardest things to do."

Of course. Aaron saw himself in Kira. After his parents had died, he'd been focused on school, on building his new life and securing his future. That had been his plan B all along. But Kira had Tyler to take care of, and she hadn't been able to tell anyone about her situation.

Maybe Aaron understood that, too. He'd been too proud and scared to tell anyone about Dale's abuse. He and Kira had both kept their secrets, coping however they could and at some personal cost.

"I should think about getting a sofa bed," he said, arching his back. His spine cracked loudly.

"You could stay with me," Steph ventured shyly, snuggling closer.

He hummed and kissed her forehead. Warmth snaked through her. "Thanks, but I want to be able to keep an eye on Gran. She'll wear herself out trying to get Tyler to say more than two words at a time that aren't 'Yes, ma'am,' or 'No, sir.'"

Steph worried about Georgette, too. She wished she could do more for all of them, especially for Kira and her brother. Money wasn't enough, even if she could get Kira to take it. What she needed to do was figure out a way for Kira to accept help without hurting her pride. Maybe convince her that she was helping others by doing the right thing.

She jerked upright as an idea struck her.

"I think I know a way to help everyone." She picked up her phone and dialed her parents' home.

AARON WAS SURPRISED at how willing and eager Terrence and Helen Stephens were about taking in the West siblings. He'd spoken to them over the phone, and they'd sounded absolutely ecstatic to host Kira and Tyler for however long they wanted.

He didn't have any reason to be suspicious or wary, but he felt responsible for the welfare of his new charges. It seemed wrong to pass them off to someone else when he'd declared he had no problem with them staying.

But it made sense all around. Helen and Terrence were mostly retired, had lots of space in their lakeside home so the siblings could each have their own bedroom, and they were located close to both Kira's and Tyler's schools. And despite being a gossip, Steph assured him that her mother also knew how to be discreet when it came to serious matters.

"Mom's not *that* bad," she admitted. "She collects more information than she spreads."

Still, he worried the move might make Kira and Tyler feel unwanted and unwelcome. And he couldn't be sure the Stephens were a good fit.

"Mom and Dad need someone to focus their attention on," Steph reasoned when he voiced his concerns. "Since I left, I think my mom especially needs someone to coddle. And if those kids need anything, it's someone to make them feel like the center of the universe."

"Not to mention how it'd take pressure off you?" Aaron asked, lifting a brow. Steph shuffled her feet.

"I'd be lying if I said I didn't have a stake in this. The last time I was at my parents', Mom and I had a big fight. We patched things up over the phone, but the argument's not over. I'll admit Kira and Tyler being around would keep my parents from sticking their noses in my business, but I think this'll work out for everyone. We just need to convince Kira that my parents need them in their lives."

When they told the siblings about their plan, Kira was predictably reticent. But Steph managed to persuade them to at least visit.

"We can't make you stay anywhere you don't want to," she said as they drove out to her parents' home. Tyler and Kira rode in the backseat of her mini SUV, with Aaron in the passenger side. "But I hope you'll consider it. My parents are getting older, and with the hours I work...well, I'm worried something could happen while I'm not around."

"But I'll be working, too," Kira said.

"I've been thinking about that," Aaron said. "We really do need you at the bakery over the summer. It's our busiest season. So I want to offer you a deal. You keep working through the summer break when you can. If you want to do summer school, we'll work around your schedule. If you need to do another semester in September, we'll shift you back to part-time on the weekends."

"But I can't afford rent on the trailer home if I'm only working part-time." Kira's voice cracked, on the edge of panic.

"Once you've got your diploma, I'll give you a raise. You'll have earned it. I promise you'll have enough to pay the rent."

That was only partially true. Aaron would supplement a portion of the rent without Kira knowing. He'd make arrangements with the landlady from the trailer park. It was unlikely Kira had anything saved up for college, but he was determined that she and Tyler both go. It would put a strain on his own finances, but he'd figure it out for them. They deserved that chance.

Everyone fell into contemplative silence, and soon, they were pulling up to the Stephenses' enormous home. It wasn't as impressive as the clubhouse at Greenfields, but it was still a sight to behold.

Helen and Terrence greeted them at the door, huge, welcoming smiles on their faces. Tyler's awe showed clearly on his face. He broke his silence entirely when they got to the back deck.

"Kira! A pool!" he cried, running toward it and stopping at the edge as if suddenly remembering he wasn't in swim trunks. Longing filled his huge brown eyes.

Kira hushed her brother and beckoned him back.

"Do you want to go for a swim?" Helen asked enthusiastically. "We have swim clothes for guests upstairs. It is awfully hot today."

Tyler looked up at his sister wistfully, but didn't beg or plead or whine. Kira looked as though she

were weighing the propriety of using their hosts'
pool. As the adult in her family, she probably felt
obligated to sit and make conversation with the
grown-ups. But it was blistering out, and she finally said, "It does look nice. If it's all right with
Mr. and Mrs. Stephens…"

"Yes!" Tyler hopped up and down.

"Come on up with me, Kira. We've got bathing
suits for girls, too." Helen took them back into the
house while Terrence gestured at Steph and Aaron
to sit and have a cold drink.

"They seem like good kids," Terrence mused.
"Very polite, if a little quiet."

"That's about as vocal as Tyler's been since we
took him in," Aaron said as Steph poured a glass
of lemonade for him. "We're hoping he'll open up
more. We really are grateful that you're willing to
do this, sir."

Mr. Stephens lifted a hand. "Just Terrence,
please. We're practically family now, Aaron."

Steph jolted, splashing lemonade over the table.
She wiped it up rigidly. Aaron pretended not to notice her discomfort and didn't acknowledge Terrence's meaning. "About Kira and Tyler…"

They talked awhile about the West siblings' situation. Helen soon joined them while Kira and Tyler
slipped quietly into the pool. At first, neither of
them did much more than sit in the shallow end, but
soon, they were splashing and laughing and leap-
ing off the diving board while the adults cheered

them on. Aaron had never seen Kira so happy and
carefree. It was as if she'd shed ten years. After a
while, Lucena brought out sandwiches and snacks,
and the kids ate heartily, famished by an afternoon
of much-needed fun in the sun.

By the end of the day, Aaron was certain the
Stephenses would have no problem taking care of
Kira and Tyler. And it was clear, too, that Kira's
more stubborn, independent streak would ensure
they wouldn't become dependent or spoiled. They
were respectful, unselfish kids, and they even insisted on helping Lucena with the dishes.

They drove home after a hearty spaghetti dinner,
stuffed, slightly sunburned and thoroughly worn-
out. The siblings fell asleep in the car, Tyler with
his head resting against his sister's shoulder. In
sleep, free from the stress of figuring out how her
next paycheck would feed them, Kira looked like
the child she really was. Aaron nudged Steph to
look in her rearview. She smiled.

"I think they'll like it at my parents'," she whispered, and placed her hand over his across the console.

"Your parents really liked them, too. I hope it'll
work out."

His heart settled on a soft bed of happiness and
contentment. This whole day had been filled with
family, home, children...none of them his, but the
dream was so tantalizingly close. He wished he
could gather this moment in his arms and live in

it forever, holding Stephanie's hand as they drove home. The burnished remains of the sunset tinted the sky, bronzing the two worn-out kids sleeping in the backseat. He glanced at Stephanie again and felt the ache in his chest keenly.

He wanted this…with her. Like he'd never wanted anything else.

THEY HELPED MOVE Kira and Tyler into the Stephenses' home later that week. Summer was in full swing and now that some of the pressure was off Kira, she smiled much more often. She even flirted with the younger men who came in. That was nice to see, if a little alarming. It seemed Aaron couldn't shut off his paternal instincts now that he'd turned them on. He supposed he'd always look out for the West siblings.

As he'd hoped, Georgette's Bakery and Books was quickly becoming a destination, with locals enjoying fresh baked goods while reading their latest book purchase on the new patio. Aaron even managed to set up a couple of author events for early fall. Meanwhile, Georgette enjoyed a much more sedate schedule, baking only on the weekends and occasionally on weekday afternoons. It seemed she'd finally learned how to take a break.

With both Kira and Georgette around, Steph was able to take time off. Aaron had worried she'd burn out working twelve-hour days all the time. Not that she'd ever complained. Still, it was nice to see her do something other than work—ironic, considering he'd once thought she was lazy.

He shook his head. She was anything but. He realized now how badly he'd misjudged her. Whatever he'd thought he felt for her when he was a teen paled next to what he felt for her now. He admired her for her work ethic and compassion, her sense of humor and the way she somehow always made things work out for the best.

He watched her from the bookshop as she smilingly served customers. He'd always thought the way she talked on and on with folks slowed things down and cost them business, but now he knew her chatter was half the reason people came in. Everyone knew her name, or they would by the time they left the building. This place was as much about Stephanie Stephens as it was about Georgette.

When she finished up with her last customer, Aaron marched over. "I want to take you out on your day off tomorrow," he declared. "After your visit to the retirement home, I mean."

She tilted her chin to one side, studying him curiously. "Oh? Where to?"

"I'm thinking a movie, dinner, a walk on the beach. Is that too cliché?" Call him a romantic, but it was what he'd always dreamed of doing back in high school—go on a *real* date with Stephanie Stephens with hand holding and candlelight and long walks. Staying in near a bed was great, but he wanted…well, more.

She grinned. "Sounds perfect. But what about the shop?" They used the word *shop* now collectively to include both the bookstore and the bakery. Aaron liked it.

"Kira and Gran will both be in tomorrow, and Wednesdays are usually slow. I trust Kira to take care of things on her own, too." The teen had been working extra hard to earn back their trust, and she'd insisted on repaying the money she'd taken for Tyler's medicine, despite Aaron's protests. He knew she'd never steal from them again. "You and I have earned a day off."

Steph laid her fingertips against his chest with a seductive grin. He was gripped by the urge to sweep her off her feet and kiss her, or climb onto the roof and launch his feelings into the sky like a kite, wild and light and carefree.

Was this love? Something held him back from labeling it as such. All he knew for sure was that he'd never thought he would feel so deeply for her.

CHAPTER TWENTY-ONE

THE FOLLOWING DAY, Aaron picked up Steph after her visit to the retirement home, and they drove into Welksville to catch a matinee of the biggest, loudest, most explosive 3-D action blockbuster they could find. Afterward, they went for a long walk on one of Silver Lake's beaches.

They talked about Kira and Tyler, about how Steph was already getting regular phone calls from her mother asking whether she thought Kira would appreciate one kind of meal over another, whether Tyler was partial to blues over greens, whether she should allow them to redecorate their rooms to make them feel more at home.

"Sounds like she's ready to smother them," Steph said drily, digging her toes in the warm sand.

"It won't hurt them to be spoiled a little. Kira will put her foot down if they go over the line." He took her hand. "Thanks again for arranging that."

"I'm almost afraid of what Mom'll do when those kids move out again." She knew what her mother was like, after all. She chewed on the inside of her cheek.

"What's wrong?" Aaron asked.

She struggled to put her fears into words. "The way my parents raised me...I mean, I'm grateful for everything I have, but I'm worried that with everything they're giving them, Kira and Tyler will feel obligated to my parents to fulfill the dreams I never fulfilled for them."

"Hey." He stopped her and squeezed her shoulders. "You're not defined by what you haven't accomplished. Anyhow, Kira's way too smart to fall for that kind of manipulation."

"I don't know... *We* kind of manipulated her."

"For her own good, and Tyler's. And she knows it."

Maybe. Still, she couldn't help a niggling sense that she'd done wrong by those kids somehow. Interfered in a way she shouldn't have. She admired Kira's strength and didn't want to undermine it. Perhaps that was why she still felt conflicted. She'd never faced the kinds of challenges Kira had faced, had never tested her mettle in the face of adversity. Hadn't she wanted the same kind of independence? The same confidence in her own abilities to manage her life, as Kira had?

But this is different, she told herself. *Kira needed our help and didn't know it.*

Aaron took her hand, and they walked on, letting the waves wash over their feet. A group of children were building an enormous sand castle, complete with walls and a moat that filled as the surf rolled in. She saw the wistful way Aaron watched them and wondered if he was thinking about the day he'd have kids of his own. She looked back at the group of children and imagined a little boy with a mop of dark brown hair like Aaron's, and bright blue eyes like hers. She pictured herself sitting with him under that tree over there, bouncing a baby girl with gray eyes and blond hair on her knee…

She glanced up into Aaron's face. He was looking down on her with the same wistfulness, and for a moment she thought he might have read her mind and gotten caught up in the shared fantasy.

They both leaned in at the same time for a kiss that sealed an unspoken promise. All this time, she'd struggled to find something interesting to say, but now here they were, communicating everything they needed in a simple touch of lips.

She was in love with him. She couldn't deny that now.

He breathed deep as they pulled apart. "Don't pinch me," he murmured.

She leaned back, perplexed. "I wasn't planning on it."

"Good. Because I never want to wake up from this dream." He kissed her again, and she let herself sink into his embrace as the sun warmed their shoulders and the water lapped at their toes.

They went for an early dinner at the Good Fortune Diner. Over a plate of chicken balls with sweet and sour sauce—which Aaron claimed was a rare and exotic Chinese-Canadian delicacy that the Cheungs must have smuggled over the border—they had the same conversation they'd had on their first date, only this time they actually talked.

She wasn't sure why it was easier now—it just was. Rather than compare interests and find they had nothing in common, they simply told each other about what they liked. She knew he was hanging on her every word because he asked questions and didn't interrupt her to tell her what he thought. He listened and promised to try everything she suggested—music, food, TV shows. And when he started talking about something he'd read, instead of shutting down, she focused and asked him questions when she didn't understand what he was talking about. He was happy to explain and never made fun of her for not knowing something. After all they'd shared, she knew he'd never set out to hurt her or make her feel stupid. All they'd needed was to stop treating each other like the enemy and open themselves up.

He walked her back to her apartment. Warmth bloomed within her as anticipation built. She knew where she wanted this night to end, and she hoped Aaron would stay over. It felt like the proper next step to take.

And she knew without a shred of doubt that she wanted to take it.

"You know," she said, dragging her fingertip

from his chin down to his navel, "I have this great dessert upstairs I think you should try."

"Really?" He arched an eyebrow. "I thought working at Georgette's you'd be sick of sweets."

She gave her lowest, sultriest laugh. "Not this one. It involves a lot of whipped cream and chocolate sauce."

"Mmm. I like both those things."

"That's good. Because I think you'll also be interested to know that it's served on me."

He gave a growl and pulled her up against him, kissing her deeply right there in the middle of the sidewalk for the whole town to see. Steph melted into a sigh.

"When you do that…" Aaron's words evaporated as she traced the tip of her tongue around his lips. He shuddered, and a new urgency took over as he grabbed her hand and tugged her forward. Laughter burst from Steph, buoyant and light, as they half ran to her apartment.

They neared her door, and she took out her keys, but then spotted something that made everything inside her stop and go cold.

She had mail.

AARON HAD NEVER seen someone react to mail the way Steph had. She practically jumped back when she saw the envelope—too small to be a package, too big to be just a letter—peeking out of her mailbox. Her face paled as she reached for it.

"What is it?" he asked.

"My exam results." She leaned heavily against the still-locked door.

Aaron's heart thumped. "Well? Open it."

She stared at him as if she couldn't comprehend his suggestion. Instead, she fumbled with the keys and unlocked the door, then jogged up the stairs to her apartment, kicking off her shoes as she entered. Aaron followed. He wished he'd thought to keep a bottle of champagne in her fridge for this moment. What a fantastic way to cap off the day.

She sat on the couch and stared at the envelope in her hand. Slowly, she slipped a finger beneath the flap and ripped the top off, hissing when the jagged tear sliced into her flesh.

"Dammit." She sucked on her finger.

Aaron offered to get a knife and a bandage, but she waved him off and tore the envelope the rest of the way open. She unfolded the papers within.

It seemed to take a long time for her to read the results. But he knew what they were the moment she closed her eyes.

"I didn't pass." The letter dropped onto her lap, the crackle of the heavy paper like thunder in the sudden silence.

Aaron blinked hard. Had he misheard? He took the letter from her and scanned it. Maybe she'd read it wrong...

You have not met the minimum requirements to earn a New York State High School Equivalency

Diploma. In order to earn a New York State High School Equivalency Diploma...

It took a moment for him to shake off his own shock. He'd been certain she'd pass. Even though he hadn't studied with her, even though he had no idea what kind of system she'd set up for herself, he'd believed she could do it.

He'd had absolute faith in her.

She sank against the couch and let out a shaky breath. "Well, I guess that's it, then."

"Hey." Aaron wrapped her in a hug. "It's okay. You can do the test again."

"No." She shook him off. "No. It was all for nothing. I can't—" She choked on her words and put a hand over her mouth as she got up and went to the kitchen. Aaron followed.

"It's not the end of the world. Lots of people fail, I'm sure. We'll just have to work at it, figure out where your weak points are—"

"Weak points?" She laughed humorlessly. "*Everything* is my weak point. Look at these marks." She waved the letter at him. Her scores on each section of the exam were clearly listed for him to wince at. "I'm so stupid."

"Steph, don't say that."

She yanked the fridge open. "I worked *really* hard. I studied for months. I went through all the online videos, did all the exercises. I did everything I was supposed to do. But I still failed." She wrenched the twist-off cap off a bottle of white wine and poured some into a plastic tumbler. The liquid splashed across the counter in her shaking grip.

Aaron's gut sloshed almost as much as the wine had. He took the bottle and tumbler out of her hands and set them behind him on the counter. "Listen to me." He settled his hands over her shoulders. "This is just a little setback, I promise you. We can work on this together."

"Why do you even care?"

Her words came out sharp, hard and they cut him to the core. "I care because it's important to you."

She shook her head violently, hair whipping around as if she might actually be trying to unscrew her head. "No. It's *not* important to *me*. I only did this because of *you*." She jerked out of his hold. "All I wanted was to show you—show everyone—that I was smart enough to get my diploma…to live my life on my own. Clearly, I'm not, so I guess you were right from the beginning."

A sharp pain went through him. "Steph…" He didn't know how to reassure her. "Maybe you have an anxiety issue. Or you could be dyslexic. All we have to do is figure out what your problem is and—"

"See? You *do* think I have a problem." She pointed an accusing finger. "You still think I have a learning disability."

"If you get tested, then we'll know for sure. Lots

of people have problems like this and they deal with them. If you really want your diploma, there are ways around whatever issue you have."

"I only wanted my diploma because I wanted you to respect me!"

His chest ached. "Of course I respect you," he said, pleading with her for calm. Wildness crept into her eyes, as if she were an animal trapped in a corner.

"Then why is a piece of paper so important to you?"

He struggled to keep his voice even. "You know why. We went through a week of this with Kira. A good education is a ticket to something better, and a high school diploma is the most basic requirement for practically every job out there. What are you going to do at your next position otherwise?"

"My 'next' position?" The color disappeared from her lips. "Are you going to *fire* me?"

Uh-oh. He hadn't meant *you* to be personal. He'd meant *you* as in *everyone*, Steph included. It irritated him that she still expected different rules to apply to her, as if minimum requirements were for everyone else. "No one's going to fire you. All I'm saying is—"

She cut him off with a slash of her hand. "No, I get it. Kira gets her diploma. She gets a raise. Steph doesn't and she gets canned. That's how the real world works, am I right?"

He curled his fingers in frustration. "Steph, don't make me the villain in this. I'm trying to help you."

"By telling me I'm dumb. You've never believed in me. It's easier to see me as stupid and helpless, isn't it?"

"Will you stop and listen to yourself?" He recognized this now. Her defensiveness. She was attacking anything that might threaten the status quo. She ran from anything that challenged her because, why not? She could afford to. "I didn't say any of those things. All I'm saying is that your diploma is a foot in the door anywhere you go. You can't rely on Georgette's forever. What if something happens? What if the business goes under? You don't have a plan B. You don't have other skills to fall back on. You have to be prepared. Anything could happen. Your whole life can be ruined in the blink of an eye."

"And you think you're *so* smart because you've planned for everything that's going to happen?" she said with a sneer that reminded him so much of the girl she used to be. Cruel. Self-satisfied. Just like Dale.

His throat grew tight as blood pushed up into his head. "We don't all have mommy and daddy to run home to," he retorted waspishly. She recoiled. He plowed on restlessly, a wrecking ball on its unstoppable downward swing. "That's what real life is, Steph, a string of disasters waiting to happen. Right when you think everything's fine, bam!"

He smashed a fist into his palm. "Everything you thought was safe and sacred is ripped from you, and you're left to fend for yourself."

Air sawed in and out of his lungs in hot rasps. He knew he was magnifying his own past, his own worst fears and projecting them onto Steph. Knowing it didn't make him stop, though. "You've never faced that, though, have you? You've never had to worry about where you were going to be sleeping night to night, whether someone was coming to take you away, how you were going to afford rent and groceries. Because you let your parents take care of everything when the going got tough."

Her eyes filled with hatred. "At least I *have* parents."

It was a clumsy blow, slow and imprecise, but it made him flinch nonetheless. She didn't need to remind him he was an orphan. She didn't need to kick him where it already hurt.

And she seemed to know it. Her tears dropped like diamonds. "If you think the only way I'm going to have a future is if I have a diploma, then I guess I don't have a future—not at Georgette's and not with *you*." She marched to her door and opened it. "Get out."

The air was sucked from his lungs, but almost as quickly was replaced with scalded pride. She was being stubborn and emotional. Things hadn't gone the way she'd hoped, and now she was throwing a tantrum.

Classic Stephanie Stephens. He shouldn't have expected more from her. She took the easy path because there was always one there for her. He'd challenged her to try again, to be better, but instead of fighting, she was getting rid of any and all reminders of her failure. He might as well be a colicky horse.

He'd been right at the beginning—she couldn't change.

"Fine." His dismissal didn't have the conviction he wanted it to have. As he walked out, he said over his shoulder, "I'll mail you your last paycheck."

He forced himself not to look back, choosing instead to imagine that her silence meant she was gaping in shock. She could try to take back her hasty words, but it was time for her to realize there wasn't always an easy fix for all her problems. Life was unfair. And Stephanie Stephens needed to grow the hell up.

He was storming back to his grandmother's before he realized it, his vision clouded by murky, churning emotion. Fury was a large part of it, but also sadness and frustration. He wouldn't let sympathy in, though. This was tough love. No, not love. Just a cold, hard lesson in reality.

If she wanted to quit that was her choice. She'd done it before; she knew what the consequences were. If the shop meant as much to Steph as she claimed, she would come crawling back the same way she had the first time.

He couldn't say whether he would take her back, though.

CHAPTER TWENTY-TWO

"IT'S SO NICE to have you back in the house," Helen enthused. "Especially with Kira and Tyler here. They're wonderful to have around, but it's even nicer with you in the mix."

Steph sipped her too-sweet lemonade without responding. Inside, she was withering. Going back to her parents' home after her blowup with Aaron had been a terrible idea. It'd been a knee-jerk reaction—as if her parents would somehow make everything better.

They hadn't, but not for lack of trying. The day after Steph had kicked Aaron out, she'd called home, told her mom she'd quit and begged her to let her stay over. She couldn't spend another minute in her apartment with all the memories she and Aaron had made there. It was too painful. Helen had welcomed her home with open arms. Over the past week, she'd done everything in her power to make her daughter forget Aaron and Georgette's, including taking her on an overnight shopping spree in New York City.

In her idleness, Steph brooded. She didn't know

what she was going to do with her life. The first time she'd walked out of Georgette's, there had been a sense that she *could* do something else. Anything else. Anything she put her mind to. But she didn't *want* to do anything. She felt as though she faced a dead end, and her spirits sank lower and lower.

On top of all that, Kira was a constant reminder of what she'd left behind. Steph must've been entirely out of her mind when she'd made the decision to move back in.

"I'm only staying a few days," Steph said to her mother. "Just until I know what I'm doing next."

"There's no rush, dear. We've got plenty of room, and I know Tyler and Kira love having you around."

It sure didn't seem that way. Every morning as Kira left for work, she'd glance tentatively at Steph and hurry out. Steph was making things awkward for the teen, and it wasn't fair to her. She wondered what Aaron had told the girl about their falling-out, if anything.

"There are my girls," Terrence said as he walked in from the house, beaming. Tyler trailed after him, looking dazed but happy. He was carrying a bag from an electronics store.

"Did you two have a good time at the mall?" Helen asked.

"Great!" The eleven-year-old pulled out his purchase—a handheld video game system and three new games. "Is it okay if I play these now?"

"Knock yourself out." Terrence ruffled his hair, and the young boy took off.

"You're spoiling him," Steph said disapprovingly. "Kira's not going to like that."

"I don't make money so I can keep it in the bank. Anything to put a smile on those kids' faces is worth it." Terrence sat on the patio chair next to Helen.

Steph's scowl softened. Her parents spent money to make others happy, which in turn made them happy. She couldn't really fault them for giving Tyler and Kira a few gifts.

Yet she thought of her own upbringing and the way her parents' gifts had grown more and more extravagant as the void in her life had become more apparent. She'd felt that way all through her shopping trip with her mother. In fact, she'd barely bought anything. New clothes and accessories didn't hold any meaning when she hadn't earned them.

When she realized her mood was turning bitter, she stopped herself. None of this was her parents' fault. She'd made her own choice to come back here, exactly as Aaron had said she would. She could whine about independence all she wanted, but it was something she had to achieve on her own.

"I have some news about Darlene West," Terrence said. He glanced around before lowering his voice. "That PI I hired tracked her down to a clinic

in New Jersey. She was arrested for drug posses-
sion and was sentenced to court-ordered rehab."

Steph gasped. "What does that mean for the
kids?"

"According to the PI, she told the judge she'd left
them with their father. Either no one's checked up
on that—which I find unlikely—or else she gave
them a fake contact or something. Otherwise they
might have charged her with child abandonment.
But kids can slip through the cracks a lot of the
time."

"We can't be sure the authorities won't come
for them," Helen said, brow wrinkled. "But in the
meantime, don't tell Kira or Tyler. It'll just upset
them."

Steph's brow wrinkled. "Mom, they'll want to
know where she is."

"What good will it do? If Darlene is getting
clean, maybe it's best she focus on that. When she's
ready to take responsibility for her children again,
she'll come back. It's no secret where they are."

"I agree with your mother," Terrence said. "Look
at those two. They're happy for now. They've been
dealt a bad hand in life. If we can save them a few
early ulcers, they're all the better for it."

Steph blew out a breath. "But Darlene's their
mother. Kira and Tyler are *her* children, not yours.
I know you're trying to do what's best for them,
but they can handle this."

Helen gave a pithy wave of her hand. "Kira's seventeen. Still a child."

Something inside Steph snapped. Heat boiled through her and spilled over in a sudden torrent of words. "Seventeen is *not* a child. Kira has taken more responsibility for her life than I *ever* have, and you don't have the right to keep her in the dark about things that concern her. You don't get to run her life!"

Helen looked stricken. "All I'm trying to do is save those poor kids from more worry and heartache. We'll tell them about Darlene, of course, but only when they're ready."

"It's not your decision to make. How do you think Kira will react if she finds out you've been hiding this from her? All that time not knowing has eaten away at her." Her anger deflated, and emptiness took its place. She sat back, drained.

Helen took off her sunglasses and exchanged worried looks with her husband. "This isn't like you, Stephanie. You haven't been the same since you came back. What's wrong, baby? Tell us what happened at the bakery this time."

This time. Those two little words made her flinch as if scalding caramel had splattered her and was hardening against her skin. She clamped her teeth together. She didn't know how to tell them about her feelings for Aaron, or why she'd pushed him away. Worse, she was afraid that if she said anything about the breakup—if there'd been anything to break up from the start—Helen would simply pat her on the shoulder and thrust her toward another man.

"I had to leave." She sucked in her lip, knowing that wouldn't be enough of an answer for her parents.

"Well, that's your decision to make, of course," Helen said. "And if you want to talk about it, that's up to you, too."

"We just want you to be happy," Terrence agreed.

It was nice to hear, but somehow a little disappointing. "I'm going to need to find something else soon if I want to keep my apartment," she said, mostly to herself. Maya had offered her a job at the consignment shop after she'd called and told her about the exam results and the fight she'd had with Aaron. Maya had been sympathetic, but Steph could sense her disappointment. It was the reason she'd politely turned down her friend's offer. She couldn't risk alienating her further. "My rent's due soon."

"You don't have to worry about that," Helen said. "We've been taking care of that."

Terrence looked up sharply as Steph stared at her mother. "What do you mean?"

"Oh, baby. Did you think you were paying your rent on your own? We've been putting money in your bank account."

Steph's father rubbed his temple, looking awkward. "You weren't supposed to tell her about that, Helen."

"She would've figured it out sooner or later," Helen said pithily. "Don't look at us like we've done you wrong, baby. You never would've accepted help, so we had to give it to you without you knowing."

Steph felt as though the earth had shifted beneath her. Her vision wobbled. All this time believing she'd been independent and earning her own way through the world…it'd all been a lie. Her parents had been propping her up financially from the start.

Why had she never noticed? She'd done all her own banking. Not that she looked at her statements often. She paid for almost everything with cash, rarely using her credit card so that she always knew what she'd spent. She withdrew cash from the bank when she needed it…but it had never occurred to her that what was in her savings had been maintained by some mystery influx.

Her sheer ignorance made her cringe. She knew she should be grateful, but all she felt was cheated. Slowly, the embers of resentment kindled.

"Why?" The single word encompassed everything.

"You're a *baker*," Helen said, part pitying, part exasperated. "You barely earn enough to feed yourself, much less pay for an apartment and gas. We just wanted to make sure you always had enough."

Steph seethed. "I would've made it work."

Terrence made a face and tilted his chin modestly. "With all due respect to Georgette, you're worth a lot more than she pays you. You don't even have benefits, much less health insurance."

Well, of course not. Georgette would never have been able to afford a group plan. Besides, Steph had health insurance under her parents' policy...

Oh, my God. Everything Aaron had said was true. She'd taken her safety net for granted. She'd never been truly on her own. She'd never even thought about moving out of town. Why would she when she was safe and sound here? When everything she knew and loved was here? Where her parents assured her she was safe and loved and would never let anything harm her?

She'd made that choice. *She'd* shrugged off that final high school credit and allowed her education to lapse. *She'd* let the years pass and hadn't pushed herself to do more. To be more. Even though she'd known she could.

"I can't believe it. All this time..." She covered her mouth as if to suppress a scream.

"Aw, baby." Terrence rubbed the back of his neck. "I'm sorry we've upset you. We only did it because we love you."

Helen hummed in sympathy. "You've been through enough as it is. Let us take care of everything. You don't need to worry anymore."

Suddenly, all the years of good intentions and

coddling and shielding collapsed around her, burying her in her own self-perpetuated failure. She'd never asserted herself enough to show them she could endure when things went south. "But I want to worry. I *should* worry. Mom, I'm thirty years old. I can take care of myself."

"I'm sure you can." Her tone was skeptical, and it sharpened Steph's anger to a fine point.

She sat up straighter. "I did my high school equivalency exam." The words came out clipped, the consonants brittle. Her parents looked up, startled, but she wasn't done yet. She took a deep breath and locked gazes with them. "I failed."

Saying the words was like dropping two massive bombs. Somehow, she'd expected them to blow up in her face, but they didn't. They were duds.

I failed.

"Oh...oh, honey." Helen automatically reached for her, her face a study of upset and befuddlement, as if her daughter had announced she'd stabbed herself with a seafood fork for no apparent reason. "Why would you put yourself through that? You don't need a diploma."

"I *wanted* it." Never mind why. "I studied and worked really hard, but I still failed. Aaron and I got into a big fight about it—" She paused. "No, that's a lie. *I* picked a fight with him over it. He thought I should retake the exam. I didn't want to. We...broke up." Hearing herself say it out loud, she realized how petty she sounded. Her mother didn't see it that way, though.

"Well, then, maybe it's for the best. He shouldn't be forcing you to do anything that would upset you." She cupped Steph's cheeks and peered into her face worriedly. "No wonder you've been looking so piqued lately, straining your eyes like that. I bet you haven't been getting enough sleep, either. We'll book time at the spa, all right? Get those wrinkles out before they ruin your pretty face."

"A man who doesn't appreciate you for you isn't worth the time." Her father's casually tagged-on statement launched Steph's self-awareness into the stratosphere. Only weeks ago he'd been singing Aaron's praises. And now he was shrugging him off because Steph had given up on him. As if he were another lost investment. A whim she'd flaked out on.

Suddenly, it became clear to Steph that no matter what she said or did, her parents would never do anything to upset her, to tell her she was wrong or had made a bad decision. They'd fix everything for her when things went awry. But it wasn't their job anymore, even if they felt otherwise. No one was responsible for her needs except her. Kira knew that and had made do; and now Steph understood what she had to face.

"No." She stood. "No, I don't need more shopping trips or spa visits. I don't need you two to take care of me like that."

"Darling, we're your parents. Of course we're going to take care of you."

Steph shoved her hands through her hair. "Well, then it's my fault that I let you."

They stared at her. She felt itchy all over, as if she wanted to tear off her skin and crawl out of the shell she no longer fit. Her brain throbbed as if it were ready to burst from her skull.

"I don't know what you expect us to do," Helen said with a touch of asperity.

"I want you to tell me the truth." She took a deep breath. "What is wrong with me?"

"Wrong? Nothing's wrong. You're perfect, baby." Her father reached out to her, but she shied away.

"No. I'm not. No one is. I'm talking about my grades in school. I want to know why I was always behind and couldn't do my homework like all the other kids. Why I always passed even though I failed most of my tests and exams."

Her parents gave each other a telling sidelong glance. Steph's stomach pitched.

"What does it matter now, Steph? Tests and exams aren't a measure of the person you are. Anyhow, that was all so long ago, and you've shown everyone you're perfectly capable."

"I *am* capable. But I want to know—I need to know… Did you two suspect anything was wrong? Did anyone ever say I might have a learning disability?"

The silence that met her was deafening. Of

course people had. Aaron had asked her right from the start, and he couldn't have been the first to suspect. All those whispers behind her back... Had she really brushed them off as people's opinions? Helen laughed faintly. "Where on earth would you get that idea? Who's been putting those thoughts in your head?"

"Helen." Terrence's face was hard. He gave her a slight shake of his head and looked at Steph imploringly. "We didn't want to tell you anything that might upset you or make you feel different."

The breath left her lungs. She gripped the edge of the patio table and sank back into her chair.

"Terrence, I don't think she—"

"She's an adult and she's our daughter and she's asking for the truth. I won't lie to her anymore." He faced Steph. "Early on your teacher brought us in, told us she had some suspicions about your behavior and how you were performing in class. But you have to understand," he rushed on. "We weren't raised like that. You did your work or you didn't. And you were so popular and had lots of friends. It wasn't as if you were eating paste and drooling in the corner of the class."

Steph stuffed down her outrage long enough to ask, "When did you know this?"

"First meeting must have been...what? Grade two? Three?" He looked to his wife for confirmation, but she'd clamped her lips tightly together, agitation and disapproval clear in the tightness rippling across her face.

"You knew all that time and you never got me any help?" Steph's nerveless fingers groped at the hem of her shirt.

"Now hold on a minute. We were doing what we thought was best. We wanted you to be happy. Separating you from your friends would've hurt you."

"The teachers wanted to have you tested, but they had to ask us for permission first," Helen rushed to add. "We weren't going to let them ruin your life by making an outcast of you. Besides, teachers aren't concerned with anything except keeping overall GPAs up. It's a numbers game. But we both know when it comes to being a good person and a productive member of society, grades don't count."

"And how, exactly, did you expect me to be productive? By getting married and pushing out a litter of grandchildren for you?" Steph squeezed her throbbing temples.

"You've always wanted to be a mother. Why wouldn't we support you in that?"

"Didn't you ever think that I might have had other dreams? You should've trusted me enough to make my own mistakes and decisions and do better." She felt sick. "I would still have been the same person whether or not I was getting help."

"You can't know that." Helen crossed her arms and shook her head. "You have no idea what it's like to ride the short bus, Stephanie. Children can be cruel."

Steph paused, wondering if her mother was speaking from experience. Had her mother been shielding her all this time?

"We did try to get you help, you know," Terrence said defensively. "We hired a private tutor, but you got tired of her."

"Tutor? What are you—" Steph's jaw slackened. The mysterious evenings her parents spent away and the kindly babysitter who'd taught her so much but who'd become annoying when she'd started challenging Stephanie's abilities... It all snapped together. "Kitty was a tutor."

"A specialist. We brought her in all the way from New York City. I had to put her up in a hotel in Welksville when she came." He wiped his hand down his mouth. "Your mother—we didn't want anyone to know you were struggling. So every week we took off for the club and let her work with you for a few hours."

"But then you sent her away...because of me? Because I said I was *bored*?"

"Well, it was clear you weren't getting anything out of it," her mother put in, still infuriatingly calm, as if she still didn't see what they'd done wrong. "Why put you and your father's wallet through all that if we couldn't fix you? I accepted you for who you were."

Steph covered her mouth. She wanted to scream.

Her mom just didn't get it. It wasn't about being *fixed*. Even if she didn't understand her particular problem, she knew this much. "Why didn't you tell me she was a tutor?"

"Baby, we didn't want you to know there was anything wrong."

"Of course I knew something was wrong!" she shouted. "How stupid did you think I was?"

"Maybe we've done you wrong," Terrence said, hands splayed, begging for calm. "But it doesn't change facts. You grew up to be a smart, caring, wonderful girl with a will of your own and the means to do anything you want. We're proud of you. Can't you be proud of yourself?"

The words hung in the air, and she tried to grasp their meaning and the love that propped them up. She thought about the years of feeling lost, left behind, stupid and slow and embarrassed. She thought of all the energy she'd wasted putting on a facade of not caring, of pretending not to hear the talk behind her back in high school, of having to cheat to stay afloat. She thought about all the times Aaron and others had tried to tell her she might have issues. All the times she'd dismissed it…

Her parents might be guilty of denial, but she was the one who'd denied herself the chance to get help.

"No." Her heart closed. "I can't."

Because she hadn't tried hard enough, and didn't think she was strong enough to disappoint herself yet again. Because she'd failed to achieve the one thing that meant something to her. The one thing that could've justified a meaningful relationship with Aaron.

And if the diploma was all that mattered to him...maybe he wasn't the man for her.

She didn't hear her parents' pleas as she got up and drove away from the house. She was too numb in her fury and desolation. Too stricken by her naïveté and self-delusion. She couldn't even blame her parents for hiding the truth from her because deep down, she'd known and had always known, and she hadn't done anything about it. This was all on her.

She'd wanted to take responsibility for herself and be independent; well, now she was. She hadn't realized how lonely it would be.

She didn't know how or why she ended up at the B Bar Ranch of all places. Maybe she was following the internal compass that always led her down the smoothest road. She pulled up as Wyatt Brown strode from the barn, giving her a puzzled but not entirely displeased look.

"Not that I'm not happy to see you," the rancher said, tipping his hat up when she rolled down the window. "But what are you doing here?" His gaze roamed over her. The slight narrowing of his eyes told her he'd figured out she'd been crying.

"I'm sorry for imp...implying...imposing." She clenched her teeth at her misspeak. It'd been so long since she'd faltered like that. "I was wondering if I could go for a ride on Junebug." Junebug was the mare he'd saddled for her on their horse-back riding date.

Wyatt assessed her for an agonizing moment as if searching for the catch. She prayed he wouldn't ask her what was wrong. He notched up his chin. "I was about to go for a ride around the fences. Why not come with me? Halfway, at least. It's a pretty long ride."

She exhaled in relief. In minutes she was caught up in the distraction of tacking up and soothing the excited mare. Junebug took off at a quick trot the moment Steph spurred her on. When they were clear of the stable yard, she let the horse have her rein, but Junebug wouldn't break into the gallop Steph yearned for. Instead, the mare waited for Wyatt and his horse to catch up and then followed his lead sedately.

Steph wanted to feel free, to have the wind whipping through her hair and lose herself in the exhilaration of flight, but she couldn't bring herself to kick the horse into action. It would've been too cruel to make the horse do more than she wanted.

She wiped away a tear, then another, cursing as they flowed freely past the tight knot in her chest. Wyatt's horse came to a halt as Junebug sidled up next to him. "Everything okay?"

"It's…dust…" She sniffled and tore her borrowed gloves off, palming away the wetness, but still the tears came. "It's really dusty…"

The first sob burst from her, startling Junebug. And then she was crying, silently, her face stuck in what she imagined was an ugly mask of a silent scream. Wyatt dismounted swiftly and helped her down. She slid out of the saddle and fell in a crumpled heap against his chest.

"I'm sorry." She felt utterly wretched. "I'm sorry. I had a…a fight with my parents. They told me…" She ran out of words. What good would it do telling Wyatt? He didn't care about grades or learning disabilities or a lifetime of denial.

Her mind blank and her heart empty, she squeezed her eyes shut and craned her neck up, closing the distance between them.

"Whoa, whoa, whoa." Wyatt took a step back, staring at her with confusion and a little anger. "Obviously, you're upset. But that's no reason to be throwing yourself at me."

Numbly, she searched herself for a response. None came. She hadn't *wanted* to kiss him. She was simply resigned to her fate: marry Wyatt and raise his children in that giant house of his. It was all she could ask for. All she could expect of herself. All he'd wanted from her, too, which was why his rejection confused her. "What's the matter? I thought…" She trailed off. Her pride should've been bruised, but all she felt was relief.

The rancher cut his grim gaze away as he turned to his saddlebag and brought out a bottle of water and a package of tissues. "I have my pride, Stephanie. And I appreciate you coming out here to find solace. There's no better place to find it. I can be a shoulder to cry on. I can be a confidant. I'm even content to be a friend, if that's all it comes to. But I'm no rebound guy."

She was struck by the intensity behind his words, and at once felt ashamed for putting Wyatt in this position. "I...I'm sorry. I didn't mean—"

"I don't think you did, either. And I'll be damned if I let you make any mistakes while you're still working things out with Aaron."

She winced. "You know what happened?"

He scratched the stubble on his jaw. "I was by Georgette's earlier in the week. Aaron was more broody than a cathedral gargoyle. A man stews like that for two reasons—his car or his girl, and I've seen that clunker he drives." He chuckled drily. "Whatever you did to him, you got the message across. That's for sure."

"How do you figure *I* did something?" she asked, irked. "Maybe *I* dumped *him* because of something *he* did."

"And what did he do?" He raised an eyebrow and waited.

Expected me to be my best. Held me to a higher standard.

"Nothing." She felt bad now for even suggesting it. "You're right. I said some awful things to him. I pushed him away."

They got back on their mounts. As they rode the

fences, she told him about failing her high school equivalency exam and the fight with Aaron that had followed. Then she told him about her parents' revelations regarding her learning disability.

When she was done, the rancher looked off into the distance thoughtfully. "I'm not judging, 'cause your folks are good people, but I don't think it was right for them to hold that information back from you. Frankly, I'm surprised your teachers didn't insist on getting you tested. I'm pretty sure there are laws the school would've had to follow."

"Well, the thing is, my parents donated a lot of money to my elementary and high schools for extracurricular functions and stuff. My dad even sponsored the principals for membership at Greenfields. If he wanted something kept quiet, believe me, he could do it." Bitterness filled her. Money certainly had a way of greasing the gears.

"That doesn't let anyone off the hook," Wyatt said.

"I know they meant well, but I had a whole lifetime to work on this, to do something about…" She gestured at her head, still coming to grips with the idea of a learning disability she could've addressed decades ago. Her heart sank. "Maybe they're right. Maybe I should just ignore it."

"Well, now you're trying to stuff the genie back in the bottle. It doesn't work that way. The real question—" he tipped his chin up at her "—is what do you *really* want?"

Her thoughts went straight to Aaron, but she didn't say it out loud. The rancher seemed to glean her answer from her stilted silence. He notched his cowboy hat down and sighed. "You already know in your heart."

"I guess I do." She stared at the slack reins in her hand. Junebug plodded on, content to follow the worn track bordering the fence.

"Well, then, what're you going to do about it?"

She huffed. "What am I supposed to do?"

"You're asking me?" He raised an eyebrow.

"I thought you wanted to be helpful."

"And I thought you wanted to take control of your life, Little Miss Independent."

He was right. She'd been looking to him for answers, just as she'd gone to her parents for an easy solution to her problems. She didn't realize how automatic a response it was.

Junebug nickered and strayed from the track into the grass. She stopped to graze, and Steph let her.

"You're right," she said. "I guess I have been coasting. Looking for the easy path."

"The easiest path would've been to marry me from the start," Wyatt said wryly. "But you didn't because you have more ambition than that. I don't blame you. You're a talented baker, Stephanie Stephens, and one smart cookie."

She felt only a little guilt that Wyatt had come out of this on the losing side. But as her thoughts again turned to Aaron, she decided there was no comparison. She loved Aaron Caruthers and every geeky, sexy, infuriatingly brilliant inch of him.

"I guess I do know what I have to do," she said, spurring Junebug onward. The mare resisted as she stubbornly cropped the grass, but Steph tugged on the reins and gave her a firm kick to the flank. The horse pushed forward reluctantly. "It's not going to be easy."

"Nothing worth doing ever is. Now would be a good time to ask for help."

She peered at him, confused, and he chuckled. "You're awfully good at asking people for answers but not help. You're something of a paradox, you know."

"Am not." She knew what a paradox was. "And I ask people for help all the time."

"So ask me." He grinned. "'Cause I happen to know some folks who can help you."

CHAPTER TWENTY-THREE

AARON TRIED TO focus on the inventory list, but the lines of numbers and titles blurred together. He had to blink rapidly and take a few deep breaths to keep from zoning out as he'd been doing for the past two weeks.

It wasn't just that he hadn't been sleeping well. His seven-cups-of-coffee-a-day habit had ensured he was alert and extra irritable. And it wasn't just his worries about Gran's health since she'd been waking up at her ungodly morning hours again to do the baking.

No, his mind had been drifting...no, not so much drifting as making a beeline for Stephanie Stephens. What was she doing now that she'd quit? How was she paying the rent?

Stupid question. Her parents would pay it, of course. They'd never let their precious little princess go hungry or homeless.

He immediately chastised himself. That was a mean and unworthy thought. What the Stephenses did was none of his business, and he couldn't begrudge them for taking care of their daughter. Why he remained so bitter about it he didn't understand. Maybe it was the state of things that had him so on edge.

The fact was despite Georgette's new lease on life, she was slowing down. Without someone like Steph to take over the daily running of the business, the bakery would soon deteriorate. And without the regular flow of customers, the bookshop would soon follow.

He was at once angry and sad that his grandmother hadn't planned for this eventuality. She couldn't have expected Stephanie to stay forever. There should've been more redundancy. Kira would eventually go off to college, he was certain. And even if he could convince Gran to hire someone new, it would take years to train them, and Georgette might not have the energy to teach them everything she knew. He swallowed, trying to stem the sudden tears that filled his eyes.

Gran would die one day. That was the bald truth he faced. After his parents had been killed in that car accident, Gran had become his whole family. He'd dedicated his life to making her proud, making sure neither of them would ever be left with a gaping void in their lives again. Now he wondered if he'd gone about it all wrong, leaving Everville and getting a job pushing papers while sending her a monthly check. He should've been *here*, learning the trade himself, making sure the bakery that was his family's legacy would last.

A worn and stained red binder landed with a thump on the counter in front of him. Georgette placed both callused hands over it and shoved it forward.

"What's this for?" he asked, nonplussed.

"It's my recipe binder."

"I know that." He opened the binder to the first recipe. Chocolate chip cookies. He couldn't help but think back on that first lesson Steph had given him, summarized on a piece of slightly crinkled lined paper, written in Gran's neat printing, the blue ink faded. "Why's it out of the safe?"

"I'm giving it to you." She folded her hands in front of her. "I want you to type out these recipes and make them into a cookbook."

His brow furrowed. "You want to what?"

"I've been hearing a lot about self-publishing. I guess that means printing your own books. I think it's near time to retire, but I don't want my recipes to go to waste. I've spent too much time perfecting them to let them disappear into the ether." The stern set of her mouth reflected the acknowledgment of her mortality. "I think if we print out a few hundred copies, people will be willing to buy them."

He pressed his fingertips along the bridge of his cheekbones. "Gran, you don't have to do this."

"No. But I want to." She leaned forward. "Do you know why this bakery has been here as long as it has? Because it makes people happy. Your grandfather and I didn't start the business because we wanted to make money. We did it to share our creations with others."

"But...you can't just give your recipes away." He stabbed the binder with an accusing finger. "This is your life's work."

"*You're* my life's work, Aaron. You've grown up to be a strong, independent, successful man with dreams and the will to pursue them. I'm proud of you." She patted his arm. "Besides, I'm not giving away anything. I said people would *pay* for the book, didn't I?" She gave a tut-tut. "I may not be mercenary, but I am still a businesswoman."

She turned to go, but Aaron stopped her. "This is because Stephanie left, isn't it?"

Gran sighed, turned to face him. "You can't hold on to things forever, Aaron. Or people."

"I didn't mean to drive her off," he said quietly.

"She would have left here one day. I don't think she realizes how talented she is. I would've been a fool not to hire her when I did." She gave a dry chuckle. "On second thought, maybe I am a little mercenary."

"You don't blame me for breaking up with her?"

"That depends. Do you?"

"A little." He sighed resignedly. "A lot. I said some things I shouldn't have. But *she* kicked me out of her life. I just did what she wanted and left."

"Out of anger and frustration," she pointed out. "Because it was easier than fighting for her and then being disappointed if things didn't work out the way you've always hoped they would."

Leave it to Gran to get to the heart of his feelings. He forked his fingers through his hair. "I thought I could keep myself from being hurt," he admitted, realizing how petulant he was being. To save himself from further humiliation, he'd shut Steph out. He hadn't wanted to be that desperate, eager-to-please loser—the one Dale used to beat up. But in his effort to keep from being that weak ever again he'd become a coward.

"I'll admit," Gran said when he didn't respond. "When I heard you were coming back here for good, I was hoping you and Steph would develop a good working relationship." Georgette plucked at her apron, dusting flour off the front. "I was a little shocked when you two started dating. But if she made you happy, who was I to interfere? As long as you could work together, things were fine."

"It didn't work out that way."

"No. It didn't. But I shouldn't have expected it to, nor could I have predicted her leaving the bakery when things soured between you. But that, to use a baker's reference, is the way the cookie crumbles. I wasn't going to step in either way. This is *your* life, Aaron. You can't live it in fear, trying to predict the next bad thing that'll happen in the name of preserving what you have." She expelled a breath. "*Live*, Aaron. Enjoy life to its fullest. Live the way you *want* to." With that, she left him with her binder.

His heart hurt, but he knew she was right. He'd made the conscious decision to act like a jerk by turning away from Steph when she'd needed him most. He'd chosen to protect his own heart rather than try to help her through a difficult time. He'd accused her of running when things got tough. Hadn't he done the same?

At the end of the day, Aaron caught up with Kira. "How have things been for you and your brother?"

"Great," she said brightly. "Mr. and Mrs. Stephens have been really nice. I kinda wish they'd stop buying Tyler toys and stuff, though. I mean, it was enough that they got me new glasses—" she tapped her stylish frames "—but it feels wrong to accept all these gifts from them."

"You can put your foot down whenever you want, but I think they enjoy spoiling you."

"I know. They keep saying so, and it's hard to turn them down. Mrs. Stephens especially." She chuckled ruefully. "I've had to tell them to stick to a budget. Mrs. Stephens really loves shopping."

"She's not pushing anything on you, though?" he asked, concerned. "Not making any demands of you or making you uncomfortable?"

"No, nothing like that. I know I'm complaining about nothing. Like, poor me, look at all this stuff someone is buying me." Kira shook her head. "I can handle her. Mostly, I think she's kinda lonely."

"So...has Steph been back to see her parents at all?" He didn't want to involve Kira in their drama, but he was itching to know.

"Yeah, she's there." She pressed her lips together tightly.

Her reticence was out of loyalty, he guessed. She didn't want to gossip about the family who was hosting her and her brother, and he didn't blame her. "I've tried to call, but she hasn't picked up her phone."

"She's been busy. She and Mr. Brown—" She cut herself off abruptly.

Something thumped him in the chest. "Mr. Brown? As in *Wyatt* Brown?"

"He's been coming by a lot. That's all I know. I mean, they haven't done anything, you know..." She made empty gestures. "I don't think they're—"

"It's okay." Shock gave way to pain. Had she already turned to another man for the security and love he'd denied her?

No. He couldn't believe Steph had simply given up on them. On what they'd had. Her parents might have forced it on her...

But then, Steph was more assertive than that. He knew that now. She wouldn't cave to their whims. She was her own woman. Otherwise, why would she work at the bakery? Why would she have moved out? She could have lived a pampered life at home and had all her needs taken care of.

No, Steph was a smart, independent woman who made her own choices.

And apparently, she was choosing to be with Wyatt.

He shook off the despair clawing at him. He was not going to brood and wallow in self-pity. She'd picked *him* over Wyatt. She'd called Aaron's name over and over when they made love. She could've had the rich, handsome rancher at any time, but she'd chosen Aaron.

Kira cleared her throat. "You know, you guys were a cute couple. Not that it's my business, but I think you two are good for each other. You should try to make it work."

He smiled crookedly. "Thanks. I will." But first, he needed to offer Steph something better than a book or a raise or a meaningless promotion. He needed a grand gesture to show her she meant more to him than old books or chocolate soufflés could relay.

He needed to make her wildest dreams come true.

"WHAT DO YOU mean you're moving out *for good*?" Helen's voice rose to fretful new heights.

It was the *for good* part her parents were still trying to grasp. Steph didn't think it was that hard to understand. They'd come home to find Wyatt, Maya and Tyler helping her pack up and empty her room. They were already half done by the time the elder Stephenses realized what was happening.

"I mean, I'm taking what I need and I'm donating everything else to charity after Kira and Maya go through and take what they want." She dumped an armload of clothing from her closet on the bed and started sorting out the pieces she thought she'd still use. Most of them were too fancy for her to wear anywhere. Anywhere she actually wanted to be, anyhow.

Maya snatched up a silk Vera Wang dress from the discard pile. "You're crazy to let me have this for nothing," she said, but stowed the takings into a clear plastic garbage bag. "I really ought to be writing you a consignment slip."

"I owe you for all the time you spent helping me study." She tossed her a Versace number, and Maya squealed with delight. "And I may need your help again soon."

To her parents, she said, "I'm moving back to my apartment. If I stay over, it'll be in the guest room. You can move Kira into this suite if you like. Or turn it into a library. You've always said the light in here would be perfect for reading."

"Stephanie, if this is because of what's been happening…" Her father cleared his throat. "Not that I think you're making a rash decision—"

"Daddy." She laid a hand on his shoulder. "This is what I want. I need to do this on my own."

"That's what you said the first time." Helen sniffed.

"Do you want to keep the furniture?" Wyatt asked as he marched back in with Tyler. They'd been taking boxes down to his pickup truck.

"No, it can all go to charity. Unless you want to keep it, Mom."

"Why would I? I don't want reminders of how little my own daughter needs me." She blotted her eyes melodramatically.

Steph chuckled wryly. She was too excited to be frustrated. She squeezed each of their shoulders in reassurance. "Mom, Dad, I love you. And I'll always need you. You're my parents. And you guys have done so much for me. I don't even know how I'd live without you. But that's the problem. I've let myself depend on you even when I thought I was on my own. I want a real chance now to figure things out for myself and deal with my problems on my own."

"With a little help from your friends," Wyatt sang, leaving the room with another box.

"You're not helping!" Helen shouted after him and huffed. "I thought he was on *our* side."

"He is. He got me in touch with some specialists who can help me deal with my LD." Saying it out loud didn't feel as alien as it once might have. She knew she had a long road ahead of her, but it wasn't a death sentence. It was something she could deal with. "I have a real shot at getting my diploma now. It's going to take time and work, but I know I can do it."

"And in the meantime, what? You'll work at some burger joint for minimum wage?" Helen wrung her hands.

"Or waitress or bartend or wash dishes. Whatever it takes. Yes, Mom. I would do that."

"But why? Why would you slave your life away when we can take care of you?"

"It's not slaving away if it's my choice. I don't want to be totally dependent on others for my happiness. I don't need you to take care of everything for me." She took a deep breath. "What I do need from you is a loan."

"A loan?" Her father raised an eyebrow.

"Not now. For when I go to college."

Her parents stared at her openmouthed.

"It's too early to talk about it, I know. But once I get my diploma, I want to look into certificate courses, or maybe get a degree."

Helen's face puffed up and turned beet red. Tearfully, she yelled, "Wyatt! You ask this girl to marry you or so help me—"

"Sorry, Mrs. Stephens," he shouted from the hall. "I already tried that tactic, and she said no. My ego can't take much more bruising than that."

Maya snorted a loud laugh as she hauled a garbage bag of clothes out to her car.

"College, huh?" Terrence stroked his chin. "Well, well. My little girl really is all grown-up."

"I was grown-up a long time ago, Dad. But I needed a chance to figure that out for myself." She could see the approval slowly warming his gaze. Concern still lingered there, but that was to be expected. They'd always worry about her. "I'll pay you back, of course. With interest."

He clapped her on the shoulder. "I know you'll be good for it," he said. "All right, sweetheart. We'll do it your way. No more money infusions into your bank account."

"Terrence!" his wife cried.

"This is what she wants, Helen. And you've never been one to deny her." He picked up a box and started to carry it out. "Why start now?"

Steph mouthed a thank-you as he exited, leaving her alone with her mother. "Are you going to be okay with this?"

Helen pouted, hands clutched in front of her. "It didn't end the way I'd hoped."

"You don't know that it won't," she said. "I still want to have a family. I'm even going to start saving for a place of my own, with a nice backyard where the kids will play. In time, once I've met the right guy…"

She trailed off and bit her bottom lip. She'd already met him. Despite their vast differences, Aaron was the only man she could picture sharing a family and a lifetime with.

There was a commotion downstairs, and the pounding of footsteps as Maya stuck her head above the banister. "Steph! You better get down here!"

"What?" She hurried outside to where Wyatt's pickup truck was parked in the driveway. A familiar station wagon had pulled up nose-to-nose with it. And the man she loved was standing toe-to-toe with the rancher.

"Aaron punched Wyatt in the face," Maya whispered fiercely, almost gleefully. "I think he might have hurt his hand."

Steph was immediately worried for Aaron's safety. But though the rancher was taller and broader and had more muscles, *he* was the one backing away, hands raised in surrender.

"It's not what you think, Aaron," he said, rubbing his jaw.

Aaron clearly wasn't listening. "I'm not letting you sweep her off to your ranch, Wyatt. She's got so much potential. You can't let her give up on her dreams. She wants to run Georgette's, and if you think I'm going to let you keep her from that—"

"Aaron!" Steph stepped forward. Aaron's gaze snapped to her. The intensity burning there did all kinds of crazy things to her body. Slowly, his fury melted from his features like ice cream sliding off a slice of piping-hot apple pie.

"Like I was saying," Wyatt said with sardonic cheer. "I was just helping her move her things back to her apartment. Now, I'm going inside to leave you two to it." He slapped Aaron hard on the back and gave him a menacing smile. "Go get 'er, slugger."

The rancher ushered everyone else back into the house, winking at Steph as he passed. Maya whispered, "Good luck." And then they were alone.

"Hi." Aaron cleared his throat and flushed a becoming shade of pink. "I…um…overreacted. I guess I owe Wyatt an apology."

"He'll be fine." She kept her expression neutral, trying hard not to hope, to set herself up for disappointment.

"Oh. Okay. That's good." He rubbed his knuckles and shook out his hand. "Listen, Steph, I'm sorry I tried to push you to retake the equivalency exam. I'm sorry I made you feel bad about yourself. I've always put too much stock in grades and numbers and official papers because…well, that's how I've always measured my successes. I always need to know I'm on the right track. But I don't need those things to know that you're a good person. The best person to run the bakery."

She laughed softly. "You know that's a lie."

She'd come to terms with that. She'd worked at Georgette's long enough to know what she hadn't dealt with. If she ever wanted to run the bakery on her own, she had to take the initiative and learn *everything* she needed to know about how to run a bakery.

Aaron rubbed the back of his neck. "Well, I figured I would still have some say in the family business. But the fact is the bakery needs you. *I* need you. If running Georgette's is what you still want to do, then I want to help you make your dreams come true." He took an envelope out of his back pocket. "Here."

She took the papers out. She scanned the contents and looked up, confused. "This is a contract."

"It's more than that. It's a legal agreement that splits ownership of the building fifty-fifty. I convinced Gran to sell the business to me, but she'll only do so if you agree to run it with me." He tapped the part that listed her as the co-owner. "All you have to do is sign and the bakery portion is yours."

She stared, clinging to the remains of her pride. "Why?" If this was him giving her something she hadn't earned and didn't deserve, simply to appease her...

And then she saw it in those big, sad eyes: pain, acceptance and that tiny hint of bitterness. And she suddenly knew what he was going to say, because she'd faced the same kind of acceptance, too.

"Gran's tired, Steph. She's letting go bit by bit, and there's nothing we can do to stop it."

The truth hurt. Her eyes grew damp, and she nodded. "Yes."

"She's content to let go, but I'm not. Without you, everything she built with my grandfather will disappear." He released a labored breath. "It was never my dream to own a bakery. But it is yours. And all I want in life is to see you achieve your dreams. You're the one who deserves to run Georgette's."

Her heart swelled. Yet something kept her from feeling true happiness. "And what about you?" she asked. "What do you want in life?"

He gazed up at her mournfully. "I want you back, Steph. I know things weren't perfect between us, but that was my fault. I kept you at a distance. Part of me was sure you'd hurt me and...well, I was ready to jump ship to keep my heart safe." He made fists at his sides. "I know I don't deserve a second chance. You've given me plenty of them already. But with this, at least—" he gestured at the contract "—I know I can offer you the chance you deserve."

A hiccup of a sob burst from her. "No." His face fell, and she reached for him, taking his hands. "I was the one who pushed you away. I never felt worthy of you, Aaron. When I failed my exam, I thought I wasn't good enough for you. I was sure it was the only thing that mattered to you."

His face was pale. "None of that matters to me. Not a bit." His lips trembled as he clasped her hands. "I love you for *you*."

Her heart soared. She threw herself into his embrace and wrapped her arms around him.

"I love you for you, too," she said hoarsely, then gave a watery laugh. "Even when you're a big jerk."

"As long as I'm *your* big jerk." He rested his forehead against hers. They kissed then, fully, deeply, with their whole beings. She held on tight, breathing him in, knowing no matter how things turned out, they would always be there for each other.

"Will you forgive me?" he asked.

"Only if you can forgive me. Not to make you jealous or anything, but Wyatt really has been a big help. He's been arranging meetings for me with a learning disabilities counselor, and I'll be starting a special program next week. I'm hoping to retake the equivalency exam before the end of the year."

Aaron stilled and drew back. "You don't have to do that. Not for me."

"Not for you," she agreed. "I want it for me. I'm going to get that diploma. And then I'm going to college. So I have to say no."

"Wait...no? No to what?"

"No to ownership of Georgette's. I'm not ready yet. I appreciate your confidence in me, but I want to learn how to deal with my issues first. The counselor said there are ways I can make things easier. Things I can do that won't make me so nervous under pressure."

Aaron's face relaxed into a full, open smile of acceptance. He kissed her briefly, hotly, once more. "Whatever you decide, I'll back you up on it. I know Gran will, too."

And wasn't that all she really needed? Not charity or pity, not people to hold her hand all the way through life, but the simple knowledge that she was not alone, that the people around her trusted her and were ready to help her if she needed it.

Aaron swept her up in another kiss, but she pulled away as his hands started to roam. "Enough of that. I've got work to do and we've kept the others from loading the truck."

He rolled up his sleeves. "Try and stop me from helping."

She grinned. "Don't hurt yourself. I'm going to need you in one piece for later."

"Oh?" His lips tilted up.

"I've got to keep studying, you know, or I'll lose it. If you're willing, I'm hoping you'll drill me."

He waggled his eyebrows. "Oh, I can do that."

"In math, you dirty bird!" She punched him in the arm, laughing.

"You can count on me. I know all kinds of incentives to get you excited for homework."

"I have all the incentive I need. Now hurry up. There's work to do."

* * * * *

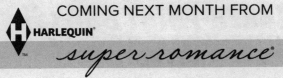

COMING NEXT MONTH FROM

HARLEQUIN®

super romance

Available April 7, 2015

#1980 TO LOVE A COP
by Janice Kay Johnson

After what Laura Vennetti and her son have been through, she's avoided all contact with the police. Then her son brings detective Ethan Winter into their lives. Immediately Laura can see how different he is from her late husband. And the irresistible attraction she feels toward Ethan tempts her to try again.

#1981 MY WAY BACK TO YOU
by Pamela Hearon

Married too young, divorced too soon? Maggie Russell and Jeff Wells haven't seen each other in years, but as they reunite to move their son into his college dorm, they discover the attraction between them is still present—and very strong. Yet so are the reasons they shouldn't be together...

#1982 THOSE CASSABAW DAYS
The Malone Brothers
by Cindy Homberger

Emily Quinn and Matt Malone were inseparable until tragedy struck. Fifteen years later, Emily returns to Cassabaw to open a café. Matt, too, is back—quiet, sullen and angry after a stint in the marines. Emily's determined to bring out the old Matt. Dare she hope for even more?

#1983 NIGHTS UNDER
THE TENNESSEE STARS
by Joanne Rock

Erin Finley is wary of TV producer Remy Weldon. She can't deny his appeal, but Remy's Cajun charm seems to hide a dark pain—one that no amount of love could ever heal. And her biggest fear is that he'll be around only as long as the lights are on...

HSRLPCNM0315

LARGER-PRINT BOOKS!

GET 2 FREE LARGER-PRINT NOVELS PLUS

2 FREE GIFTS!

✦ HARLEQUIN®

Romance

From the Heart, For the Heart

YES! Please send me 2 FREE LARGER-PRINT Harlequin® Romance novels and my 2 FREE gifts (gifts are worth about $10). After receiving them, if I don't wish to receive any more books, I can return the shipping statement marked "cancel." If I don't cancel, I will receive 4 brand-new novels every month and be billed just $4.84 per book in the U.S. or $5.24 per book in Canada. That's a savings of at least 19% off the cover price! It's quite a bargain! Shipping and handling is just 50¢ per book in the U.S. and 75¢ per book in Canada.* I understand that accepting the 2 free books and gifts places me under no obligation to buy anything. I can always return a shipment and cancel at any time. Even if I never buy another book, the two free books and gifts are mine to keep forever.

119/319 HDN F43Y

Name _____ (PLEASE PRINT) _____

Address _____ Apt. #

City _____ State/Prov. _____ Zip/Postal Code

Signature (if under 18, a parent or guardian must sign)

Mail to the **Harlequin® Reader Service:**
IN U.S.A.: P.O. Box 1867, Buffalo, NY 14240-1867
IN CANADA: P.O. Box 609, Fort Erie, Ontario L2A 5X3

Want to try two free books from another line?
Call 1-800-873-8635 or visit www.ReaderService.com.

* Terms and prices subject to change without notice. Prices do not include applicable taxes. Sales tax applicable in N.Y. Canadian residents will be charged applicable taxes. Offer not valid in Quebec. This offer is limited to one order per household. Not valid for current subscribers to Harlequin Romance Larger-Print books. All orders subject to credit approval. Credit or debit balances in a customer's account(s) may be offset by any other outstanding balance owed by or to the customer. Please allow 4 to 6 weeks for delivery. Offer available while quantities last.

Your Privacy—The Harlequin® Reader Service is committed to protecting your privacy. Our Privacy Policy is available online at www.ReaderService.com or upon request from the Harlequin Reader Service.

We make a portion of our mailing list available to reputable third parties that offer products we believe may interest you. If you prefer that we not exchange your name with third parties, or if you wish to clarify or modify your communication preferences, please visit us at www.ReaderService.com/consumerchoice or write to us at Harlequin Reader Service Preference Service, P.O. Box 9062, Buffalo, NY 14269. Include your complete name and address.

HRLP13R